Jeannette, best
wishes

Gordon

D1825019

CRISPIN'S SPUR

CRISPIN'S SPUR

Gordon Wardman

Secker & Warburg
London

First published in England 1985 by
Martin Secker & Warburg Limited
54 Poland Street, London W1V 3DF

British Library Cataloguing in Publication Data
Wardman, Gordon
Crispin's spur.
I. Title
823'.914[F]   PR6073.A7223/

ISBN 0–436–56170–0

Phototypeset in Great Britain in 11/12½ pt Baskerville by
Inforum Ltd, Portsmouth
Printed and bound in Great Britain by
Biddles Ltd, Guildford and King's Lynn

For S.M.C. with love

Anarchism was not infrequently a kind of penalty for the opportunist sins of the working-class movement. The two monstrosities complemented each other.

V.I. Lenin

Each man kills the thing he loves.

O. Wilde

The hell I will.

J. Wayne

1

The passageway that connected the lavatory and kitchen in the back of the house to the meeting room below the shop was in darkness. It was nine o'clock at night. A light bulb screwed into a wall socket at the foot of the stairs should have gone some way towards lighting the passage, but it had died some months before and nobody had got round to replacing it.

As Jim moved forward with due caution he felt something crunch under his shoe. He shuddered as instinctively he held back the full pressure of his shoe sole from the splintered shell and its rubbery contents. Jesus shit, why couldn't evolution have left the bloody things in the sea where they belonged? Another snail with its roof caved in. Hope it's fit enough to crawl away and die, because no bugger is going to sweep it up here. What a frigging hole this is. A pure disgrace to the movement.

Jim opened the door and stepped back into the meeting. What he saw at that moment ran through his head in the form of a string of clichéd epithets. Conspiratorial. Claustrophobic. And overlong. Five men sitting round a table and a sixth chair which he had just vacated. A few beer cans on the table. A cloud of cigarette smoke hanging round a naked bulb on a frayed black cord.

There was no carpet – no furniture come to that, except the table and chairs and a beat-up duplicator on a stand in the far corner. But, incongruously, propped up against one wall and covering its entire surface area to give the effect of a mural, was a painting of scenes of working-class life and struggle executed

1

on a sheet of what seemed to be hardboard. God knows how they had got it down there, or why. Nobody seemed to remember; it had been there a long time. Like some of his comrades, thought Jim, casting an affectionate eye over them. They looked at home. They had served their time at meetings much like this one.

Jim Carson was twenty-five years old. Tall, slim and clean-cut, he carried himself as if his shoulders were broader than they actually were. In a well-pressed suit, with his shirt collar buttoned down and his tie carefully knotted, he looked like someone who was starting to carve out a career for himself. Which, in a way, he was.

Jim was a lot younger than his companions. Grouped round the table, he saw in them an image of collective middle age – thinning hair, paunches, stained teeth, bloodshot eyes, bristling nostrils. Not a pretty sight. They really ought to look after themselves more, he thought. It was their duty.

'All right, Jim?' asked Alan, who was chairing the meeting, as Jim sat down.

'I just squashed a snail out in the hall there.'

'Cunt was probably a spy,' said Martin, who was sitting on Jim's right. 'They've found a way to put microphones in them these days, you know. Don't let the horns fool you.'

'OK, comrades,' continued Alan, whose sense of humour was underdeveloped, 'let's give a resumé of where we've got to.'

They had been at the discussion for three hours already and were getting nowhere fast. Six activists, clear on what they wanted but unsure of how to achieve it.

'There's no disagreement that HQ's perspective of coordinated attacks in a number of different regions is correct. Nor that ROF Hardcoats is the obvious target in this region. What we're stuck on is how to get to it, particularly in the time-scale, for all the reasons that we've been over tonight.'

It was a fair, if brutal, summary of three hours of argument and discussion. The ordnance factory at Hardcoats, on the outskirts of Northburn about thirty miles from where they were meeting, made tanks and had done so for years. What made it an attractive target for sabotage now was the recent controversy surrounding the leaking of a document to the press which

2

showed that the new type of light battle-tank in production there, intended primarily for the home market, was a particularly versatile weapon which could be adapted for domestic counter-insurgency operations.

ROF Hardcoats was situated in an accessible urban area, a suburb of a northern city. Its workforce was routinely screened for political and trade union militancy. But since it employed over a thousand workers with all the human diversity that implied, it could scarcely have been regarded as impregnable in normal circumstances. However, circumstances were far from normal and the Party had an organizational – and hence political – problem on its hands.

Internal political disputes around the adoption of the Party's new line, followed by some damaging defections coupled with a series of untimely arrests arising out of weakened security, had all but destroyed their organization in the Northburn area. In one sense this did not make a great deal of difference, since the kind of unit or cell neeessary to carry out an unprecedented attack of this type would have to function outside the Party's normal structure anyway. Indeed, it was possible for an incorrigible optimist to see the parlous state of their local organization as a positive advantage – it would be the last place anyone would be expecting an attack and there would be less targets for reprisals afterwards.

But the fact remained that the attack was not going to launch itself. Somebody had to do the groundwork, and the question was who they could call on with the necessary local knowledge to set up such an operation. On this the six of them were stuck. Several names had been volunteered, chewed over and discarded as unreliable or inexperienced or tainted in some way. It was stalemate.

Except that an idea had half formed in Jim's mind while he had been out in the lavatory. He formulated it now as a question.

'Comrades, you remember when we went over our recent organizers in the Northburn area? I think I could summarize it as a list of brief-lived hopes, cut short by arrest or political disagreement or proven incompetence.'

'There were some wankers, and some that were unlucky,'

said Martin, passing Jim a cigarette and lighting one himself. He liked the young man, liked the way his style veered between enthusiasm and pomposity. It reminded him of himself years before. He could not sound that serious about anything these days. 'None of them lasted long though.'

'Well put,' said Jim, pausing to light the cigarette. 'Now from what was said, I gather that before the present unsettled period – going back, say, ten years – we had a fairly prolonged and stable stretch under a comrade called. . .' he paused, and his tone became interrogative, 'Cliff? Or. . .'

'Chris,' Alan supplied the answer, 'Chris Powell. Yes, Chris was organizer there for a good few years; well thought of sort of comrade, did a job of work.'

There were a few nods round the table.

'Obviously I was still at school then,' said Jim, flattering their experience with a smile. 'I gather that this Chris resigned after disagreements which were, well, a bit to do with personalities and a bit to do with politics. Is that right?'

'Not far out,' said Frank, who was sitting on Jim's left. Frank had a gentle manner that seemed slightly incongruous, given the context. 'To be honest, I felt sorry for old Chris. They made him out to be a second Uncle Joe, but he was right politically, really, he could see how things were going. He was just a bit ahead of his time.'

'Being right too soon is one way of being wrong,' said Alan quietly. It was a ruling.

'What happened to this Chris?' asked Jim.

The comrades were listening. Even Alan, whose expression during meetings was as unrevealing as a poker player's, was obviously paying attention. Jim's idea had some substance. There was a pause to evaluate it. Then Alan spoke again.

'Well, Jim, he left the area. Went down South somewhere. He's still in the Party, but not active, as far as I know. Do you have any more information about him, Martin?'

'I had some contact with him after he left – the odd letter or phone call – but it's a year or so since I've heard from him now. He gives a bit of conscience money to the Party but, like you say, Alan, he's not active down there. He's running an antique shop

4

in Kent with his missus. Calls it Pharaoh's. That's the name he uses now – Crispin Pharaoh.'

'Jesus Christ,' said Bill, coughing absent-mindedly into his cigarette. Bill was a stocky, hard-bitten man, with firm ideas of what constituted appropriate proletarian economic activity.

'Would he be any use to us?' Jim persisted.

'He was a good comrade,' said Frank kindly, 'but you know, Jim, ten years is a long time in this game. Take a comrade away from his roots like that and he changes. An antique dealer is going to think like an antique dealer, not like a working-class activist. That's basic Marxism, isn't it? It's a good suggestion, but I'm not sure how much use the comrade would be to us now.'

'It's a bit since Chris hung up his gunbelt, is what Frank is saying,' Martin glossed.

'I don't think we should dismiss Jim's idea out of hand,' said Alan. Everyone looked at him. It was an unexpected, but perhaps decisive, remark. 'For a start, we're exaggerating the time-scale. It's not ten years since Chris hung up his gunbelt, as Martin puts it, but seven or eight at the most. And in those years things have moved on a lot. We wouldn't even have been talking about blowing up a factory eight years ago, would we? Chris may, as Frank says, have lost touch with his roots in that time. That's quite possible. On the other hand, it's just as possible he may feel that subsequent events have vindicated his stance politically. Let's face it, we don't know. It might be worth finding out, comrades, instead of sitting here speculating. I think Jim has a point. Chris could be our man.'

'Yes, it could be worth a try. After all, we've been kicking it round for three hours and we haven't come up with anything better.' It was Lou speaking, for the first time since Jim's return. Lou was tired and his head ached. Half way through a crucial election campaign in his trade union, probably the most important in his career, and it felt like he had flu coming on. This meeting was getting nowhere and he wished it was over.

The others caught his mood and fell in with it.

'Yeah, why not?' said Bill tersely, making it a de facto majority. 'Stop him pansying about, eh?'

'Gunbelts it is,' said Martin.

5

'It looks like you've talked yourself into a job, Jim,' said Frank.

That was indeed the unspoken assumption. He had won the comrades into giving his idea a try. Now it was up to him to see it through.

'I've never been to Kent,' said Jim.

'Pretty place,' said Lou. 'Churches and hop-fields. Very green. You'll like it. It'll be good for your education.'

'It's not quite that bad,' said Bill. 'There's some engineering on the Medway and I think there's still a couple of pits down near Dover.'

'But your man Chris has got himself firmly entrenched in one of the other bits,' said Martin, laughing, 'selling frigging cuckoo-clocks to the natives.'

Its climax passed, the meeting was relaxing into disorder, with chuckles and the sounds of ring-pulls on cans. Alan moved to wrap it up.

'Let me put this as a proposition then, comrades. Martin and myself brief Jim tomorrow evening on everything we know, or can find out by then, about Chris Powell, or Crispin Pharaoh as he now calls himself. Then Jim can travel down to Kent the day following and make contact with him. If we aim to reconvene this meeting at the same time next week, we should be in a position to report to you what the score is and either work out the details or look for another plan. Agreed?' Nods and murmurs round the table. 'All right then, let's call it a night.'

It did not take the meeting long to break up. They made their way, single file, up the stairs into the shop, relying on the light of a street lamp outside its window. The shop had once sold books but was now rarely open for business, though it still had some residual stock displayed. It was located in the sort of run-down area where a shop that seldom opened, but was used for storage or as a workshop, did not stand out as unusual.

Times had changed, and quickly. Even Jim could remember when the Party had needed shop fronts. Now it needed them like a hole in the head. The Party was not actually illegal, yet, but most of its activities were. It was in a state of transition, a political limbo.

They stepped out of the shop into the semi-clandestine night

6

and went their separate ways. Security considerations had destroyed the old, matey tradition of taking a drink together after meetings.

Jim moved away quicker than the others, rapidly walking the quarter mile or so to where his car was parked. He did not even bother to look over his shoulder. He felt excited about the enterprise ahead.

2

Crispin Pharaoh was drunk – profoundly, soul-searchingly, and yet slightly ridiculously, drunk. He had been drunk all day. It felt the natural way to be – not good exactly, but natural. In fact it seemed to him that he had been intermittently drunk for as long as he could remember – years, decades, lifetimes – with any sober interludes an unreal irrelevance. All fucked up inside his head. Situation normal, as the old saying went.

It was a Sunday. Although a life-long atheist, the day was of some significance to Crispin. It meant that the shop was shut. Moreover Mary, his wife, was visiting her sister who lived in London. Often, these days, she visited relatives or friends without him on Sundays. None of their children lived close by. Crispin had no real friends in Carlton, the village where they lived. What did it all add up to? A day of social isolation. A good day for serious drinking.

He had, in fact, woken up half-pissed from the night before. A large whisky and soda lay unfinished by his bedside. He inspected it with a professional eye, noting the slight sediment in the bottom of the glass, evidence of a dissolved ice cube. That's one thing I miss down South, he thought, decent water. The stuff here is full of shit. It's a damn good job I never drink it neat. He drank the whisky slowly, with considerable pleasure, feeling the euphoria creep over him. No worries. The day was written off in advance. Fuck it.

7

His next step was to take a bath, drinking a can of lager, cold from the fridge, as he did so. Whisky was a good start to the day, but a man needed a solid breakfast to settle his stomach. A radio on the window-ledge blared out pop music through the steam at a volume just below the pain threshold. Crispin tapped out a rhythm on the side of the bath with the can. This is the life. Today I can be as antisocial as I like. When the wife is away Crispin can play.

Dried, he inspected his naked body in a full-length mirror. A little flabby, its covering of hair turning grey. Not hopelessly decayed yet; probably in good average shape for a middle-aged male in an advanced capitalist society, with its poisons of rich food, sugar, nicotine and booze to contend with. But it saddened him nevertheless. It lacked the tough, muscular quality it had had in its prime. It would not look so good now anywhere its appearance might be thought to matter. Not wanted on beach or building site or in boudoir. The trouble is, thought Crispin, once we discover we can get through life without fighting or working and that women will take us as we come, we lose the will to keep ourselves in shape. You've had it too cushy too long, old lad.

He dressed in jeans and a pullover and spent the rest of the morning sprawled on a settee, drinking gin and orange juice and reading the papers through a boozy haze. The papers, as usual, contained little that he had wanted to know. Reading them was a silly habit, he decided.

At midday he walked down the road to the pub and stayed there till two, drinking beer slowly and picking at some sandwiches. He made the sort of polite conversation required of him, hid his drunkenness as well as he could and fought down the impulse to become abusive towards the stupid, middle-class people around him. How's business, old chap? Did you see the Princess on the box last night? Up your arse, squire. How in Jesus' suffering name did I end up in this dump? I feel like Joe Hill, whose last request before his execution was that his body be taken over the state line for cremation because he did not want to be seen dead in Utah. Except that Carlton has Utah beat.

Back home again, afternoon blurred into evening for Crispin,

8

dug into his settee in front of the television, working his way through the gin bottle. He was no longer particularly conscious of being drunk. At one stage he found himself in tears during the dénouement of a Disney movie involving dogs, small children, wide open spaces and the dawning awareness of death.

'Jesus shit,' he said out loud, wiping his eyes with his sleeve, 'the fucking gin is getting to you, you old cunt.'

After that he switched the television off and played records instead. The selection he chose was a mixture of labour movement hymns, revolutionary songs from round the world and folk ballads about mining disasters and lock-outs. Listening to them, his emotions ranged from boredom to irritation to depression. Neither their content nor their associations suited his mood.

El pueblo unido jamas sera vencido – the chorus of the Chilean battle anthem seemed to come to him from a world so far away as to be unreal. A world of linked arms in urban streets. A long way from his present situation, recycling pretty junk for people with more money than sense or taste among the green fields of exile. Santiago was closer to Northburn than Northburn to Carlton at that moment.

He tried to review his career. He had been brought up in the labour movement, moving naturally through its practices and institutions, finally deploying the experience he had gained as a trade union and political activist to reasonable effect as a full-time revolutionary organizer in Northburn. That was back in the good old days when a political agitator could still get a listing in the yellow pages.

Ironically, in view of what had happened to him since, at the time when he had been removed from his position after an internal power struggle, the underlying political reason had been that he was too hard-line in his attitudes. Not sophisticated enough for the modern world. That looked doubly sick now, with the Party semi-illegal, many of its militants in custody and Crispin, the prophet vindicated, miles away servicing the bourgeoisie. Time for a comeback, eh? he thought, realizing that he had, in fact, spoken the words aloud. He poured some more gin into his glass. The orange juice had run out and he could not be bothered to go to the fridge to get ice, so

9

he drank it neat. It still tasted as if it had been diluted – vaguely warm, and effortless to drink.

But there was, in reality, no way back as far as he could see. When he had fallen from power he should have had the courage of his convictions, taken a job, any job, in Northburn and carried on the struggle. But he had felt too tired and frustrated at that time to face what he knew might be years of internal struggle conducted in his spare time, while, if he was lucky, he scratched a living in a factory. He had already had a bellyful of that sort of fight, where yesterday's friend becomes today's enemy and you end up trusting nobody. He had wanted out.

Well, he had got out all right. His was the ultimate middle-aged fantasy – new career, new area, even a new name. It had taken some nerve for a man with no capital, no knowledge of the business except what he had gleaned selling bric-a-brac on a market stall to raise cash for the Party, and who had never been to Kent except as a holiday-maker. He had made some sort of point, whatever the cost.

And where had it left him? Nearly fifty, maudlin drunk, a competent shopkeeper who had once been a seasoned and respected revolutionary, estranged from his roots, cut off from everything, in fact, which gave life value and purpose.

'That's right, lad, make your speech.' He was talking aloud again. He got up, unsteadily, and opened the door that led out into the garden.

Outside it was a cold autumn night. The sky was absolutely clear, the moon full and silver, the stars blinking in recognizable, half-remembered constellations. A hedgehog moved, snuffling noisily, at a surprising pace across the leaf-strewn lawn. Things far and near going about their lawful business.

He suddenly felt cold, standing out there in carpet slippers in the night air, contemplating the unimaginable distance to the stars. He recognized the drift of his thoughts only too well as he turned to go in again. Meditations on death. Speculations on self-destruction. Summoning up the nerve to kill himself.

Suicide was wrong for a revolutionary, a crude negation of the principle that change is constant and to be welcomed, a denial of the potential for change still remaining in himself. But he had thought of it a lot recently. Thought also of comrades he

10

had known over the years who had taken that dreadful step.

And dreadful it had always been, he remembered, mechanically pouring more gin. One had cut his throat, another had jumped from a window in a tower-block, a third, almost unbelievably, had stabbed himself to death with a kitchen knife. Messy, violent deaths, proclaiming self-hatred, designed to punish both victim and whoever was left to mourn.

He could not die like that. Could not leave his wife to find him butchered, or his children to brood on the consequences as they grew nearer to their own deaths. And, to be less pious about it, there was the obstacle of his own cowardice to overcome. Faced with the cutting edge or the concrete far below, fear could be guaranteed to override disgust. No, if he was to die by his own hand it would have to be quietly and painlessly – an overdose to carry him imperceptibly into oblivion.

He switched the television back on. Adventure under a tropical sun. Did he have any tablets in the house? With the right stuff it wouldn't take much, not with the load he had on. He had done the hard work already.

He went through to the kitchen and rifled through the cupboard where they kept medicines. Scores of bottles – witch hazel, cough mixture, kaolin and morphine, indian brandee, herbal pills for rheumatism, but nothing more deadly than a strip of aspirin tablets. He had been sure there were some Mogadon in there somewhere. Mary had obviously hidden them or taken them with her. Fucking good lass, he said ironically, registering how slurred his speech was, you've missed your big chance.

An eyebath, caught by his sleeve, fell and shattered on the tiles. He searched for a brush and dustpan. Failing to locate them, he started to pick up the tiny shards of glass with his fingers, cursing the dingy light and his failing eyesight. They were spread over a surprisingly large area of the floor. As he stood up to throw them in the bin, he noticed his thumb was oozing blood. He had obviously cut himself without noticing.

He made his way back to the living room sucking his thumb and then plunged it into his glass of gin. To his surprise it did not sting.

'Fuck it, kid, you've got leprosy,' he said, sitting down on the

11

couch. His voice sounded drunk and far away. The tropical sun still beat down on the adventurers. His eyelids were heavy. It was easier to focus on the screen with one eye shut.

The sound of the signal tone from the television, a single piercing note indicating that the evening's programmes were over, woke him up. It was just after 1 am. Fuddled and tired, he dragged himself up to bed. No energy left for destruction. No time for any further thoughts of failure. Tomorrow was a working day. He had a business to run.

3

Wednesday morning was winter at its best, crisp and clear and hopeful. Jim drove with confidence through the deserted backstreets of Southdale, past boarded-up factories with their fading For Sale signs, until he reached, quite abruptly, the roundabout which took him on to the southbound carriage of the motorway. The road to London was, at that point, slightly elevated, giving him an excellent view of what was left of industrial Britain for a mile or so, until he passed into something more resembling open country.

He was glad to be on his way. Tuesday had been an anticlimax after Monday's meeting. Alan and Martin had been able to come up with precious little new information on Chris. His briefing had consisted, therefore, of not much more than a general political pep talk spiced with scraps of fatherly advice, the details of Crispin's present address in a village called Carlton and directions on how to get there, the names and addresses of two reliable comrades in the same general area whose help he could call on, and some hopelessly anecdotal information on the power struggle which had removed Chris from his position in Northburn – information Jim had largely ignored since few of the participants were personally known to him. Well, the facts he had, plus the travelling money, were all he needed. He could take it from there.

Crispin as a person, the blood and bone behind those facts, was the bit that intrigued him. His record, which Jim knew in outline, was one to be proud of. A strike led, bitterly fought, and carried to victory while he was still an apprentice. A reputation as a public speaker established before he left the youth section. A gold medal awarded for winning recruits in his early twenties. And so on up the ladder, tried and tested in a dozen kinds of struggle. Until he lost a battle. For being right too soon. Then, bang, he was up and away. Off selling antiques and never seen since. That was the puzzling bit.

Puzzling and disturbing. Because he had to assume that the old revolutionary from Northburn was still there somewhere, buried under the rubbish, and that he, Jim, had the political force to rekindle the spark. After all, he had staked his reputation on doing so, in the face of varying degrees of scepticism from his comrades.

Ah, fuck it, he thought. Nobody had any better ideas. I've reactivated supposedly hopeless cases before. There's generally still something there, when you get behind the defences they've erected to justify their inactivity. All it means most times is that nobody has put the argument properly. I bet nobody has spoken to Crispin in years. The old bugger is probably raring to go. Or will be when I've chatted him up a bit. Hurt pride becomes habitual, unless someone breaks the spell. I'd probably be rusty myself if I'd been poncing about down South. I'd need coaxing back into action by a bright young lad too.

He had forgotten how flat and boringly rural much of middle England seen from a motorway could be. Enemy country personified. Calculated to take its vengeance on working motorists by putting them to sleep at the wheel for the few moments necessary to send them and their vehicles to their doom.

He decided to stop and break the tedium at a service station. There he sat for half an hour in a large cafeteria, drinking coffee and smoking and looking the waitresses over. It was not really a hell of a good way to pass time. Just another sort of tedium, another penalty for living in the wrong sort of society. Nothing in these damn places seemed right. Even the records on the jukebox sounded like they were being played slightly too fast, just to make a few extra coppers' profit. And the waitresses were strictly only for the lonely.

He thought a bit about his own career in the Party. Different from Crispin's, for sure. He had come up in downbeat times; he had only seen the tail-end of the great mass movements and working-class actions which Crispin would have taken part in, and taken for granted. He had seen the other side – deindustrialization, declining class identity and morale, increasing authoritarianism and repression, internal battles of striking bitterness within the Party. And now a whole new ball game. Armed resistance. Well, those were the times he had lived in. All the way through he had been the Party's man. That much he had in common with Crispin. That was his starting point.

It was time to move on. He drove into London, from where he made some phone calls and arranged to spend the night with one of the comrades whose name he had been given. He was called Paul Lodge and he lived some ten miles from Crispin.

After that he took his time driving into Kent. The scenery came as a surprise to him. Rich-looking country, even at the back end of the year. Land worth fighting for. No wonder the ruling class had grabbed it all.

He had arranged to meet up with Paul at six o'clock in a pub on what had once been the main road from Dover but was now abandoned to the natives. Jim's prejudices led him to expect fake oak beams, brass ornaments and commuters, with perhaps the odd fox hunt thrown in. To his surprise the pub turned out to be scruffy and patronized by men in working clothes. And the beer was drinkable too.

Paul Lodge turned up after a few minutes and at once made him feel at home. A tall, burly man in his mid-thirties with an impressive beer gut, he wore national health standard-issue black-framed glasses which gave his face a boyish appearance. A lorry driver by occupation, his conversation was a rapid-fire mixture of obscenity, humour and sharp political observation.

'Now then, Jim, you cunt, what have you brought us, a bootful of coal or a basket of pigeons?'

14

'I've got some tripe sandwiches, if you're peckish.'

'What do you do with them, shag them or eat them?'

'Suit yourself. You have to catch them first.'

'I gather you want to catch Crispin Pharaoh?'

'Is he hard to catch?'

'No harder than herpes, and about as much percentage. Planning to take him back to clog-land are you?'

'Not for good, Paul, we just want to borrow him for a while.'

'Feel free, my son. Crispin has been about as much use to us as a spare prick at a wedding.'

'As bad as that?'

'Oh, we tap him for money and he's quite generous. Blood is a bit harder.'

'It's blood I need.'

Paul looked straight at him. 'Yes, I'll believe you.'

'What's the best way to approach him, Paul?'

'He'll be at home now, I should imagine. We can give him a ring and I'll introduce you.' He dropped his voice. 'From here would be safer. I get some funny bastards listening in on mine at home.'

There was a pay-phone in an alcove off the bar. It just about took Paul if he left his belly outside.

'Mary, hello darling, is your old man in?' He put his hand over the receiver and turned to Jim. 'She's just going to get the cunt out of his coffin.' He turned back. 'Now then, Chris, I've got a visitor staying with me who wants to meet you. Lad called Jim Carson. Bit of a cowboy. Picks between his toes. But he's kosher. I'll put him on.'

They changed places. Jim came straight to the point.

'Crispin, I have to speak to you on some Party business. Can I come and see you at your shop tomorrow?'

The voice on the other end came as a surprise. It was strong, with a harsh edge and a marked northern accent. Not your average Kent village antique merchant. Jim's spirits rose.

'Yeah, I close half day Thursday. Why not come round then – say, one o'clock?'

'Fine'.

'You sound like you come from my part of the world, lad.'

'I do, as it happens. Southdale.'

15

'Good. I look forward to seeing you then.' He did not sound 100% convinced of it.

They went back to their table.

'Thanks.'

'What did you make of our Crispin, then?'

'He didn't sound too bad. A bit cagey maybe.'

'Well, you were coming on like a frigging Gestapo. No finesse, you northerners. Get him up against a wall and fuck him till you get what you're after, eh?'

Jim laughed. 'Just obeying orders.'

'I shudder to fucking think. Look, Jim, do you fancy going back to my place now? My missus will cook us some food and we can have a chat about things, as much or as little as you want to say. We can get some beer in if you want a drink.'

'Sounds good. I've got a bottle of whisky in the car.'

'You're on. We'll get a few cans to take out and get going, then.'

They stood up, strangers who felt confident in each other's company.

'What's for tea then, jellied eels?'

'Cheeky cunt. Don't forget your bearskin.'

4

There was nothing that Crispin could see to choose between the two vases. Nothing that would have made him dither about for half an hour like this lady. It was mid-morning and they had the shop to themselves.

He had been working for some time on a hangnail, and now it had started to respond to his attention by sending spasms of nervous agitation through his body – a sensation so painful that he thought for a time he was going to have to make an excuse to leave the shop. Fingers, toes, penis, nipples, every extremity tingled. His breath was short and he felt pains in his chest.

Crispin knew what it was about. Unusually, he had not had a drink since Sunday and although the first, soul-wrenching devastation of the hangover had passed, he was still a bit strung-out. He fought the feeling down. This was no time for me nerves, doctor. This was a time for swift, decisive action.

'Mrs Snee, if you'll be guided by me, my dear, this is the one for you.' He turned the vase in question round in his hands. 'Both nice pots, of course, but this is the one you should take.'

Mrs Snee smiled coyly. It was what she had wanted to hear, the climax of a skilfully prolonged play of love.

'Yes, I'm sure you're right, Mr Pharaoh. Your feel for what will suit me is always so perfect. I'm sure you can see how they will be when I've got them settled in at home. It's a real art you have. Could I take it now, and drop in to pay you on Saturday?'

She always did this. She had the money, of course; probably had a handbag stuffed full of it on her right now. But she liked to think that this worldly-wise north country antique dealer regarded her as a specially trustworthy and privileged customer. Humouring her fantasies was all part of the act like the Romany name and the carefully casual dress.

'Of course, Mrs Snee. Pay me whenever it's convenient for you.' You empty-headed old bitch.

After Mrs Snee had departed in triumph, he went through to the back of the shop and poured himself a glass of malt. It was a sensible move: once he had got the whisky down him he felt infinitely more settled and more rational.

He was not sure what to make of last night's phone call. Paul Lodge was a conventional enough middle-cadre type, who no doubt despised him as much as he would have done had their positions been reversed. But, from the brief words he had exchanged with him, he had placed Jim Carson in an altogether different category. He had leading comrade stamped all over him – young, keen and pushy leading comrade – and he came from Northburn or somewhere thereabouts, to boot. Trailing clouds of puritan glory no doubt. Whatever Jim was after, it was more than an arm and a leg, that was for sure.

But just exactly what he could be after intrigued him. The Party had gone through a period of intense factional struggle, emerging weakened and altered, and Crispin was not at all sure

17

where its self-destructive urges were leading it now. Except, apparently, to send leading cadres from Northburn way to knock on his front door. Now that was a turn-up for the books. He smiled to himself as he permitted himself a tiny drop more of the malt. Come back, Crispin, all is forgiven. Come back and get fucked again.

In the course of the next two hours he had three callers. One of them was the milk-man and the other two did not buy anything either. When Jim turned up it was obvious he was not a customer. He wore a collar and tie and he strode through the shop as if its contents would contaminate him if he lingered.

'Jim Carson?' asked Crispin, coming to meet him. They shook hands, looking each other over as they did so. Jim was very much as Crispin had pictured him – a smart, energetic youngster, with no hint of doubt in his eyes. Crispin came as more of a surprise to Jim – bigger and tougher-looking than he had expected, apparently in better shape than his contemporaries on the regional leadership. 'I'll shut up shop now you've come. Then we can have a chat through the back.'

They sat facing each other across a kitchen table in the back room, under the pendulum of an antique clock, as Crispin poured out two whiskies.

'Paul Lodge get you pissed last night?'

'We had a few bevvies, yeah.'

'Get that down you, then.' They drank. 'Now tell me what sends you here from sunny Northburn.'

'Southdale, actually, but it concerns Northburn.'

'Ah yes, Southdale, you said on the phone.'

'Well, Crispin, the regional leadership met on Monday – '

'It has been known,' Crispin cut in drily.

Jim laughed despite himself. 'OK, just so you're clear on who I'm speaking for, being as how I was still dodging the school-board man when you left Northburn.' He took a sip of whisky. Crispin found himself warming to him. 'The thing is, we're trying to set something up in Hardcoats. All the cadres around there have pissed off or got themselves arrested. We need someone reliable with local knowledge to help us. You were my suggestion. I sold the idea to the other comrades, which is why I'm here.'

18

'Well, I'm flattered someone your age has still heard of me. Hardcoats was never really a Party area. Rather petit bourgeois. What are you trying to get going there?'

'It's not so much the place, Crispin, as the factory – ROF Hardcoats.'

'That fucking place. Best thing you could do with ROF Hardcoats is burn the bugger down.'

'That was more or less what we had in mind.'

Jim had caught him in mid-swallow. He sprayed whisky across the table.

'Jesus fucking Christ, you're not serious?'

'Well, it's a bit more complicated than – '

'OK you're serious. Then you're crackers. Not you personally, the Party. Alan is in charge there now, isn't he? Jesus, from opportunism to adventurism in one easy move. Take a tip from me. Go home and tell him to get stuffed before you all end up dead.'

'Hang about. I'll accept that this is new territory we're getting into, Crispin, but we're talking about the Party responding to objective changes in the political terrain – a deepening of the crisis, in fact a very rapid and qualitative deterioration in political conditions.' Crispin nodded to show that he was not disputing this background analysis. 'What we're asking of you is that you lend us your local knowledge. We would not expect you to be involved in the actual operation.'

'The operation being what exactly?'

'A sabotage exercise at the ordnance factory to highlight the fact that production there is being geared towards tooling-up for domestic counter-insurgency. You may have seen the documents about that leaked in the press?' Crispin nodded. 'This exercise will be one of a number in different parts of the country, timed to coincide with the anniversary of the introduction of the Domestic Emergencies Act on February 1st. It's not terrorism in a vacuum, Chris. There'll be strikes and demonstrations on the same day.'

'By sabotage you mean what, exactly?' asked Crispin, sticking to the point.

'Explosives.'

19

'The Party has suddenly developed an expertise in this field has it – sort of political dynamite?'

'Well, we have experts, yes.' This was pure bluff. Jim had been given no details at all of the possible logistics of the operation. The question had never arisen at Monday's meeting, and Jim had not given the matter much thought since. He assumed the Party would provide, as always. But he had to admit that Crispin's sarcasm made him just a little uneasy.

'So all you want me to do is open a few doors for you? Then your commandos can do the rest. Is that it?' The sarcasm in his voice was becoming more marked.

'I'm not saying it's going to be easy. If it was – if we were talking about any old factory – we wouldn't need your help. But you can see why Hardcoats would be of enormous propaganda value, can't you, and why it's worth trying to overcome the difficulties?'

Crispin poured more whisky in silence. Out in the shop a clock struck at random. It was about the daftest proposition he had ever heard. He was not even sure why he was listening to it. The fact that Jim himself appeared to be horribly sane and the certainty that his scheme had the full backing of the Party only strengthened its unreality. There must be some damn funny things going on inside the Party if this was what was coming out. Perhaps this is what happens when you spend so much time fighting each other, he speculated. First you get paralysed into inactivity. Then, by the reaction, you do something loony. Like pushing the auto-destruct button.

And yet part of him envied the young man sitting opposite, sipping his whisky cautiously. He was not really arrogant, not like an old and powerful person could be arrogant, but he was sure he was right. He could not really see the problems, only the potential, only the objective.

And he was *doing* something. That was important, for Christ's sake. Most of the things Crispin had ever done – the scores of pickets he had stood on, marches he had taken part in, leaflets he had written – had probably ultimately achieved nothing politically. But doing them had been important. You can't be a revolutionary unless you do revolutionary things, often and repeatedly. How often had he heard comrades, half-jokingly, say something like, 'Give me a gun and I'll do a job of work for you'. And then he'd persuade them to do something more mundane, like stand on a corner in the pissing rain selling papers. And the argument, the clinching argument, would be – *do* this for the Party. We need you to do this task. Never mind why. Don't question whether it is effective. Just do it. Because theory without practice won't work. As he had found out to his cost of late.

'Look, Jim, it's not really for me to argue with you about how sensible or viable this scheme might be. You would only come back on me and say I was out of touch, and of course you'd be damn right. How long were you intending to stop in Kent?'

'I've got to report back to the regional leadership next Monday. You could say I've got until then to persuade you.'

'That's honestly put. I suppose Alan and Co think you're flogging a dead horse with me anyway, do they?'

'Like I said before, it was my idea. They went along with it for lack of an alternative.'

'I'll bet.' He took a sip of scotch. 'You can stop with Paul a day or two?'

'Yes, no problem.'

'OK. Well, here's my offer. I could spend a little time with you over the next few days giving you a run-down on everything I know which could be of use to you. For what it's worth.'

'It would be worth a lot, and I'm grateful. Of course what I also want to do is persuade you to make a trip to Northburn. You've never been back, have you?'

'No, if I was into holidays, I would take them in Spain, like any good antique dealer. Frankly, Jim, there's no way on God's earth I'm getting drawn into this lunacy. I'm an old man and bombs are bad for my health. Look, let's go and have a pint now. Then we can fix up to have a further discussion later. I'll also suggest one or two places you could visit while you're here. Ever been to Kent before?'

'No. First time.'

'I suppose the comrades told you to visit Betteshanger colliery and other scenes of historic struggle?'

'They also warned me you were a cynical old bastard.'

'Well put, our kid. Come on, let's have that pint.'

21

Outside, Jim cast his eyes over the main street while Crispin locked up the shop. Deserted now, he could picture it full of sightseers in the summer. It was tailor-made. Even the bank was mock half-timbered, with a tub for flowers at the door.

'Pretty, isn't it? Won third prize in the best-kept village award last year. What do you think?'

'I think we're bombing the wrong place, Crispin.'

5

When Crispin let it be known to Mary that he might – just might, you understand, love – be thinking of paying a short visit to Northburn with Jim, and could she manage the business without him for a couple of weeks, it probed an unexpected nerve of anxiety in his wife. It seemed uncanny, not to say downright unfair, that after more than twenty-five years of intimacy the old bastard should have retained this capacity to surprise her.

Of course she knew at once that his apparently tentative statement meant that he had already firmly resolved to go to Northburn and probably for months rather than weeks though he assured her, when questioned further, that all he had definitely agreed to so far was to travel up with Jim for a meeting in Southdale on Monday night to discuss a proposition. All very reasonable, on the surface, though she surmised from his manner that what was involved was rather more than a routine request for a bit of help with a campaign. God, wasn't he old enough to know better? Not that she had any rational cause to feel worried for his health or safety. Chris had been born a lucky bastard, and he had always survived everything that fate had thrown at him so far. There was no reason to assume he had lost his touch. It went without saying that she knew she had no chance of stopping him from going.

She realized her husband had taken a fancy to Jim from the

word go, and when he came to dinner on Friday night, flowers and wine in hand, she saw why. The young man was bumptious and cocky, but he had charm and he was no fool. In fact he was a good approximation of Crispin at the same age – a damn sight more like him than their own son, come to that. Not that the comparison had any meaning. The complexity of life, theirs as much as anyone else's, was designed to ensure that we all turned out different. Their son was what he was. Nature gives you so much and lets you fight your surroundings for the rest.

Mary did not resent Jim's influence on her husband. She grasped its essential superficiality. Chris was not the sort of man to be swayed by a comrade half his age, however persuasive. The plain fact was that he had been rootless and dissatisfied for years. His drinking, and the bouts of suicidal depression which it increasingly seemed to induce, disturbed her though, inhibited by long proximity, she had never got round to raising the matter with him. Jim's visit had simply acted as a catalyst, allowing him to grasp whatever idea had been floated and present it to himself as a solution to his problem. Stupid, of course. How could you find a solution in the world of politics to the process of ageing and the fear of dying? It was, she decided, a typical masculine delusion, a by-product of the cult of collective activism. But harmless, she guessed. Or, at any event, less harmful than drinking yourself to death. Because what would happen to me then?

Right now she just wanted him to come to bed. Propped up on pillows in a dressing gown, fresh from the bath, cigarette newly lit in her mouth, Mary peered at the cover of a novel, wondering where she had left her glasses this time, and reflected on her present need for human warmth and touch. The confused communication of marriage. You go to bed early. Signal clear enough. By the time he joins you, you've fallen asleep unaided. Signal also clear enough, but contradictory. Signals crossed. Double bind.

But not this time, she decided. Positive reinforcement coming up. I'll go downstairs and drag the dozy pig back to my lair. Signal repeated and copied. And if he won't come, I'll get the cat and stroke that instead.

She found Crispin sitting crosslegged on the carpet in the

living room, surrounded by a sea of political ephemera –
leaflets, press cuttings, notes for speeches, posters, pamphlets,
rule books of trade unions long vanished into amalgamations,
badges with portraits of heroes dead or forgotten, endless lists
of names and addresses.

'You know, love,' he said, looking up, 'I must have better
archives than MI5.'

'I didn't realize you still had all this stuff. I haven't seen it in
years.'

'Me neither. It's all good stuff, mind. The trouble is I can't
find the one thing I'm after.'

'What's that, sweetheart?' she asked, sitting down beside
him, turning over one or two papers in an instinctive gesture of
solidarity.

'My old phone book from Northburn. My secret weapon. My
ultimate deterrent. Guaranteed to blow all Trots, time-servers,
class traitors and revisionist wimps to hell and back.' He cocked
his thumb over two extended fingers of his right hand and shot
his wife at close range.

'That tatty green cardboard thing?'

'No sense of beauty. Everyone who is anyone is in that
notebook. It took me years to amass all those numbers.' He slid
his hand under her nightdress. 'You'll catch your death of cold
walking round with no knickers on at your time of life.'

'I'm surprised you still notice. But if it will get you up to bed
any quicker, I can tell you that your precious phone book is in
the bottom drawer of the dresser in the kitchen, where it's been
ever since we moved here.'

'Shit, that's right. I remember now.' He was on his feet and
through to the kitchen as he spoke.

'I haven't seen you this enthusiastic in years,' she said as he
returned, holding the dog-eared, hard-backed notebook with its
alphabetical indentations.

'Enthusiastic men make better lovers,' he commented, head
bowed, busily flicking through the pages.

'Then leave your souvenirs till the morning and come to bed,'
she said, standing up and putting her arms round his neck.

'OK. I'm just going to the bathroom before it's impossible.'

They went to bed and made love, and everything was perfectly satisfactory. Later on, with Crispin abandoned to sleep, she lay in the shared warmth, thinking of the future.

It was a fact of life that the more time ran out, the less real thought you gave to the one indisputable proposition, that it was not going to last for ever. A quarter of a century spent with this man. You ought to know him by now, Mary. He's been a good boy too long, making a living selling junk and drinking himself into never-never land between times. He must be bored stupid. He wants another crack at the game, whatever it costs. He can smell blood in the air and he's going to follow the scent.

Well, I don't give a sod for Northburn or any of his so-called comrades up there any more. Do what you like to them, Chris, and take your time. But come back in one piece, huh? We've still got things to do together.

6

Washed and shaved, standing six feet tall in his socks, Y-fronts and dressing gown, Crispin went through his wardrobe, selecting his outfit for the day. Jeans were out, sweaters were out, denim jackets and silk scarves were out, everything with a taint of antique dealer was out for now. Give me clothes fit for an activist, he said out loud. A good cloth jacket, well-pressed strides and a new shirt. And a tie. Red ties for funerals, but any colour will do for this trip. I haven't worn a tie in years. Blow the dust off and hope you can remember how to do the knot. Goodbye to all this frigging middle-aged bohemianism.

This one will do nicely. An old favourite, narrower than currently fashionable. And to go with it, a belt with a large ornamental buckle and heavy cuff links. I always dressed smart for a campaign; flashy, even, some comrades reckoned. No way am I going back looking like a scruff now.

He put the jacket on and inspected himself in a mirror. Not bad, you old poof. The phone book he had searched for the night before lay on a bedside table. He slipped it into his pocket. Just enough weight to make the jacket feel lived-in, and Crispin feel dangerous. Dressed and armed he went downstairs, to the smell of bacon and coffee.

'Two minutes, love,' Mary called from the kitchen.

He crept up behind her as she turned the rashers in the frying pan and squeezed her buttocks.

'Behave yourself.'

'I'll just clear those papers away while you serve up,' he said, walking through into the living room, where the archives were still spread on the floor from the night before.

Hurriedly he swept the debris back into files, envelopes and boxes, which he piled up in a cupboard. It's always a let-down, he thought, going back through these souvenirs – the leaflets, the press cuttings, the newsletters – hundreds of thousands of words, most of them with your name or mark on. And somehow what you are looking for is never there. The incidents that actually stick in your mind, and the comrades you shared them with, have always slipped through the net, doomed to be as mortal as yourself. Memory and history talk to each other in foreign languages. More fruitful to create some new moments than to try to recapture the ones that are gone.

He sat down to his breakfast opposite Mary who was drinking a cup of tea. Dieting again.

'What time do you expect to get back tomorrow, love?'

'Hell knows. Teatime maybe. I'll phone you from the station, eh?'

'OK. I'll come and pick you up.' She paused. 'Then I suppose you'll be back up to Northburn fairly soon for a few weeks.'

'Yeah, I'd imagine if we sort out things to my satisfaction tonight, I'll be off again in a few days.'

'Nervous?'

'Yeah.'

'It's been a long time.'

'I always was nervous before something like this. It's a good sign. Shows you're on your toes.'

'Well, take care. I don't really want to know what you're up to, Chris, but watch your back. You may be a crazy old drunk, but you're the only man I've got.'

26

If you did but know, my love.

'And I still screw pretty good for a geriatric, eh?'

'Not so bad.'

They held hands over the grease and the rind, waiting for the sound of Jim's car. When it came, Chris did not wait around. He leaned across the table to kiss her, and then went straight out to the car, closing the front door behind him. Like he had always done it in the past. The best way.

It was a damp, miserable morning. Conversation between the two men was minimal as they drove through Kent and into London. Respecting Chris's mood, Jim kept his thoughts to himself and played cassettes of traditional jazz to fill the silence in the car. Eventually it was Chris, conscious that he was being antisocial, who broke the ice.

'You've no thoughts of getting married, then, Jim?'

'Not unless I have to.'

'Probably just as well, if you're set on making her a widow.'

'Looking at the people I know who're active in the Party, I'd be more worried about paying divorce lawyers.'

'Yeah, there's always been a lot of that around.'

Jim decided it was time to tackle the underlying subject of their exchange. He pushed the eject button of the cassette player.

'Let me ask you a question, Chris. You were a full-timer for the Party for a good few years. Did you ever use violence in that time?'

Crispin thought about this for a moment. When he started speaking his eyes were fixed on the passing motorway verge, as if the signs for The North were some kind of gigantic cue card.

'I don't think I've ever struck a blow except in self-defence, personally. Oh, I turned a blind eye once or twice when comrades decided to kick the shit out of someone particularly objectionable – but that tended to be the coalfield comrades, and miners always had their own way of doing things. Bloody forbearing of me, when I come to think of it – at that time I used to get death threats at the rate of about one a week. I've been roughed up times many and seriously assaulted a couple of times, but I just kept on putting it down to experience. I suppose I'm suspicious of violence really, Jim. It tends to reduce the solution of complex political problems to a question of taking out this or that individual, instead of the real task of building a mass movement. It can become very élitist. You know the sort of thing I mean: "We are the Party of the armed vanguard – only armed vanguards need apply".'

'You presumably don't include the use of massed force – say on a picket – in your suspicion. I mean, there was far more of that sort of thing in your day than mine, wasn't there?'

'Oh sure. I never thought of that as violence. If you have a lot of police facing off a lot of workers, you're bound to get a bit of argy-bargy. I never thought much about that, as long as it was just a spot of shoving and a few arrests. These days it's all got a lot heavier; the police treat every group of workers on the streets as a riot, and the law backs them up. I can understand you wanting to have a go at them. A proper go, I mean.'

'But you don't approve?'

'I've got nothing against revolutionary warfare. It's got to be the normal road to socialism – Vietnam, Cuba, Southern Africa, right back to Mother Russia. I'm not sure we're at that stage in Britain yet, mind, but if we are, then so be it. No, what I'm against, Jim, is what used to be called propaganda by the deed – the individual acts of heroic terrorism that are supposed to galvanize the masses but never do. It's been tried in every generation from Bakunin to Baader-Meinhof, and failed every time. All it provides is a justification for more repression which the workers go along with, with the result that it sets us back years.'

'I wouldn't argue with that, Chris, but it's very easy to smear genuine, popular, armed struggle in its early stages with the terrorist tag. The point is you have to start somewhere. Castro and Che must have looked like a small bunch of isolated adventurers when they first started up in the Sierra Maestra. But they went on to make a revolution, didn't they?'

'Yeah,' Crispin admitted, 'against the Party's advice too in the early stages, as I remember. Well, you know the lesson to draw from that, don't you?'

'Right. Make sure you win or they'll damn you for ever.'

Crispin laughed, and Jim knew he had touched the right nerve in the man's experience. He had half turned round now and was looking at Jim.

'Let me just sound a note of warning, Jim. I've always felt the way to socialism lay through mass working-class action, guided by a working-class revolutionary Party – a Marxist, internationalist Party. A few years ago now I started to see that concept being derided in our Party as outdated and sectarian. We had to be fashionably anti-Soviet, form alliances with dykes and poofs and headbangers and take up every daft, trendy cause going. Well, we did all that – over my dead body, but we did it – and where did it get us? You know where it got us – fucking nowhere, or nowhere near socialism, anyroad.'

'Sure, they should have listened to comrades like you.'

'Then listen to me, Jim, because I think you're going from one extreme to the other, and in doing so you're going to make the same mistake again. It's dialectics, kid.' Crispin was leaning forward now, resting a hand on the dashboard. 'Adventurism is the opposite side of the coin to reformism. They're the left and right sides of opportunism. It doesn't matter which way it falls, because it's the coin that's bloody bent.'

'The difference is that we're talking here of selected acts of violence as part of an overall strategy of mobilizing the working class. The other strategy simply rejected the working class altogether.'

'Bollocks. How do you mobilize workers by blowing up their factory?'

'How do you persuade them that it's a bad idea to forge the instruments of their own oppression?'

'With great difficulty, in the case of them bastards at Hardcoats, I must admit.'

Crispin sat back again, lit two cigarettes, and passed one to Jim.

'Ta.' He smoked in silence for a minute, weighing up whether it was the best time to put the important question. 'But you've decided to go along with this, haven't you?'

Crispin paused. What a shrewd young bastard, he thought.

'Yeah,' he said after a minute, 'I've got to salvage something for us from this mess.'

Jim grinned in delight.

'Go on, you old chuff,' he said, 'you're looking forward to getting back into struggle, admit it.'

Crispin grinned back.

'Yeah, you're not wrong there, kid.'

7

I'm getting old, Crispin thought; even the North seems to have changed. A quarter of a century ago it must have been, when I was first driving down these same streets in Southdale to the same meeting place, a room above or below the Party's book-shop.

The bookshop had been past its best even then, a relic of the glorious days of popular unity against fascism, when workers saved their coppers and bought books and pamphlets in great numbers in order to learn the truth. Good days, so they tell me. Young Jim, sitting next to me here, probably thinks I go back to then. No, son, I'm not quite that ancient. I came in with the Cold War and you-never-had-it-so-good affluence and working-class militancy, and I stayed around long enough to see the decline into déclassé confusion and creeping authoritarianism. The good old days were before my time. In fact, take that as a general lesson of history. The good old days are always just before your time.

Just how has it changed, then? he pondered, looking out at the darkening streets. They're still dingy, as streets go; even the cobbles are intact in some cases. And the factories are still there, even if they have sprouted Closed and For Sale signs.

Smoke. In a word. It was the absence of smoke that summed up the change. A warning that he had lived through a profound revolution in technology. At one time you could have told where you were with your eyes closed, even if the car window had been wound up, just by the smell that hung in the air and caught in your nasal passages. But not any more.

Cities used to mean smoke. Trains smoked. Factories smoked. Houses smoked in their endless terraced ranks. And the people grew to match their environment, never seen without a cigarette or pipe in their mouths. Hang a shirt on the line to dry in them days, and it came in dirtier than it went out. My Christ, they'd cleaned up cities like this since then. It was all central heating, new technology and No Smoking signs now. I might as well be back in the rural idiocy of Kent for all the smell of industry I'm getting.

'Jesus, Jim, it looks dead as fuck round here.'

'It is, comrade, it is.'

'Workers all used their redundancy money to buy themselves little fish and chip shops, or started window-cleaning rounds, have they?'

'Absolutely. They're all part of the broad democratic alliance now. Your working class is dead. Didn't they tell you, Chris?'

'Except for this one last factory you want to blow up?'

'Well, yeah, we have to complete the historic process.'

'Ride the tide of history with the surfboard of dialectics.'

'That sort of thing.'

Jim parked the car a good half mile from the shop on a piece of derelict land inhabited by heavy goods lorries and builders' skips. As Crispin climbed out and stood up, easing the stiffness in his joints, he felt something familiar hit him – the cold. He had experienced plenty of cold weather in winter in Kent but this was different: the real, authentic, cutting, cruel, ball-shrinking urban cold.

And it brought back a rush of memories. Campaigning was about learning to endure that cold. Feeling it numb you, killing concentration, choking conversation as the dawn broke on a picket line. Or as you hawked papers to a sceptical population with frozen fingers. Or marched with aching arms, holding a tightly spread banner against an oncoming wind. It was the unappreciated physical side of being a revolutionary. You had to be tough to take it. He had known that cold kill activists, wear them down over the years, taking its toll along with the missed meals and the endless cigarettes and the drinks taken at all hours.

So at least the cold is still there, he thought, pulling the collar

31

of his car coat up over his cheeks and bending his head as he walked into the wind, along the familiar streets to that familiar building.

'Bringing back memories?'

'Yeah, one or two. I must have been to some bloody meetings at this place. Meetings of the regional leadership. Getting my monthly orders to take back to Northburn. I'll bet it's just the same. Different faces, same old song.'

He was not far wrong. They were waiting for them in the downstairs room. He had forgotten how bleak that room was, a caricature of revolutionary austerity.

Crispin looked them over, trying to put names and characters to faces. Alan, the chairman now, he barely remembered. Martin he knew well enough; a bit of an opportunist, but with a ready and redeeming wit. And Frank. He was a nice guy, thoughtful, quite sound politically, someone he remembered with affection. He could not put names to the other two – one was a big-built bloke who looked like he would go a few rounds; the other a nervous young man of about Jim's age whose hands twitched as he smoked. Well, it took all sorts to make a revolution.

'Remember this place, eh, Chris?' said Martin.

'Fucking right,' he said, shaking his hand. He gestured towards the quasi-mural propped against the wall. 'Still got that monstrosity, I see. I ought to do you a favour and take it off your hands.'

'How would you get it out?' Jim asked.

'Saw the bugger in half.'

'I think that was how we got it down here in the first place,' said Frank, 'in the old days, eh, comrade?'

'We were all more artistic then,' said Crispin, winking at Jim.

Alan took charge at this point.

'Well, it's good to see you here safely, Chris. Do you like to be called Crispin Pharaoh these days, or would you prefer Chris Powell while you're back up North?'

There had to be something to this Alan, Crispin decided. It takes a certain talent to ask a question like that with a straight face.

'I answer to Crispin Pharaoh. But both names shorten to

32

Chris, so use that.'

'OK. Now you know Martin and Frank. And Bill?'

'No.' He shook hands with the tough-looking man. The grip was predictably overdone. Come on, he thought, grinning slightly, you didn't really think I'd be limp-wristed did you?

'We've had apologies from Lou, who's involved in an important union election.' Crispin registered the name vaguely, at the same time thinking how they spoke in clichés. How many times must he have described a union election as 'important', as if they were in a habit of getting involved in any other sort? 'Steve Brown is here from the National Executive, to give their viewpoint.'

My God, thought Crispin, shaking hands again, so that's who the youngster is. I must be teetering on the brink of the grave. Policemen started looking young decades ago, and even hospital sisters looked young sometimes these days. But when the Executive member comes down from the mountain with his tablets of stone and he looks that young, you had better watch out. I can remember when they used to scare the hell out of me, even on the telephone.

Crispin was conscious of a hiatus. Nobody seemed to know what to do next. So, for the hell of it, he took the initiative, aware that he was being sized up, made the subject of the inevitable questions – What's he like? Has he changed? How will he handle this? Can he deliver?

'Comrades, it's been a few years since I last sat here. So, just for old time's sake, perhaps I should kick things off?' Alan nodded approval. 'When Jim approached me on your behalf to ask for my help in this project, I must admit I thought you had all gone crackers. I'm still, frankly, sceptical, and I'll be very interested to hear what the National Executive member has to say when his turn comes round because, of course, I am a bit out of touch with developments in Party policy.

'But for all my reservations, I do feel, having given the matter some consideration, that I have some kind of duty to respond to this request positively, especially since it does seem that the success of this project could depend on my local knowledge, such as it is.'

And I bet that surprises some of you bastards, he thought.

'Young Jim has obviously used all his eloquence on you, Chris,' said Frank. 'What's your domestic situation these days, comrade?'

A humane question.

'I'm twenty-five years wed, Frank, and more. My lass will back me, as she always has, and she can manage the shop without me for a few weeks. She won't be in a position to send me any pocket money, though, so I would need ordinary Party wages for the duration, plus expenses. Contrary to rumour, I'm not a rich man.'

'Just comfortable, eh?' said Martin. 'Don't worry, we'd see you all right. Tell us where you're at politically, Chris.'

'Not so much into violence as you bloodthirsty bastards, by the sound of it,' he said, looking at Steve Brown who was making copious notes longhand. Steve had his head down and did not respond. At least on a cardiograph the pen would have jumped, Crispin thought: he's not human, he's a frigging android. 'At the time I left full-time Party work, I had a number of criticisms of our political practice. I felt we were spending too much time on marginal issues – women's liberation, gay rights, stuff like that – making too many concessions to bourgeois democracy, not concentrating enough on the central class issues, abandoning proletarian internationalism as a principle –'

'Becoming reformist?' Frank suggested.

'Poncing about,' Bill glossed.

'Exactly. Both. That's all well known. I haven't been particularly active politically since I went to Kent, and I guess you know that too. But I have followed developments in the Party and although I haven't been involved myself directly in the inner party struggle, I did feel it had, generally speaking, been going in the right direction.'

'But you've got some reservations about this latest project?' asked Alan.

'Yeah, sure. Not because I've got anything in principle against armed struggle. Believe me, if we had been into armed struggle in my day, I wouldn't have taken any prisoners. You could still shoot all the bastards as far as I'm concerned, and good riddance. So I'm not pleading emotional pacifism now.

Moreover, I fully accept that the growth in state authoritarianism, the deepening of the political crisis, the semi-legality, to all intents and purposes, now, of our Party – all these things put armed struggle more and more on the agenda.

'But, yes, I do have reservations. I want to hear more about this particular idea. You see on the surface it does sound a bit divorced from mass struggle, a bit adventurist, a bit like "propaganda by the deed". And it's a lot unfamiliar, isn't it? You have to go back to General Ludd for precedents on blowing up factories in this neck of the woods.'

'Good local lad, Ludd,' said Martin. 'Rawfolds Mill and all that. Mellor and Booth.'

'Before my time,' said Crispin.

'Well perhaps we could ask Steve to put things into perspective for us,' Alan suggested.

At this stage Crispin lit a cigarette, adopted an expression of intent concentration, and switched off. He had already decided to cooperate, and the official rationale for his future actions did not bother him much. His motives were so confused, he would just have to work them out as he went along. Anyway, National Executive members at meetings like this had always bored the shit out of him as they dotted *i*s and crossed *t*s through good drinking time. Jim could tell him about it later; he was young enough to take it seriously.

As it happened Crispin's assessment turned out to be accurate. Steve spoke in a monotone, punctuated by regular and ineffective attempts at rhetoric, which amounted to little more than raising his voice and addressing them directly as 'comrades'. He spent one quarter-of-an-hour period giving a review of the domestic political situation since 1945, another describing the present situation, and yet another scouring the globe of the twentieth century for examples of armed struggle. None of this was particularly controversial. Crispin switched back on when Steve got down to cases.

'The operative date, as far as we are concerned, is February 1st. Which means that, with holidays intervening, time is short. February 1st is, of course, the anniversary of the introduction of the Domestic Emergencies Act. We hope to mark that anniversary with demonstrations, industrial action, and direct attacks on at least six targets, selected for their symbolic importance, throughout the country. If the National Executive approves of your plans at its meeting this weekend, you'll start work straight away.'

'Can I ask a question?' It was Jim.

'Go ahead,' said Alan.

'It's about technical arrangements. How we do it, in other words?'

Not before time, thought Crispin. Let's see the bottom line.

'Your job will be to prepare the target – find out the layout, check out any problems, and recruit whoever you need to plant the explosives. We'll supply the materials and an explosives expert when you're ready.'

I shudder to think. Probably some crazed IRA veteran they've picked up down Kilburn way.

'Have you got any questions of Steve, Chris?'

'Yeah, I hope you're intending to destroy those notes you've been taking.'

Steve blushed, putting down his pen. 'Yes, of course.'

Martin winked at Crispin. One to me.

They kicked things around for half an hour. It struck Crispin as pointless and he contributed little to the discussion. The scheme was going to go through for that most basic of reasons – inertia, the lack of an alternative. And once it had gone through, all he had to do was find the weak points of a factory he had never been inside, chat up a few people who worked there to risk their necks in order to destroy their livelihood, and then blow it up. Simple as that. A veritable piece of piss. A job for an antique dealer.

Bill read his mind.

'I want to ask Chris a straight question. It's about lifestyles. You've been eight years selling antiques down in Kent. Can you still get through to the workers at Hardcoats – or anywhere else?'

Them's fighting words, comrade.

'Bill, it's a straight question, and I'll give you a straight answer. I've been in the Party for thirty-five years. Sure, I've been earning my living down South recently – not my decision exactly, don't forget that, but I'm not ashamed of the fact. I've had as much experience of labour movement politics as anyone here. And I know that area. It was my patch for a lot of years, and it was fucking well-organized in my day, I can tell you. So don't you worry. I can talk to workers – even in a shit-hole like Hardcoats.'

'If you're saying yes to the idea, how soon could you start?' Alan asked.

'Next week. As I said before, I'll want wages and I'll want Xmas off.'

'The comrades here will set you up in a flat,' Steve said. 'HQ will pay wages for you and an assistant if you need one, plus any expenses.'

'OK. Do I get to pick my partner?'

A slight pause. What's the crazy bastard got up his sleeve?

'Do you have a suggestion?' Alan asked cautiously.

'Sure, I want young Jim.'

'Thank Christ for that. We thought you wanted another furniture salesman,' said Martin.

'I think we could spare him. How about it, Jim?'

Jim had not expected this at all; simply had not considered the possibility. But he felt irrationally good about the idea – flattered to hell, chuffed to buggery.

'Yeah, I'd like that. I think I could learn a lot from Chris.'

'And you can teach me how to commit suicide, kid.'

And this way we can keep an eye on you, thought more than one person in the room. Everyone was happy. The vote was a formality.

8

Crispin and Jim were now partners, and partners have a duty to get to know each other better. After the meeting was over, the two men took themselves off to a working men's club which offered overamplified vocalists, foul-mouthed comedians, the rituals of bingo and cheap beer. Welcome home, pilgrim, thought Crispin, some things don't change at all. Since it was the only welcome he was going to get he plunged into the spirit of the thing, laughing, clapping and marking his card with the rest of them, as if entertainment was going out of fashion. By the time he got back to Jim's flat he felt wide awake, overstimulated by nostalgia.

There was no way he was going to get straight to sleep after that; not in a strange house at the end of the day when he had made a decisive, and probably insane, commitment. Lying on Jim's couch after he had gone to bed, wrapped in a blanket, smoking cigarettes by the light of a gas fire, he reviewed the meeting at the bookshop.

It had been a strange sort of occasion – part interview by the committee, part lecture by young Steve, with a large element of Hobson's choice floating in the background. In many ways he had found the committee itself a pleasant throwback – all male, all proletarian and most of them long in the tooth – none of the strident feminists, muttering youths and bombed-out sociologists he had remembered from the tail end of his time in the game.

The bedrock of their politics seemed sound too, if a little pedestrian. In fact that latter element was probably their fatal flaw, he reasoned. It had to take a certain lack of imagination to recover from supine opportunism only to plunge blindly into wild adventurism. But it was not fair for him to judge or condemn. He had been out of it for eight hard years, during which time they had survived all the battles he had dodged. It was no great surprise if they had emerged punch-drunk or shell-shocked, and all too eager to punch that auto-destruct button which comes with every political model.

Jesus Christ, he thought, stubbing out his cigarette, we switch lines with casual drama because we've actually got quite used to the idea that we can't agree on anything for more than five minutes at a stretch. Just like the big bad world around us really, sunk, with all its confusions, in national paralysis. That's why we no longer offer a coherent challenge to society; we mirror it too well subculturally. That's why it's for the best that we fight it out among ourselves. It's our best hope of renewal, of achieving a new unity. No society can survive for very long without rules it agrees on, and it's the same in our political microcosm.

My God, there was a time when we knew that too. The Party I joined was a rock. I trusted it absolutely and after a while the Party and I became so closely identified that I was not sure where one ended and the other started. But now the Party is lost and I'm lost and I've come back to it for the comfort of being lost together.

Because what do I, Crispin Pharaoh aka Chris Powell, stand for? Exactly what I stood for thirty years and more ago. My class riding on history's back to political power. Except that just at the moment my class isn't going anywhere, because my class is deindustrialized, demoralized, disorientated, becoming more and more like its own caricature as reproduced nightly in clubs like the one just left. It was heading that way when I pissed off and left it, and it sure as hell hasn't improved since. So why have I come back? To add to the confusion? To help with the destruction? I'm asking myself how I got into this, and I don't even know.

And it's worse than that, he added, groping for another cigarette, feeling the cold on his arms as they reached into the shadows round the fire. Because if I'm honest, I've got another reason for going back to Northburn besides blind kamikaze loyalty. I want to know exactly what went wrong eight years ago. And I want to get even.

Facing that committee tonight it had all come back: not just the same regional committee as it had been eight years ago, but his own district leadership back in Northburn. And he felt the long-suppressed bitterness creeping into him. He had got the hell out of Northburn, and stayed out, because he had no desire to be either a resident opposition or a prince across the water. But that principle was breached now: he was back, and the bitch revenge was baying.

There had been seven, himself included, in his inner cabinet, and when the crunch came they had split three/four. The line-up was clear enough, though exactly what lay behind it in terms of organization he had never been able to determine – himself, Jeff and Terry on one side; Pamela, Ian, Tom and Alex on the other.

Jeff had stuck by him through all the arguments and conspiracies, making himself ill in the process. Looking back, he had probably already been suffering from the lung cancer that was to kill him a couple of years later. He remembered him now with a lump in his throat – a big-boned, rough-arsed man, his skin weather-cured from the years working on the buildings – in the simple certainty that he would never see his like again.

Terry he had never been so close to personally. But give the lad his due because he had stuck by him to the finish in that fight. Unfortunately he had drifted out of the Party's orbit since that time. Chris gathered that he had also given up his post as a trade union official in favour of some quite important job in local government but he was unclear on the details. Certainly he would be someone to look up when he got to Northburn.

Alex had also left the Party; indeed he was now a local councillor under other colours. A college lecturer, he and Chris had never seen eye to eye politically. Funnily enough, he was one man he felt no bitterness towards. His opposition had always been open, a simple reflection of political incompatibility and relatively insignificant. Alex had not been the motive force in the campaign against him.

Nor had Pamela. Indeed, in her case, he really only had

himself to blame. She had been a good ten, no, more like fifteen, years his junior and playing about with her had not been a good idea – particularly when he stopped. He should have known better. Most of the great unexplained shifts in political alignments he had seen over the years had turned out, on examination, to be traceable to changes in sexual partners. He was not even sure if she was still in the Party. He had heard that she was now married to a businessman and doing social work, which would be two good reasons to assume she was not. And probably she would not be mad keen to renew her acquaintance with a skirt-lifter from way back either.

That left Ian and Tom, one or both of whom must have been in at the start when it came to organizing against him. In the case of both men, the betrayal was deeply felt, partly because they had been so close and partly because he should have had the wit to see it coming.

Ian had been an ambitious young bastard – bright, personable, not unlike his new partner, Jim, but with a shade less charm – and he had been Crispin's protégé. He had pushed him a long way in a short time, right up to the National Executive in fact, despite his youth. He could remember taking him into the Gents at a conference, right on the deadline, getting him in a corner and giving him the hard word, arguing like hell until he had persuaded him to accept the nomination with only minutes to spare. Christ, I'd like half-a-crown for every political argument I've conducted in the piss-house; I've been at conferences where there were more delegates in the bogs than in the hall. And he had been proud as hell when Ian had gone on to win that Executive seat, and then had risen to the challenge and shone in that new setting. Only to be stabbed in the back by the sod two years later.

Well, it was all business. No point in taking it too personally. And Ian was not in a position to do him any further harm. Driving somewhere in a hurry on Party business he had met a lorry head-on and died instantly. That had been four or five years ago.

Tom was at the other end of the age-scale and Crispin had inherited him as district chairman, a post which made him literally his right-hand man, always by his side at meetings and party to all his actions and decisions. They had worked closely for years, gone out together with their wives on a Saturday night and resolved all their outstanding problems over a few pints; operated as a team without ever really examining their relationship too closely.

Well, it's funny how taken-for-granted friends can become born-again enemies, Crispin thought, stretching and scratching his armpits. They had never really fallen out in the formal sense, even when Tom's switch of allegiance became public. They acted like men, like comrades, all business and icy politeness. Mary, on the other hand, never spoke to Tom or his wife again. Someone in the family has to show some emotional honesty, he thought wryly; perhaps I'm starting to catch up after all these years.

Tom was out of the picture now, retired from his work as an engineer after a heart attack, in poor health apparently, and no longer involved in Party life since his wife's death. Crispin found himself hating him, hating him more now when he was down than he had when he had been on top, and puzzling at the intensity of his own irrational feelings.

Yes, thought Crispin, I should have sorted all this out years ago, before it started to fester. Now it's just frustration that's coming out. The realization that I've done nothing in eight years and meanwhile everything I left behind has crumbled to dust. Worse, really, than being proved right; being proved irrelevant.

It's a fucking good job you can't see inside my head, young Jim. You'd be wondering what kind of bastard partner you'd saddled up with.

He stubbed out his cigarette and lay for a few moments, hands behind his head, listening to the hiss of the gas fire in the quiet of the room. Then he stretched over and switched it off, leaving himself alone in the darkness.

9

In the natural order of things, a man would overwinter, waiting for the spring to sail for home. To travel seeking adventure in the depths of winter, and especially to seek it in old haunts and killing grounds, was perverse. But the Party had commanded and they would obey. Over the hills and far away.

Within a week, Crispin and Jim had put their respective affairs in order and moved to Northburn where they rented a sparsely furnished flat in a decaying Edwardian house near the city university. Although several miles from Hardcoats, it was an ideal base area for their purposes – run-down, anonymous, with enough of a floating population for two more to make no difference, and so few long-standing residents that Crispin was not going to keep bumping into old friends and enemies. As a bonus, their landlord spoke little English and used his son, a boy of eleven or twelve, as an intermediary when conducting his business.

Northburn lay thirty miles to the north of Southdale. It was a city which had sprung up from nothing during the industrial revolution, stabilized itself around a huge town hall in Victorian times, and then extended itself by swallowing up the surrounding towns and villages, both physically and administratively, until it reached its present size of three quarters of a million citizens. Traditionally its factories and mills had been situated to the south of the city centre, along with much of its working-class housing. To the north, beyond the university and a swathe of inner-city decay, lay the more prosperous suburbs, safe on the high ground.

Development to the east and west was less easy to categorize. Hardcoats, which was on the eastern edge of Northburn, had originally been a village. Later the name came to be applied to the suburban housing which crept round it in the 1930s, and later still to an adjacent council estate built in the 1940s.

It was also applied to the ordnance factory, which originally had been built in green fields and had taken its name from the village. Generations of workers had referred to this indiscriminately as either 'Hardcoats' or 'the ROF'. The latter title, short for Royal Ordnance Factory, was now, strictly speaking, inaccurate. The move to the right in British politics had knocked the Royal out of the factory. Denationalized, it now belonged to a consortium whose loyalties transcended the boundaries of the nation states to which it sold its products.

Hardcoats was a particularly characterless part of town. The private housing was not rated as especially desirable; by contrast the council estate, relatively speaking, was. As a result the population was homogeneous – stable and conformist. There were few pubs, no clubs, no large shops. The ordnance factory was the only industry and because it covered a large area, and was landscaped with trees and flower-bedded earth mounds it was, in practice, curiously invisible. Altogether, Hardcoats was not an obvious sort of place to start a revolution.

Crispin came back to Northburn looking for physical changes, but these were not immediately obvious. The redevelopment boom of the 1960s and 1970s, the last fling of post-war prosperity, had been visually dramatic. The deindustrialization that had succeeded it was not. A closed or run-down factory looks much the same as one in full production to a casual observer. Only gradually does the truth dawn that parts of the city are now clinically dead – factories, pubs, shops, all gone and the grass growing on them – and that the city itself is no longer concerned with production, the creation of wealth, but only with distribution; that it has become, in fact, a hollow, glossy temple of parasitic consumerism.

From Crispin's point of view, the political changes were more immediately apparent and dramatic. Not only had his own Party vanished from sight; all the little signs of political life across the board had gone too. Nobody painted a slogan on a wall near your bus stop, or pushed a leaflet full of anger through your letter box, or opened a shop where you could buy the books and newspapers which they did not stock at Smiths, or held up your car with a demonstration. And nobody, but nobody, talked about politics – in the queues or at the hairdresser's, on your doorstep or in your workplace, everywhere, except in the licenced confines of the television studio, politics was a taboo subject. Talking about it, people seemed to be signalling, will only make matters worse.

And meanwhile the police were everywhere in evidence, cruising around in their cars, looking for signs of trouble. He had forgotten about that. They did not do that in Carlton. There it was by invitation only.

For the first two days Crispin hardly stirred from the flat. Instead he spent the time reading and making notes and discussing ideas with Jim.

His method of work, if it was work, fascinated Jim. It seemed both random and systematic. Random in that he would send Jim out to get copies of every local paper and then trawl through them, looking for nothing in particular. But systematic in that whatever caught his eye would be ringed with a marking pen and the information later transferred to a notebook.

The notebooks intrigued him also. He would watch Chris divide each page vertically down the middle with a thick pen line before he started writing. On the left of the line went the raw information; on the right, his reaction to it. It was a simple technique Crispin had learnt to use at meetings when, at the same time and in a great hurry, he had to make a note of what a speaker said along with the bare bones of how he intended to reply to it. What Jim was watching were the now antiquated and obsolete skills of the orator and agitator. Indeed they were potentially dangerous skills in an era of secrecy, where notes could be seized and used in evidence against you. But it was Crispin's style, and Jim felt a compulsion to learn from it.

At the same time he nursed a nagging worry that perhaps Crispin had as little idea as he did of where to start work. He was not quite sure what he had expected Crispin to do, but he felt it should be something more positive than simply reading and making notes. He was impatient, and behind the impatience he recognized a growing element of fear which only positive action could banish.

He gave Crispin full marks for bottle as he broke in the furniture and the ashtrays. The older man seemed perfectly relaxed, in no hurry, as if the minor business of blowing up a factory would soon fall into place once he had got back on top of local affairs.

When Crispin did finally decide to break the surface and make contact with someone, it was not quite what Jim had expected either. The person concerned was a journalist on a local paper, and Crispin arranged to meet him in a pub out in the country.

'This guy Clive,' Jim asked, 'is he in the Party then?'

'Fuck no, he hasn't much politics. But he's a good journalist.'

10

The Stag at Bay had two things going for it as far as Crispin was concerned – he had never been there before in his life and neither had anyone else he knew. It also turned out to serve a good pint and a tasty steak sandwich. They got there shortly before noon and took command of a table in a quiet alcove in preparation for Clive's arrival.

Jim knew that Clive was an old drinking mate of Crispin's. When he turned up, he had no difficulty in spotting him across the bar. Clive wore his occupation like a uniform. Red-faced, dressed for sleeping on a park bench, a notebook sticking out of the pocket of his raincoat, he looked the part to the point of caricature. A small silver lapel badge in the shape of a crucifix suggested a religious orientation. Apart from that, there seemed to be nothing out of place in his friendship with Crispin. Certain trades – politicians, journalists, entertainers, criminals – do a lot of their business in pubs and make natural drinking companions. Crispin and Clive seemed an example of one such partnership.

Rather to Jim's surprise, considering the fact that they had not met for eight years, the two men got down to business straight away and Crispin's approach, if not honest, was at least direct.

'I need a favour, Clive. It's certainly out of order, and probably illegal, so just say if you can't do it.'

'That sounds like the old Chris. What do you want me to risk my job for now?'

'Do you still ignore your principles and go to all the press junketings the military, and the arms manufacturers, lay on?'

'I leave most of them to the youngsters now, Chris. When you've tried on one helmet, or played with one machine gun, you've seen them all. Anyway, we tend to be below the salt for the champagne and smoked salmon; they palm us off with beer and sandwiches.'

'You're breaking my heart. You've seen the controversy about this latest contract at Hardcoats?'

'Sure. Your lot have just discovered that tanks can kill our workers as easily as someone else's. That makes sense, you know. Being a pacifist I'd worked that one out years ago.'

'We're catching up with you, Clive. I've been asked to do some research on the Hardcoats situation for the peace movement. I need some background information.'

'Secret plans you can microfilm and send to Moscow?'

'The usual sort of thing, yes.'

Both men laughed.

'I hope you're not corrupting this young lad you've got with you.'

'Jim's corrupting me. At least that's the theory. Go and get some beer in.'

By the time Jim got back with fresh pints, Crispin was inspecting a rough lay-out plan of the Hardcoats works, which Clive had sketched on a beer mat.

'And you can get me details of what work is being done in which shop?'

'Sure. I got all that sort of detail and more when they showed us round. And all the hand-outs about the new work will

47

be around somewhere, untouched by human hand, I should imagine. I can dig that stuff out for you this afternoon and put it in the post.'

'I'd appreciate it, Clive. It's for a good cause, believe me.'

'That I do not want to know. You're a good bloke and I'm happy to help you out. But I'd sooner remain in ignorance about the details.'

'Then I don't need to worry if you'll crack under torture. One more thing you might be able to help with. I don't think the management would talk to me, but someone from the unions just might. Do you know who is convenor there these days?'

'No, not off hand. It's not the sort of place that throws up newsworthy militants, as you well know, particularly now they have the no-strike clause. I guess our industrial reporter would know; he's a mine of useless information. I'll ask him if you like.'

'Please.'

'I'd have thought you could ask one of your engineering members.' The eyes were probing.

'The fact is, Clive, I'd be just as happy if not too many of my old friends knew I was here.'

'OK. That's your business. Is that it, then?'

'That's it.' He held up his hands, palms outwards, as if to prove the point.

'Then let's talk about something more pleasant than weapons of war. How is Mary?'

Jim half listened as the two men shared the accumulated news of eight years. It surprised him that old friends could leave these pleasantries until their business was completed. But both men had been well trained. They knew that the work of a two-hour lunch, properly handled, takes ten minutes. Better, then, since the two-hour lunch is an institution worth protect-ing, to get business out of the way while the head is clear. That way nothing gets overlooked, the institution is not discredited and the serious drinking does not get interrupted.

'Come in for a warm, have we?' Jim asked, rattling his empty glass on the table.

'Cheeky young bastard, isn't he?' said Crispin, standing up to get his round in.

'How long have you been working with Chris?' Clive asked,

as Crispin moved through the growing lunch-time crush to the bar.

'Not very long. He's breaking me in.'

'Well, you look like you can handle it. He's a hell of a character is Chris. I don't know what he's like as an antique dealer, but he used to be dynamite as a political organizer.'

No pun intended, Jim thought.

'Oh, he still is. How did you come to know him, Clive?'

'Partly professionally. And partly through the anti-racism movement. I came into that through the church. Some of the political people were suspicious of us – as we were of them – but not Chris. He was always 100% non-sectarian, very open, and I enjoyed working with him. You know, he's a man I'd trust. Honest, and that's rare. Also he liked a pint, which helped.'

'This guy is a fervent alcoholic,' said Crispin, rejoining them, 'don't let him convert you.'

'We were just talking about the old days, fighting racism.'

'Yes, they were good days,' said Crispin. 'All sorts of different people, working together openly for a common end, which is exactly the way it should be. Now we're all hiding in our different foxholes. It seems a fucking long time ago.'

Jim caught the sadness in his voice. He wanted to be working again with decent men like Clive against a clear and simple evil. Instead he was pushed into conning them and compromising them, for the sake of a cause he only half believed in. And, it had to be said, doing it very well. With all the flexibility of a great revolutionary.

Jim felt light-headed with the drink. He sensed that the others were more sober than he was. He wanted to tell Clive what a clever operator Crispin was and how essential it was for world peace, or whatever turned Clive on, to make this explosion in Hardcoats. And he felt ashamed, realizing that these men had gained more than a head for drink with their maturity.

Well, make allowances for yourself, he thought, because you're only a young lad, and this Crispin Pharaoh is a very cool customer, a real expert. You're just getting the hang of working with him; baffled or exasperated one minute, full of uncritical admiration the next. Just like being in love, kid.

He had become aware of someone over by the bar who kept glancing at them as he fed money into a fruit machine. It was the sort of person who looked at home in a bar – well padded and hail-fellow-well-met and not inclined to stare at strangers without a good reason. He finished playing the machine, drummed his fingers on it for a few moments, appeared to hesitate, then made his decision and approached their table. As he did so, Jim kicked his partner on the ankle to alert him.

'It's Chris, isn't it? Remember me? I used to work with Terry in the union. Are you living back up this way again?'

Crispin's face showed nothing but innocent pleasure as he rose to shake hands. Jim guessed that the Terry he referred to must be the former union official, now a town hall manager, whom he had heard Crispin mention as one of his leadership in the old days.

'Sure, I remember you, Ernie. I'm just up for a day or two on some family business. What are you up to these days?'

'Working for myself, to tell you the truth. I've got a little garage business near here.'

'Still see anything of Terry?'

'A bit. I'm seeing him tomorrow night as it happens, for a jar. Fancy coming?'

'I'm a bit tied up tomorrow, Ernie. Tell him I'll give him a bell before I go back, though.'

'You ready for another?'

Everyone was, and they drank as a foursome for another half-hour until Clive had to get back to work, and then a while longer until his business called Ernie. If Crispin felt any irritation at being recognized, he did not show it. For that matter, he did not give away a damn thing about what he was actually doing either. His conversation was an exercise in good-humoured evasion.

By the time they were on their own, the pub had emptied considerably.

'First in, last out,' said Crispin.

'Where does meeting Ernie leave us?'

'There's no problem. It just means I'll have to get to Terry before Ernie makes him curious and he starts asking round about me. I wanted to look him up anyway. I'll just bring the date forward.'

'Happy with Clive?'

'Yes, I think I got what I wanted.' He drained his beer. 'Time we were going, kid.'

Standing in the stalls in the Gents, Jim realized that he was slightly distanced from his surroundings; on the way to being drunk, in fact.

'Fucking hell, I feel a bit pissed.'

'Christ, lad, it's me that's supposed to be out of practice with the northern ale. Do you want me to drive?'

'It might be an idea,' he said, fishing the car keys out of his pocket and then proceeding to drop them on the floor.

'Have a piss on them before you pick them up, there's a good lad,' said Crispin, 'they've probably got germs on them by now.'

11

With the first blow struck and some ale on board, Crispin was in an expansive mood. He drove at a steady pace while conducting a monologue that was part commentary on the passing scenery and part reminiscence.

One story got a bit involved. Something about a meeting out this way, and a young comrade giving Chris a lift there because his car was off the road, and then boozing after the meeting until past midnight because no bugger had ever heard of licensing laws out that neck of the woods, and then as soon as they set out for home the comrade's car packing up on them. And Crispin wanted to doss down in the back until morning once he had established that there was no garage open in miles, but the young comrade was just recently wed and naturally if he stayed out all night his wife would think he was carrying on with another lass, so he persuaded Chris to hitchhike with him. And didn't they walk all fucking night, getting back at dawn, not a fucking lift in sight? And didn't the comrade then insist on Chris coming in to help him square his wife up? Christ, and they did, too. You wouldn't believe it, Jim, on my life. Woke her up. Half-five in the morning. Made her listen, while Chris told the story. Then the two lovebirds went to bed, leaving Chris with a cup of tea and terminally sore feet to wait for the first bus.

At which point in the story, Crispin drove through a red light and was promptly flagged down by a police car which U-turned across the road behind them.

Crispin stopped and wound down his window. Two officers had got out of the car and were approaching them on either side, so Jim wound his window down too. This is it, he thought, fucked before we start. But keep cool. They don't seem to be armed, so they're probably just on traffic duty. Crispin can handle this. Jesus, I hope so.

'Is this your car, sir?'

'No, it belongs to my passenger.'

'What's the registration, then?' said the other policeman.

Jim found the words to tell him.

'Can I see your licence?'

Crispin passed it out of the window.

'Right then, Mr Crispin Pharaoh, what did you do just then?'

Jesus, thought Jim, he actually has a licence in that name. This is unreal.

'I went through a light on red.'

'Yes, you did. And why was that?'

'To be honest, I didn't see it till it was too late. I don't know this road very well.'

'You were talking to your friend, weren't you?'

'Yes.'

'Instead of concentrating on the driving.'

'Yes.'

'I keep having to scrape up idiots like you. When they crash into something hard and solid while they're chatting to their pals. Have you two been drinking?'

'Yes.'

'Is that why you're driving instead of the owner?'

'That's right.'

'Do you have your documents?' asked the second policeman.

Jim took the insurance and MOT from the glove compartment and handed them over.

'They're in order,' said the policeman grudgingly.

'Step out a minute, please, sir,' said the first policeman to Crispin.

Out of the car, Crispin stood taller than the officers. Jim caught snatches of the conversation as they lectured him. Crispin's style was magnificent, neither too aggressive nor too subservient. He was playing it by the rules. Challengers and victims get arrested. Crispin did not. They did not even test him for alcohol. Eventually they allowed him to get back into the car.

'On your way, gentlemen, and in future, watch out for red lights.'

'Thanks.'

'You were fucking cool,' said Jim as they drove off.

'Couldn't afford to bugger up a national campaign of terror and destruction, could I? I wondered about trying to bung them some money, but they seemed to be straight lads, so I just kept my fingers crossed their shift was almost over.'

And then to Jim's amazement, Crispin launched into another anecdote as if nothing had happened. In this story a coach-load of engineering workers had got stranded on the motorway on their way back from lobbying the TUC at Blackpool, all because the bugger who booked the bus did it on the cheap and ended up with one that conked out at the first opportunity. So while they were waiting for the replacement coach to turn up a few of them, full of Blackpool beer, had got out for a piss. Then someone had spotted blackberries growing on the motorway verge. Huge, juicy blackberries, like you remember from childhood, growing in profusion because, naturally, not many people came to pick them on a motorway. And, you might not believe this, but they all started to pick them, like kids on an outing, putting them in carrier bags to take home.

Until the cops showed up, and fuck, did they bawl us out? Straight up, I thought they were going to bust the lot of us. Of course we had crossed three lanes to get to the blackberries. And one of the lads did shout fascist pigs at the cops when they turned up. Not very tactful, that, in the circumstances. So that back there wasn't so bad, Jim, kid. By comparison it was easy.

And it really did not seem to be an act. As far as Jim could judge, Crispin was genuinely not bothered about being stopped. It was just an interlude in a journey down memory lane. The latest anecdote sounded amusing, but Jim found he could barely concentrate on it. He was shaking and sweating with tension, realizing now how little it would take to sink their enterprise. Supposing it had been a few weeks later and they had been loaded for action? They could have wrecked a whole national campaign in one go, and taken the entire Party down with them. This type of struggle was a whole new ball game – requiring different standards of behaviour, different levels of discipline – to traditional legal activity in the labour movement.

He wondered whether Crispin, with his background, grasped this point. Probably not. You can't teach an old bolshevik new tricks. But it had to be said that he had the nerve for it. Sheer brass neck. As cool as fuck.

Crispin seemed to read his mind.

'Tell you what, though, kid, I think I'm going to have to restrain my natural, law-breaking, anarchistic tendencies this trip. I wouldn't fancy facing Alan and Co, not to mention leading comrade Steve Brown, God bless him, and having to tell them I'd set back the revolution six months by going through a red light.'

'Imagine if we'd been carrying the explosives.'

'Yeah, it doesn't bear thinking about. We'd have ended up hanging by our thumbs for sure.'

'The whole committee, eh?'

'Steve accusing me of Maoist tendencies between screams of pain.'

'Maoist tendencies?'

'Aye, back during the Cultural Revolution, red lights meant go in China.'

12

The best kind of bastard to have on your side, Jim decided, was definitely a lucky bastard. Because when Crispin got a big brown envelope in the post the following morning, courtesy of Clive and his employers, it turned out to contain not only a plethora of up-to-date information about Hardcoats, but also the name of the convenor. He was called Ted Atha. And many years before, he had served his time alongside Crispin Pharaoh, then Chris Powell, in a well-respected engineering works long since gone to grass and rubble and dreams of progress.

'He's a cunt,' was Crispin's verdict, 'but he's a lazy, conceited, stupid, grabbing cunt. That's four possible ways we can get to him.'

But Ted could wait until tomorrow. The priority, in Crispin's mind, was to get to Terry before Ernie did, and he had duly fixed to meet him that afternoon in a drinking club in the town centre, stressing to him over the phone the fact that his visit to Northburn was not to be widely publicized. Jim got the distinct impression that, whatever Terry's past credentials, he would be only too keen at this stage to play down any connection with Crispin.

The club, which was small and dingy, was attached to a Catholic church and was presumably intended primarily as a private watering hole for its congregation. But there are many paths to God, and sudden conversions have been known to happen. By the usual process of deals and understandings, the club had acquired an afternoon clientele of people who worked in, or around, the town hall, and had both the facility and the inclination to slip out for a drink when the pubs were shut. Thus did two revolutionaries end up bending the law in company with a motley collection of barristers, bureaucrats, police officers and other notional converts to the Old Faith.

It sounded like a nightmare venue for their purposes, and Jim had expressed misgivings. However, precisely because it did not occur naturally, it was the sort of setting where privacy could be created and respected in a small space, and once they had got sat down round a corner table over a bottle of beaujolais, they found they could talk freely, if quietly.

Terry was the sort of youngish middle-aged man who looked like he had made it in whatever he did, that whatever being harder to determine, but had paid a heavy price for doing so. Most of his hair had gone, and his neck bulged over his collar. He smoked incessantly, holding the cigarettes in podgy fingers with too many signet rings on them, talked a lot as if trying to convince himself of some truth, and his eyes had a tired, rather dead look.

'What exactly do you do, over in the town hall?' Crispin asked, when they had completed the formalities of shaking hands and pouring wine.

'I push bits of paper and bodies around in roughly equal proportions. I'm responsible for personnel. I suppose that doesn't sound very exciting, put like that, but it's a living.'

'You've done well.'

'I felt that what the council was doing was progressive. When they offered me the chance to get involved, I took it. I miss the union in some ways, I wouldn't deny that, but I feel I can achieve more where I am now, in terms of the things I believe in. You probably don't agree.'

The latter remark was offered as a question, but Crispin chose to ignore it.

'I suppose you left the Party?'

'Oh, well, yes, a long time back, Chris. I wouldn't say my views changed really, mind, not all at once, anyway; but after all the business with you, the Party went sour on me somehow. Not only that, it didn't seem to be doing anything anymore, if you know what I mean. Or maybe it was, and I didn't know. I guess you've heard lots of renegades excusing themselves by saying that it was the Party that changed, not them, eh? I drifted out, rather than leaving in a blaze of glory. I'm not sure they even noticed that I'd gone. You're still involved, I take it?'

'Yes, I am. I'm working on a journalistic project with Jim here. I'd be grateful if not too many people knew we were here, if you follow me. I bumped into your old mate Ernie yesterday. I had visions of him running round town telling everyone I'm back.'

'That sounds like Ernie, he never was very sophisticated politically. I'll have a word with him. Is there anything I can help you with on this project? I'm not completely clapped out yet.'

'Possibly. It's to do with government interference in the trade union movement. I don't mean the legal side, the various anti-union laws, I mean MI5 stuff. In our day you used to get the Economic League and IRIS with their leaflets and bulletins, didn't you? And maybe the local Special Branch doing a bit of snooping and phone-tapping, but all quite small beer, really. Well, now we're starting to get evidence of quite serious infiltration and sabotage, and we're doing an investigation locally.'

Jim listened, amazed at Crispin's power of invention. Brilliant. It was a perfect silencing move, involving Terry in something he was not going to want publicizing. And it sounded plausible, certainly more plausible than what they were actually doing. Who knows, he thought, we might even come up with something.

'I can't honestly say I've seen any evidence of that where I work.' Terry sounded defensive.

'It's more in industry that we've had reports. For instance, in our old union we think that number 9 and number 15 branches have been used as a base.'

'That figures. They were always right-wing branches, both of them. Number 15 was mainly Hardcoats workers, for Christ's sake.'

'Have you still got any contacts in that area?'

'Yes, personal ones, you know. I still see some of the lads.'

'Could you make a few discreet enquiries for us?'

'Sure. I don't see why not. It's all for a good cause. What am I looking for exactly?'

'Anyone suspicious, anyone who stands out. Not only people talking like government hand-outs or retired colonels, but the opposite. Loony militants mouthing it off who could be plants.'

'A Trot hunt, eh? Now I have got a few of them bastards where I am.'

'Yeah, just like the old days. Except these Trots are being paid for fucking things up.'

'I reckon some of them always were. Yeah, I like the idea. How soon do you want the information?'

'As soon as you find anything. We should be around till Xmas. I'll give you a number to ring.'

Jesus, Jim thought. He's actually got the guy recruiting for us. I don't believe it. If you want some nutters to plant a bomb, then why not try personnel?

The pattern was the same as the day before. Business completed, the conversation moved into a discussion of the old days.

'Do you still see any of the comrades from my day?'

'Not many. Most of them have gone, one way or the other. Jeff is dead, of course. A real tragedy, that. And Ian too, though that wasn't so much of a tragedy in my opinion. As for me, I suppose you would say I'd reneged and I couldn't really quarrel with that. That goes for Alex too; he reneged all right. He's doing very nicely. I see quite a bit of him, with him being on the council now. Small world. I'm not sure he'd want you to remind him of his revolutionary days, now he's training to become an elder statesman. Who does that leave?'

'Pamela. And Tom.'

'Pamela is another renegade. Lives in a big posh house with a sugar daddy and does good works on the side. I'm bloody sure she wouldn't want to be reminded of you, you old ram.'

Crispin laughed.

'Tom I haven't seen in years,' Terry continued.

'I gather he's pretty sick.'

'Serves the bastard right.'

Jim caught the overreaction. You're pathetic, he thought, watching the trembling signet rings grope for a cigarette. Slagging Tom off is not going to make you any less of a renegade, for all your self-justification. He did not like Terry very

58

much. If he could do them some good, fair enough; otherwise, fuck him.

'One thing I've often wondered in my spare moments is who really did the organizing against us.'

The 'us' was a nice touch.

Terry thought for a moment. 'Alex gave me a lot of slaver at the time, but it wasn't him. Maybe Ian, maybe Tom, I don't know. I think probably Tom. He'd have got the word from up above somewhere. Yes, he'd have kicked it off, and then, of course, Ian would have got in on the act, because he was ambitious and he'd have wanted to be on the winning side.'

Crispin nodded. 'That's how I'd read it too.'

Silence fell over the table. It did not seem to suit Terry. He cast his eyes round the club as he picked nervously at the label on the wine bottle.

'Chris, I've got to get back to work before I'm missed. It's been nice seeing you again. I'll give you a ring in a week or so. OK?'

'OK, old mate. Stay lucky.'

Jim watched him make for the door, cigarette in mouth, turning up the collar of his sheepskin coat as he did so.

'Well, you played him along, you bastard. What a cunt, eh?'

'So you didn't like my old comrade Terry?'

'I thought he was rubbish. What amazes me is how someone like that is still apparently willing to help you. You must have really been his hero.'

'No, I don't think so. I was never that close to Terry, though he did support me politically. Terry wasn't a bad bloke really. He's like a lot of comrades, I think. He's sincere enough, as far as it goes, but he lacks political depth. He drifts with the tide of events, and it takes him away from the Party. He doesn't consciously change his views, but they do change. Because the circumstances of life, and the man involved in them, and his views, are all interconnected. You have to avoid taking an idealist view of these questions. Remember what Marx said about Feuerbach, about the coincidence of the changing of circumstances and the individual's actions being revolution-izing practice? He'd have understood our Terry very well.'

Jim recognized the passage referred to, though he had never

fully understood it and was not sure he had got the point now. Crispin did not very often talk in theoretical terms. It was a side of him he did not know much about.

'So he drifts into thinking like a council bureaucrat because that's what he's doing, but put him back in a situation of helping the Party and he'll adjust his thinking accordingly, is that what you're saying?'

'It's not that conscious even. He's in a logical trap, a trap created by the logic of his own history, just as he's also in a trap created by the logic of his current situation. The fact that the two traps contradict each other is neither here nor there.' He poured the last of the wine. 'It's exactly the trap I was in down in Kent. In Carlton I'm an antique dealer, with all that that implies. I'm pissed off with the whole scene, but there's nobody I trust, or who would understand what the fuck I'm on about, that I can talk it out with. Trapped in the logic of my subculture, with no way out. Until you come along and break that trap, just as we've done with Terry and Clive and we're going to do with some more before we're through.

'Mind you, all I've done is to exchange one trap for another. I disagree profoundly with what you, with what we, are doing right now – but who the hell would understand that disagreement except ourselves? It's a disagreement within our subculture, a family quarrel, and I'm trapped inside it. I have to do this, for all my reservations, because the alternative is an alienation too awful to contemplate.'

'Damned if you do, and damned if you don't.'

Crispin shrugged.

'Heavy stuff. I signed on for life. I shouldn't grumble if the going gets rough. At least I'm back with the family. I'll tell you what, this place gets on my tits. Let's push off somewhere else.'

13

After eight years in the land of jellied eels and rock salmon, where they serve you oversized and overpriced pieces of cod wrapped up in the most wimpish of batter, Crispin had an insatiable appetite for sensibly sized and cheap portions of fish and chips, properly fried in beef dripping and eaten fresh hot from the range. And he knew exactly where to go to get them.

The shop was in a backstreet just off the town centre. Its long, stainless steel range was fronted, at peak times, by several friers, while as many as eight women wrapped orders along the counter. Behind the scenes, a back-up team kept the frontline staff supplied with buckets of chips, fillets of fish and freshly made batter mixture. It was efficiency with a human face. You could join a queue of thirty or forty people stretching out into the street, and be served within five minutes. And if you wanted to eat your scran right there and then, they even provided a corner of the shop where you could stand, with a counter to rest your paper on.

There was nothing Crispin could fault about the place – superb service, a quality product, a portion suited to everyday consumption, and all at less than half the London price. Fuck the Yanks, he thought. We invented fast food up here, along with skilled engineering and decent beer. There's not a right lot of it left, lad, so grab it while you can.

They ate their tea out of the paper, sitting in the car.

'Miss this down South, do you?'

'It's the worst bit. That and the beer. The rest is not so bad. The women are built the same way, and you get the hang of the

61

language after a while.' He gesticulated with a piece of steaming cod, emphasizing his point.

'I could use a pint after that wine.'

'Yeah, me too, I could kill one. That wine whets your appetite but you don't feel like you've had a drink, somehow.'

'Do you know somewhere we aren't going to bump into all your old mates?'

'Yeah, I think so.'

They went to an old working-class area where most of the houses had been demolished years before, leaving four pubs standing in splendid isolation within sight of each other. With more pubs than people, and plenty of room for parking, it had become a natural pilgrimage spot for boozers. There was an expectation that the visitor would spread his custom round all four pubs, taking a couple of drinks in each. Which was only fair, since each served a perfect pint – with the emphasis on pint, since these were rugby league and pool table bars where middle-class real ale freaks sipping halves were frowned on.

They spent a leisurely evening doing the rounds, supping beer and talking about working-class life, a phenomenon that seemed to have more continuity there, in what was virtually a time warp – a comforting, beery, masculine, proletarian womb – than it did walking the new shopping centres of Northburn, a democracy for those with full purses, or the prizewinning toy-town streets of Carlton. It was a necessary recharging process. They needed to convince themselves that at the basis of their beliefs lay more than golden myths and lost countries. And by closing time they had just about got there.

They drove home by a route that avoided the city centre, but involved negotiating a number of badly lit backstreets. Turning into one of these, at no great speed, Jim braked as a slight impact registered from the front of the car.

'What was that?' said Crispin, groping on the floor for a lighted cigarette that had fallen from his fingers.

'A cat. I'd better get out and have a look. I think I caught the bugger.'

'Waste of time,' said Crispin, with callous authority. 'You might injure a dog with a car, but not a cat. They move so fast, they either get away or they're killed outright. Nothing in between. Your moggy's gone, kid.'

Crispin turned out to be correct in his hypothesis. The cat, a young black one, was stretched out on the pavement several feet from where it must have struck their car. Though not obviously damaged, it was clearly dead.

'I think we've found its owners,' said Crispin, nodding towards two old ladies standing in the doorway of a house on the opposite side of the street.

'Shit,' said Jim quietly.

'Told you not to get involved,' said Crispin, picking up the cat and advancing with it held before him towards the doorway. 'You'd better park the car.'

He sized the ladies up. It was not too difficult to work out that they were sisters, and almost certainly spinsters. The house was an old drum, a rather neglected property which he assumed had once belonged to their dead parents. Their age was harder to determine; somewhere over sixty, but not necessarily much over. It was disappointment that had diminished them, more than age.

'I'm sorry to trouble you, but we hit a cat. Is it yours by any chance?'

'Yes. We never let him out, do we Elsie? He slipped past me just now when I was putting the milk bottles out.'

His big break for freedom, and he blew it.

'We braked, but he was going very fast. I think we just caught him. He's dead, I'm afraid. He wouldn't have felt a thing, I promise.'

'It's not your fault, love,' said the other lady. 'He wasn't used to going out at all. I'd left the living room door open, and he must have slipped into the hall and past my sister when she put the bottles out.'

Jim had now joined Crispin, who was beginning to feel the incongruity of the situation, conducting a friendly conversation on a strange doorstep with a dead cat in his arms.

'Shall I bring him inside?'

'Yes, if you would, dear.'

They were ushered into the living room, among the ornaments and family photographs. It was the sort of room where you felt cold unless you were standing directly in front of the electric fire. For want of any better idea, Crispin sat down on the couch, still holding the dead animal, as the two ladies hovered around him.

Finally Elsie summoned up the courage to touch the cat.

'Are you positive he's dead?'

'Yes,' said Crispin, quietly but firmly. 'I'm sorry.'

'He's still warm.' Just a hint of obstinacy starting to creep into the voice.

'He would be, love. Believe me, he didn't feel a thing.'

'He's not marked.'

'He might just be stunned,' the other lady added.

'I'll tell you what,' said Crispin, sensing the growing potential for hysteria, 'if you get me a mirror, I'll check if he's breathing.'

He had just noticed the bottle of cheap sherry on the sideboard, and the glasses on the table. The two old birds had been on the piss; probably been half sloshed for years. He wanted to get out before they made a scene.

'There's one in my handbag, Elsie.'

The call for positive action calmed them a little. The mirror was produced and he held it under the creature's mouth to demonstrate that it would not mist-up. Instead, a few drops of blood fell from its nostrils on to the glass. Good idea that mirror, thought Crispin, it's saved my strides. The blood was bright red and thick.

The sight of the blood, rather illogically, seemed to convince the sisters that their pet really was dead.

'Could you put him down in the cellar for us?'

'Yes, then we can see to him in the morning.'

'It wasn't your fault.'

'He never went out normally.'

The stairs to the cellar were inside the house. They ushered him down and showed him where to put the corpse, on an abandoned armchair underneath the coal hole.

Back upstairs, life resumed.

'Would you like a drink before you go?'

'We've got some sherry, if you'd like a drop.'

Jesus Christ, Crispin thought, now how about that for a macabre idea? Catch a falling star and put it in your pocket and don't let the bugger go. I bet we'd be the first men in a good while to have a drink here. I wonder which one is supposed to be mine? And don't you make any cracks about them being my generation not yours, young Jim. That's a bit near the bone.

'That's very kind of you,' said Jim, sounding like every mother's favourite son, 'but we'd better not. We're driving, you see.'

'Oh, of course, we forgot.'

'In fact, if there's nothing more we can do, we'd better get off,' Crispin added, turning to his partner. 'Your mother will be waiting for us.'

The ladies saw them to the door, wishing them a safe journey, and stood framed in the doorway until they had driven off.

'Well, that's one each, kid.'

'How do you mean?'

'Slip-ups. Breaches of security. At this rate, if the police don't get us, the RSPCA will.'

'You're a callous bastard.'

'Yeah, maybe, but imagine trying to explain that to the comrades. "We had to abort the mission after Jim ran into a spot of bother with two sherry-swilling old biddies and a dead moggy. Sorry, Alan, better luck next time." Fucking magic.'

'I bet Fidel never had this trouble, eh?'

'No way. You just don't get cats like that in the Sierra Maestra.'

14

They spent the day reading and rereading the information about Hardcoats which Clive had sent them. In between times they took a drive out to the factory.

To Jim it seemed a pointless exercise. What, after all, did they see? A security man in an office by the main gate. Behind that, flowerbeds and a flagpole. Then the various buildings and the landscaping around them (some of which looked like it was designed to contain and localize blast damage – Jim wondered if, at some stage, the place had been used to assemble munitions, or had they been expecting them all along?). They even saw a couple of samples of the finished product standing under tarpaulin. Well, hell, he'd seen a tank before. It was no big deal.

Crispin disagreed.

'We have to get a feel for the place before we even start to talk to anyone who works there. You have to know something of the layout of the place; if possible, right down to where the lads would slip off to for a smoke and a look at a paper. You have to know what shops and pubs the workers will see when they clock off. In fact we ought to start having a pint up there ourselves. It helps to know where the various parts come from for assembly here. It helps to know the language – like the fact that they call the chassis the "hull". We have to start to feel at home with the place.'

'Why a hull, anyway?'

'When they first started making tanks back during the First War, they based production methods on the ones they used in making battleships. So naturally they used the same words.'

'OK. Point taken. I'll do my homework.'

In the evening they had a meeting with Ted Atha, who had agreed to see them after a union meeting. He had not sounded very keen on the idea over the phone, and he looked suspicious and ill at ease when he finally showed up, half an hour late. Dressed like a bank clerk and smoking a pipe, he did not look like he could ever have been on the same side as them in the class war.

The pub he had nominated for the meeting was full of young people, loud music and flashing lights. It seemed an unlikely choice for Ted Atha, who might have been born old. But for purposes of security it was near ideal, despite the fact that they had to shout at each other over the noise.

The conversation this time did not follow the pattern of those with Clive and Terry. For half an hour they spoke of children and grandchildren, changes in the town, their apprentice days, the state of the trade union movement – the full gamut, in fact, of safe topics – like two strangers in a barber's shop.

It was obvious that neither man trusted, or even liked, the other. Jim was not sure how Crispin intended to tackle the guy, unless he had a bundle of compromising photographs in his back pocket. Not a pretty thought. He found his attention wandering off towards two well-built black girls, showing some style in the sweep of the lights at the bar. Then Crispin gave it to him.

'Well, I expect you wonder what I'm doing back in North-burn, Ted.'

'Not looking for antiques, then?'

'No, I'm interested in the tanks you're building to kill workers with.'

'Cut the crap, Chris. Why should my lads go on the dole to satisfy your principles?'

'What's really impressed me is the energy that you and your pals have put into exploring alternatives to what you're doing at the moment.'

'Yeah, I've heard all that. Earth-moving equipment for the Third World. Machines for saving whales. You haven't changed at all, Chris – all slogans and fuck the practicalities. Trouble is, old son, when someone shows me a contract, I read the small print. My lads make tanks. Period. That's what we're paid for and it's what we intend to carry on doing. What the buyer uses them for is his business. I can sleep at nights.'

Jim had an overwhelming desire to break a glass in his face. 'That's the sort of argument the defence used at Nuremburg,' he said.

'Before your time, lad,' Ted retorted, like someone who had had practice.

'And yours. But I saw the movie.'

'Anyway,' Crispin waded in like a referee, 'I want you to show me how you build these tanks of yours, Ted, old lad.'

It was hard to tell whether Jim or Ted was the more surprised.

'You what?' said Ted, taking his pipe from his mouth and laying it in an ashtray.

'I'm doing a journalistic piece. Your democratic, freedom-loving, private enterprise gaffers won't give me normal facilities

67

to see the place. So I want you to fix it for me instead.'

'And just how the hell do I do that?'

'Simple. I turn up at the gate, thinly disguised as a brother convenor from one of your suppliers, and you show me round.'

'Simple as that?'

'Unless you have any better ideas.'

'OK, so that's how. Now give me one good reason why.'

'I'll give you several. One, we are old friends. Two, we are fellow trades unionists, and I still believe, deep down, that you have some misgivings about the secrecy surrounding the new work at Hardcoats.'

Ted was picking at the bowl of his pipe with a match. But he soon stopped.

'Three, you probably would not want it too widely known that you were in contact with me. And four, like any journalist, I pay my contacts for their cooperation and goodwill – there's a monkey in this for you.'

'Five hundred?'

'Five hundred.'

'You bastards have more money than I realized.'

'It's the best wages you'll ever get for a morning's work. There's no risk, and no harm done. I don't see how you can refuse.'

'I wouldn't bet on it.'

Suddenly the music had stopped, creating an uneasy vacuum. The bell was ringing for last orders. Soon they would be putting the main lights on.

'Go on, Jim, it's your shout.'

'Same again?'

'Not for me, I've got to get off.'

'Chris?'

'Go on then.'

He joined the forming crowd at the bar. The black girls were just retreating into the Ladies. Bad timing. By the time he got back to the table, Ted had already departed.

'Antisocial bastard. What did he say, then?'

'He didn't say yes and he didn't say no. But he'll do it. He's greedy and he lacks imagination. Five hundred is a fortune in his book, enough to outweigh any scruples he might have. I'll bet gaffers have bought him for less before today.'

'Can we raise five hundred?'

'That's a job for you, Jim. Get hold of Alan. Tell him we need the money or all bets are off. He'll come across. Have you got a camera, by the way?'

'Not on me. Why?'

Crispin shrugged. 'It's a historic transaction. We better get one. I want a photograph of me paying that bastard. This guided tour is just for starters. I need something on him.'

'You're enjoying this, aren't you?'

'Damn right. I should have got into espionage years ago. I've been wasted.'

As a concession to security and the workings of fate, they had left the car at home. It was only about a mile from the pub, and they decided to walk it.

It was a cold night with odd flakes of snow in the air. Just up the road from the pub they came upon five lads in denim jeans and leather jackets fighting with a couple of skinheads. It seemed to be a grudge match; they had the two of them on the deck and were busy putting the boot in. They walked past them on either side. It was obviously a private fight. Nobody asked them to join in.

15

Money, like food, has an enormous symbolic importance in human intercourse. Between spendthrift and miser, anorexic and glutton, we thread our way, sensing the power inherent in consumption or denial. Five hundred pounds might be a sprat to catch a mackerel, but it spoke with a certain eloquence to the parties in this transaction.

To Ted it indicated that he was being taken seriously, not begged or bullied, and somehow this lent Crispin's request an air of credibility. To Crispin it meant almost the opposite, that

69

he was dealing with someone utterly contemptible and therefore totally dispensable, fit only to be bought or sold. And to Alan, and those beyond him, it was a simple request for a show of confidence and commitment. They were being asked to put their money where their mouth was. To question such a request would have been unthinkable. It was a sizeable package of responses; not for nothing is money known as the universal medium of exchange.

Jim met Alan in a motorway cafe halfway between their respective bases. He found him staring into a cup of coffee, looking slightly lost without a meeting in front of him to chair.

'There you go, Jim,' he said, passing him a brown envelope as soon as he sat down.

'Was there any trouble raising it?'

'None at all. HQ has a special budget for this. I don't have to sweat for it.'

'Bet that makes a change.'

'Just a bit.'

It was a lot of light-hearted chatter for Alan. He was obviously trying. Jim noticed, for the first time, how little hair Alan had left. Clearly a worrier.

Alan then asked him for the rundown of what had been happening in Northburn which Jim had expected he would have to give before getting the money. He gave him a fairly full account, leaving out only such details as the brush with the traffic cops and the slaughter of the two ladies' cat. Alan was not noted for his sense of humour, and there seemed no sense in helping him to lose even more of his hair.

Alan remained quiet during his briefing, his attention still apparently fixed on the crockery. When Jim was finished, he looked up.

'I'm impressed by how much you've got done so quickly. Crispin is shaping up OK then?'

'He knows what he's doing all right. He's a very strong comrade politically when you get to know him.'

'And it sounds like you're getting on well with him. Personally, I mean.'

'No complaints at all.'

'I see.'

Alan relapsed into silence, at once beyond his companion's reach. Jim had always tended to admire the comrades in the regional leadership – all twice his age and with ten times his experience – in a frankly undifferentiated way. He was struck now, for the first time, by how colourless Alan was. It was his special characteristic amongst his peers: drab in appearance and uninspiring in manner. Really, he was drained of life; dependable, no doubt, but with none of the vitality he had come to expect with Crispin, who must have been about the same age and from a similar background.

Alan stirred himself again.

'I don't quite know how to put this, Jim. It's not exactly a warning, just a note of caution. Crispin has been out of action for a long time. I guess he's like a dog let off its leash at the moment, and that's good. But don't forget his track record. He may turn out not to be completely reliable – politically or personally. So don't get too infatuated by him. I know he's a bit of a charismatic character, but this operation, as far as I'm concerned, stands or falls on your judgement – not his.'

Sod me, you're jealous, he thought. You're really worried that Crispin is going to seduce your young protégé.

'He hasn't corrupted me yet, Alan, but thanks for the tip – I'll keep my eyes open.'

'That's right. I may be worrying about nothing, but this is an important and dangerous operation, and you're a developing cadre right there in the middle of it. I don't want you swept away by Crispin's enthusiasm so you lose your sense of proportion. Don't forget, you're going to be around and doing a job for this Party when Chris, and myself for that matter, are long gone.'

'I think you might find the boot is on the other foot. Crispin is not reckless. If anything he's suspicious of our adventurism.'

Alan nodded. 'Yes, that's interesting.' He paused. 'He could be right, at that.'

'How do you mean, Alan?'

'Well, it's basic to a Marxist approach that we have to adapt our strategy to fit changed circumstances, so I don't condemn armed actions simply because they're new to me. On the other hand, and it may just be because you get more cautious as you get older, but I've got to admit to having had, and still having, some doubts about what we're doing now. So I think Crispin's caution is well placed.'

'I'm not sure I'd call it caution. More like scepticism. It won't stop him delivering the goods.'

'No, I'm sure it won't.'

Neither man sought to prolong the meeting, and Jim was soon back on the road with the money in his pocket. He thought about Alan's remarks as he drove back to Northburn. He was not sure what to make of them. It was the first time he had heard Alan express any reservations about the operation.

Crispin meanwhile was having lunch with Pamela in an Italian restaurant.

He had got there fifteen minutes early and he spent the time thus gained speculating over a martini. She had sounded both curious and enthusiastic over the phone but there was still a question mark in his mind over whether she would actually turn up. He had told her he was only going to be in town for the day, so she would not expect any follow-up or comeback if she failed to show. Nevertheless, he decided she would make the date.

The next area of speculation, assuming that she turned up, was to do with how much she would have changed. For obvious reasons, it was an altogether more significant question than it had been in the case of Clive or Terry or Ted.

At first sight, as he waved to her across the restaurant and she came, smiling, to be kissed, the answer seemed to be very little. The hair was shorter and styled differently, the hips and bust, shown off by a well-cut trouser suit, slightly more developed, the down on the face just a little more visible. Otherwise, any real change was more in her manner. Age had made her more confident. She was no longer the young woman in awe of the older man, that was the message. As he kissed her he found himself wondering what her husband was like. Older than me? Younger? Taller? Shorter? Richer? Must be richer, since rumour had it he was a businessman. Blind prejudice, I'm a businessman myself. The next point of comparison was so obvious he immediately thrust it from his mind. They had not even got to the soup yet. No point in spoiling his lunch. Nevertheless he had realized, in that first moment of greeting, that it was vitally, crucially, important for him to get this woman into bed again.

He was pleased to see that Pamela still had a healthy appetite, working her way through pasta, veal and gateau at a steady pace. Crispin, who had never liked Italian food, picked at some spaghetti and drank a good deal of chianti.

They talked freely as they ate, with no apparent sense of eight years' separation constituting an impediment. Gradually, going with the flow of the talk and the wine, Crispin began to pick up that Pamela was guiding their conversation in a way so subtle that he could not quite put his finger on it. He set it down to her new-found professional skill.

He had gone to the restaurant, like any old-time politician, with a mental shopping list of topics to be covered. He had wanted to ask if she was still in the Party, talk about her marriage with due, probing subtlety, swop stories about the good old days, find out if she knew who had initiated the conspiracy against him and, of course, ascertain if, and when, she would sleep with him. Instead they got trapped, or steered, into talking first about his work – as an antique dealer rather than a saboteur – and then about hers.

So he told her how he had half acquired and half pretended a knowledge of the antiques business, persuaded a bank to lend him the capital and, against all the logical odds, made a success of it. He explained how it was 49% psychology, 49% chutzpah and 2% skill, and she smiled admiringly, and said, yes, it was the same in her game, a little knowledge and a lot of show business went a long way, and then they laughed together, thinking of the odd things that serving your time in a revolutionary party ultimately equipped you for.

Then she told him how she had been on a two-year training course in social work at a local polytechnic that seemed to have been designed to take you to bits and maybe, if you were lucky, put you back together again, but how it had been a piece of piss for an old bolshevik like herself; she had soon got the tutors psyched and the students organized and knocked the course off no trouble. She was now doing statutory child care work, all form-filling and procedures and bureaucracy, but dabbling in family therapy on the side, which was much more fun.

'What's family therapy when it's washed?'

'Oh, it's like rock and roll – an authentic twentieth-century American art form. The theory behind most traditional social work is that you counsel people until they get what we call insight. The catch is that they don't always, or even usually, do anything positive with this insight when they've got it.'

'They're just more aware of why they're delinquent or whatever, is that it? But they still go on mugging old ladies because, what the hell, it's a living. Just like you can become aware that the working class is oppressed and exploited without actually becoming a revolutionary. You might become a drunk or a capitalist instead.'

'Exactly. There's a joke about a social worker finding an old lady beaten up in a gutter, blood all over her and her purse gone, and saying, Christ, whoever did this must have problems.'

'Sounds familiar. So how is family therapy different?'

'You aim to dislodge the whole family system from its rut and get it pointing in a new direction. Insight doesn't come into it. You can con them, bluff them, double-bluff them, form alliances, the lot. All's fair in family therapy.'

'That sounds more like a revolutionary approach. Tackle the system rather than the symptom.'

'Chris, you've missed your vocation. You've got it exactly. We ought to go into partnership. I think you'd make a good therapist.'

'I'd make a better arsonist.'

'Still full of passion and hatred, eh?'

'Especially passion.'

'That sounded like a proposition.'

'I can live with that.'

She looked up from stirring her coffee at Crispin, who was rolling a glass of brandy between his hands. She had forgotten those big, strong hands, covered in black hair. Hard to imagine them wrapped around a piece of fine Wedgwood.

'Do you still smoke cheroots in public?' he enquired.

'No, I'm terribly respectable these days. Dope occasionally, but no cheroots, not even in private.'

'I can remember you smoking roll-ups in bed.'

'Uh-huh. I feared you might. If that was a hint, rather than a random reminiscence, I've got to warn you that I'm working this afternoon.'

'Pity, I wanted to try some of that sex therapy you were on about.'

'Family therapy is not quite the same as Masters and Johnson,' she laughed. 'I'm only massaging the psyche.'

Well, she hasn't said no, he thought. Nor mentioned her ever-loving husband; that's got to be a good sign.

'I'm going to be back in Northburn quite a bit over the next few weeks. Can I look you up again?'

'I'd like that. It's nice seeing you again, nicer than I expected. You remind me of good times.'

He put on his mock-serious voice. 'Times of struggle, comrade. Always the best times.' She laughed, remembering that ability of his to see the comic side of their aspirations. 'I don't remember me struggling.'

Outside in the street he kissed her again, a little longer this time.

'What are you doing back up here, Chris?'

'Not antique dealing. It's political, and a little bit hush-hush. I'll tell you all about it some day.'

'Well, take care. Thanks for the lunch.'

'I'll give you a ring.'

He watched her walk to her car. I've seen some amazing things, he thought, but nothing beats the rear view of a good woman.

16

Crispin left Jim in the flat, drinking coffee and reading between the lines of a newspaper, and walked the short distance to the university. It was a bright, clear day, but very cold. Picket line weather.

The university had not changed much since the days when he had gone there to be patronized at student meetings and to defeat supposedly clever people in argument. Its sprawl of brick and concrete buildings, owing no allegiance to any overall plan or style, almost constituted a town within a town. The campus was well provided with signposts, but they were of the type that told you where to go but gave you no clue as to when you had got there, so they tended to add to the confusion rather than diminish it. Crispin studied a map on a board by the main entrance and then plunged into the interior in the general direction of where he guessed Alex's office to be.

Like many self-educated people, Crispin was suspicious of academics. In particular, he felt the Party had become over-reliant on their services, taking on board not only their specialist knowledge, but much of their petit-bourgeois outlook as well. He remembered with affection the days, irretrievably gone, when the Party had produced its own intellectuals, ferociously learned and argumentative working men, who could deliver a lecture on the relationship between mathematical logic and dialectical materialism at the drop of a hat and make the subject come alive for an audience of work-tired and sober comrades who did not suffer fools gladly. These were the people, the wandering scholars of an industrial society, who had

76

kept Marxism alive as a science for decades when no college lecturer had ever opened *Das Kapital*, who had ensured that Tressell remained continuously in print and who could quote Byron and Shelley in living accents. However well intentioned, the new generation of sociologists, with their badly-written books that nobody read except other sociologists, were not their equal. Crispin felt himself shadowed by the ghosts of these ragged-arsed polymaths as he beat a path to the door of Alex's office.

Inside, the office was visually barren, lacking pictures on the walls or ornaments on the desk or even books on the shelves. This had the effect of concentrating attention on Alex himself, who sat behind a desk facing the door with his guide dog at his feet. Crispin realized for the first time, as they shook hands, that Alex's disability had had an odd side effect. His other political contemporaries had aged in eight years, each in their fashion, but Alex's appearance, the long out-of-style clothes, the schoolboy haircut, the unseeing eyes, gave him a timeless air.

'You haven't changed a bit,' he said.

'How are you keeping, Chris?' There was strength in the timbre of the voice.

'Fair to middling.'

They talked for an hour, mainly about Alex's work as a councillor. He was chairman of the social services committee, and as he talked about such things as day centres for the elderly, unloading facts and figures from a formidable memory, Crispin began to understand why he had left the Party. It was not a desire for power or glory which motivated him, but a simple pleasure in doing things, a willingness to get immersed in practical detail. Crispin had never really considered such administrative wheeling and dealing to be much to do with politics at all. Sure, somebody had to decide whether and where and when to build day centres, but it wasn't politics. Politics was winning positions and turning bodies out on to the streets. And blowing up things. The science of Machiavelli, not the Webbs. He had never given much thought to what being involved in local government would involve, even on a fantasy level. But he could see now that the Party, with its dreams of massive and monolithic power, must have been a very frustrating lodging for someone who actually wanted more pensioners to be able to use a hydraulic bath or have a cup of tea in comfort.

'The old days must seem very remote to you now, Alex,' he said at last.

'Yes, they do, Chris. There were things I liked about the Party – the comradeship, the constant ferment of ideas – but I never really got used to that constant sense of being against everything, or at least everything that wasn't hopelessly remote, like socialism. I don't think I was meant to be a revolutionary.'

Under the desk the dog growled at some imagined threat.

'Do you see much of the comrades these days?'

'Only Terry, with him working in the town hall. He's a reformed sinner like me, of course. Oh, and Pamela very occasionally. I suppose I'm her employer now, technically speaking. Same as I used to be yours, technically speaking. What a strange world. Who else? Nobody, really. I haven't seen Tom in years. You and he were very close at one time, weren't you?'

'One time, yeah,' he laughed. 'Before he decided I was too hard-line.'

'Oh yes, I remember now. He took me aside and told me how you were getting to be politically unreliable. Something silly like that.'

'Did it make any difference?' asked Crispin, alert now, anxious to hear the full story.

'No.' Alex smiled, an enigmatic blind smile. 'I always found you too hard-line anyway. But then I didn't find Tom and Ian much better.'

'How long was Tom talking behind my back before it came out into the open?' Crispin persisted.

'Oh, a while. Months, I should think. It was all very cloak-and-daggerish. To tell you the truth, I wasn't that interested. I mean, I always found you politically reliable. That was the problem.'

'And Tom was behind all this cloak-and-dagger stuff?'

'As far as I'm aware. Ian was pretty heavily involved as well, but I think Tom was your main conspirator. Why, are you planning revenge?'

The dog growled again.

'I'm not even planning a comeback, Alex. No, I'm just naturally curious.'

'What are you doing back in these parts, then?'

'I'm doing some freelance journalist work, using some of my trade union contacts. It's a break from the shop.'

'Yes, it must be.'

'I'd be obliged if you didn't mention it to too many people.'

'Oh, of course.'

Crispin had heard what he wanted. He had other things to do. Alex seemed to sense that he needed to be off.

'Chris, what's the time?'

'Nearly twelve.'

'I've got a student coming at twelve. It's been nice talking to you again, Chris, but you're going to have to excuse me.'

'I've got to get off myself. We'll have to have lunch sometime.'

'That would be nice.'

They shook hands and Crispin saw himself out. It had been a useful meeting from his point of view. Alex might not have been much help when it came to blowing up factories, but he had given him his clearest fix yet on that bastard Tom. And, despite what he had said to Alex, Crispin's head was filled with thoughts of vengeance.

He caught a bus into town and then another, on which he appeared to be the only passenger, out to Hardcoats. Buses, like factories, were an endangered species. Soon they would be advertising them as a special attraction. A never to be repeated offer. Catch the last bus to the last factory. It was years since he had been on a bus. He missed the fug of smoke, the press of bodies, the coughing and overheard conversations on the top deck. Instead he sat in splendid isolation, smoking and looking out at the city, trying to clear his head of Alex and Tom and things that happened long ago, so that he could concentrate on getting his hooks into Ted Atha.

The nearest pub to ROF Hardcoats was called the Three Barrels and it was doing a fair lunchtime trade when Crispin got there. He found Ted sitting by himself at a corner table, sipping a light ale and looking uncomfortable.

79

'Hello, Ted, fraternizing with your members?' he asked, looking round at the boiler-suited clientele, with their pints and sandwiches and pub games and obscene conversation. They were having a good time, making the most of every minute away from the tedium and noise of the factory like they had done every day since the place opened, and Ted Atha looked as out of place among them as any gaffer. Some bloody convenor, Crispin thought, some frigging mass leader.

'You're late. I thought you weren't coming.'

'I got held up talking to a professor. Do you want another?'

'I'll have a bottle of light.'

Up at the bar two lads were talking about a pornographic video in ear-catching detail.

'What about that bit with the bottle, eh?'

'Fucking right, mate. That fucking cunt would let anything in, I reckon.'

Amen to that.

He set Ted's bottle of light ale next to his glass and took a couple of inches out of the top of his pint.

'So when do I get this guided tour, Ted?'

'Next week. On Thursday morning. I must be mad doing this. For Christ's sake, don't spread it around.'

'My lips are sealed.'

'What about the – '

'Not here, old son. Your members might get the crazy idea you're bent. No, we'll do it on the way out, eh?'

As if on cue, one of Ted's members was, in fact, approaching their table.

'Excuse me, Ted, but could you sign these for me, please?'

He took an envelope from the pocket of his boiler suit, and shook out a printed form and a strip of photographs, taking care to avoid touching them with his oil-stained hands. Ted put his glasses on, uncapped an old fashioned fountain pen and began signing laboriously.

'Passport, eh. Where are you off to?'

'Not sure, yet. The wife fancies touring on the continent.'

'Very nice. There you are then.'

'Ta.'

Crispin had been watching Ted's pompous pantomime with amusement. When the man had gone he laughed aloud.

'Fancy that, you a magistrate, Ted. Fucking hell, you kept that under your hat, didn't you? Bugger me, anything to dodge work. We will have to take care with this little present, won't we? How long have you been on the bench, anyway?'

Ted's face was a picture of suppressed fury.

'Coming up three years, if you really want to know. The last convenor at Hardcoats was on the bench, too. It's a sort of tradition, like.'

'Like keeping ferrets or being in the Masons. Hey, I'll bet you're in on that as well, sneaking out at nights with your little briefcase, eh.'

'If you'd stuck it out here, instead of pissing off down South to make your fortune, you'd have had to face responsibilities like that yourself.'

'Oh aye, I'd have quite fancied being a beak. I could have gaoled a few gaffers. Exemplary sentences. Thirty years for breaches of the Clean Air Act. That sort of thing.'

'Well I've got to get back,' said Ted, making a big show of buttoning his coat.

'OK.'

They stood side by side outside the pub, stamping their feet in the sudden cold. Deliberately, with exaggerated slowness, Crispin fumbled inside his coat and then drew out a brown envelope. He held it suspended in the air between them for a moment.

'You'll ring and confirm my guided tour?'

'Aye,' said Ted impatiently, his fingers closing on the packet.

'Good.' He relinquished his hold. Ted undid the top two buttons of his coat, clumsily, with numbed fingers, and shoved the envelope into the breast pocket of his jacket. Then he walked off, without further comment, and without looking back.

When he was safely inside the factory gates, Crispin crossed the road to where Jim was sitting in the parked car with a camera in his lap.

'Did you catch all of that with that fancy lens of yours?' he asked, as he got into the passenger seat.

'Yeah, I've got the whole thing, five or six shots of the pair of you. You really did it in slow motion.'

'Good. Let's get out of here and I'll buy you a pint somewhere. It's cold enough to freeze your bollocks off out there.'

17

'Amazing Scenes in Hotel Bedroom' – now that's a headline for you, thought Crispin. Or for my puritanical young partner, who is probably sniffing his disapproval of yours truly right now, as he studies revolutionary form on his jack somewhere. All very laudable. But a man must have relief. Aah. He half-gasped, half-chuckled. The female tongue is a surprisingly rough instrument when it gets to work. He ran his fingers through Pamela's hair and cast his eyes absent-mindedly over the hotel decor. Not very collectable. The last burial ground of table lamps with frilly pink shades and ashtrays too big to steal. Unreal.

Aah. Right now everything is unreal. Outside, behind the thick curtains, it is afternoon. Jim Carson is planning the overthrow of capitalism, or at least a small step on the road to same. The forces of repression, the Furies of Capital, well funded and well organized, are everywhere and ever-vigilant. If they catch us we will never see daylight again. It is a real danger, and yet so unreal it makes no sense. Thirty-five years a revolutionary, and I finally see the absurdity of my situation. Getting my cock sucked in a hotel bedroom while I wait to add my pathetic little squib to the world's great bonfire party.

I feel like a figure in one of those prints of scenes from everyday life in old Japan. Real and unreal. The ones they call *ukiyo-e*. Pictures of the floating world.

I am as trapped in this act of love in this bed with this woman as I am trapped in this whole crazy enterprise. I've lain on my back for half an hour, exhausted after sex, smoking, cuddling the girl, and now it's dues time. After all, we're paying for the room and committing adultery. Less of the frivolity. We've got to be serious.

So the etiquette of illicit passion is to do it again. Like the old days. Make a special occasion of it. Except the catch is that it's years since I've had any special occasions. I've been too old and tired and plain bored to come back for more. Sex for anything except relief is unfamiliar.

But not to her, obviously. She's gone down and caught me good and proper. No escape. The rough edge of the lady's tongue. Lie back and take it like a man. I probably taught you to do this and the funny thing is, I don't think I've had it this way since the last time I had it with you. Now I come to think of it, I can see why. It's never as good as you remember. A bit slow.

Pamela's thoughts were running on parallel lines, separated by the unbridgeable air, never meeting his. Jesus, I'm going to get a stiff neck. I'm too old for this. It's all a bit odd, a bit incongruous. And another thing. Neither the taste nor the texture is quite right. I wouldn't pay money for this in a restaurant.

She was glad when he disengaged and entered her. This way you know you're wanted. You can't argue with enthusiasm. Lying there, with him on top of her thrusting persuasively she felt, strangely, more in control. And that was appropriate, she decided. After all, she was not any longer the young girl, learning to please somebody mature and hard and experienced as she had been a decade before, but more the grown woman in charge of her destiny, meeting an old friend and lover as an equal now, with nothing more to prove.

When Crispin woke up he was alone in the luxury of the hired bed. He propped himself up on a pillow, lit a cigarette and poured some wine from a bottle by the bed. He took a good drink – it was claret and tasted none the worse for having been opened a couple of hours before. Some of the wine ran from the side of his mouth down his jaw on to his chest. Hell's bells, he thought, rubbing it into the hair with his forearm, I'm really turning grey. And my aim is not improving with age.

The door to the bathroom was ajar and from inside came the sounds of Pamela wallowing in warm water. Jesus, he thought,

I could use some of that; haven't had a bath since I left Carlton
– never enough hot water in that damn flat for more than a
strip-down swill. Well, maybe I will at that. Why not? We're
paying for it one way or the other.

Getting out of bed, he hobbled into the bathroom and
climbed into the bath with Pamela, holding his glass of wine
aloft and flicking his cigarette into the toilet bowl.

'Hello, sleeping beauty,' she said, pulling her knees up to her
breasts as he slid his legs around her. 'May I?'

'Be my guest,' he said, passing her the glass.

'Mm, ta,' she said, taking a drink. 'Tell me, do you think I've
put on weight?'

'Hell, it's been a long time,' he said. 'Here, let's have a feel.'
He took a pinch of her waist: 'No, not a lot.' Then he tickled her
behind the knees, causing her to squirm and spill the rest of the
wine over her breasts. 'Ha, I remembered you were ticklish
there. Hang on, I'll just wipe it off.' He stuck his tongue out to
give substance to the offer.

'Put it away, it's obscene. There, I'm leaving you to it.' She
stood up, shaking water over him.

'That's better. I thought you'd never take the hint,' he said,
lying back to soak himself.

'Bastard,' she said, wrapping a towel around herself and
perching on the edge of the bath.

'Can I ask you a personal question?' He fixed her with his
most authoritative look, threatening her with his eyebrows,
making her suddenly feel ten years younger and more vulnerable.

'Go on.'

'When we split up, or whatever you want to call it, did you
fancy any of the other comrades?'

She scratched her bottom uneasily. 'I can't remember. Do
you mean was I sleeping with any of them?'

'Yeah.'

Her eyes were back in play now. 'You kinky old bastard. Do
you want me to tell you all about my sex life?'

He sat up. 'No, it's just political curiosity. You started voting
against me. I wondered if anything personal was involved.'

'Oh, fuck you.' She walked out of the bathroom, coming back

a moment later, puffing a cigarette and shaking her head. 'You're something else.' She sat down again. 'I was certainly angry enough with you when you dropped me. That may have affected my voting, and it serves you right if it did, you pig. But I don't remember sleeping with any of your comrades to spite you. Jesus, Chris, what do you take me for? Anyway, for the record, the answer is no. I didn't fancy any of them – a right boring bunch of old fanatics, as I remember them. Just like you sometimes.'

'I'm sorry.' He had assumed what she took to be an expression of appealing innocence.

'Is that all that interests you – my voting record eight years ago?'

'No. No. It's just a daft obsession of mine. I've spent eight years wondering exactly who started the moves against me. It had to be either Ian or Tom, but I could never quite figure out which. I know it's stupid to bother. I mean they were both little guys with bigger guys on their backs anyway, but it's been going round in my head all these years.'

'Well, get this, one of them is dead, the other not far off it from what you tell me. I never slept with either of the pigs, you're boring my tits off, and if you want to redeem yourself, you'd better get dressed and take me out for something to eat.'

'OK. OK.' A suitably chastened Crispin padded into the bedroom picking up the towel Pamela had discarded and started to dry himself.

A naked Pamela confronted him, tin of talcum in one hand, knickers in the other.

'Anyway, for a reputed political genius you must be pretty dense not to have worked it out between those two.'

'Meaning?'

'It was Tom, Chris, no argument. Ian was like me, he started off thinking the sun shone out of your arse. Then I got riled and he got ambitious and we both got even. But it was Tom who was there to pick up the pieces. And I can tell you why. He never liked being number two to you. He reckoned you never appreciated him politically. Probably right, too. Anyway, he was the man who organized the opposition. You should have rung me years ago and saved yourself the heartache.' She pulled the panties up tight round her crotch to emphasize the point, and picked up her bra.

'Yeah, I wish I had.' He rubbed the towel into his groin. 'I'll take you to your favourite restaurant now to make up for the lost years and lost opportunities.'

'OK.' She leaned across and kissed him. 'It's been good seeing you again. You haven't lost your power over me. So don't bore me with politics tonight, huh?'

'No, I'll be the perfect lover.'

Wine you, dine you, fuck you all over again, then return you safe and sound to your boorjie husband.

Then fuck that bastard Tom at the first opportunity.

18

He had not said anything to him, but basically Jim was pretty pissed off with his partner. Here they were, Christmas looming up, a deadline of February 1st looming up beyond it, and Crispin was off shagging with his bird, in some bloody posh hotel for shit's sake, leaving him to do the work.

He did not so much mind that in itself – Crispin had done his share and more and he did not begrudge him his fun, not too much, anyway – but, and it was a big but, this was not just a day off for rest and recreational purposes. It was all tied in with what was emerging as something of an obsession on Crispin's part with what had happened eight years ago – who had set him up and why – an obsession which, in Jim's view, threatened both the focus and the security of their operation.

There was no earthly justification, for example, for seeing Pamela. If he wanted sex they could pull something somewhere, but not an old comrade, intelligent, no longer politically committed, married to a businessman – it was bad news all round. The whole operation was hair-raising enough, when you came to think of it, without Crispin making it worse. You could hardly trust the likes of Terry or Ted Atha, but at least the risk you took with them was justified politically by the help they could, albeit unwillingly or unwittingly, provide. But with Alex and Pamela, superannuated reformists on the make, the risk made no sense at all.

Next it would be Tom, he could see that one coming, and God knows where that would lead. Well done, Crispin, you've tracked down the guilty man; now what do you intend to do with him? Give him a good telling off? Beat him up? Kill him? He was steaming up a cul-de-sac. Revenge politically has no end: there's always someone further up the line to blame. Crispin ought to know that by now. Business is business. Never take it personally.

What had really got up his nose had been Crispin suggesting that he should take the day off too, with a clear hint of, 'and get yourself a woman, lad, it'll do you good'. So to spite himself he had insisted on getting on with some work. Suit yourself, had been Crispin's response, why not check up on whether that cunt Terry has got any information yet?

And, of course, he had agreed. Riding up now in the lift to the eighth floor of the civic buildings, eyeing a couple of girls with files under their arms chattering as they stood by the row of buttons, he began to regret his decision. He should have listened to uncle. He hadn't had a sniff of cunt since he'd come to this town.

It was an old revolutionary dilemma. Life without sex was unnatural, but chasing it was politically suspect, a sure sign of petit-bourgeois frivolity. Monogamy was the obvious solution and recommended as such by every commentator from Lenin onwards. But how did you develop and preserve any sort of long-standing relationship in the face of a revolutionary's lifestyle – never at home, obsessed with external events, uninterested in domestic life? It was a mystery to him how Crispin was still married after so long. It was certainly unusual in a comrade his age who was at all politically serious.

The girls got out at the eighth floor too, but they turned left while he went right to the enquiry desk. A quick glance at retreating VPL. Another of the million chances of the day-to-day world blown.

Terry insisted on giving him a guided tour of his department, which Jim found as cursory as it was puzzling, before taking him into an empty conference room.

'I'm glad you came,' he explained, 'you're safer than Chris. There's always the chance somebody might know that old bastard, he got around plenty. I gave you the tour because if anyone new turned up to see me I'd naturally show them round, wouldn't I?'

'Very impressive set of offices,' said Jim laconically.

Terry disappeared for a few moments and returned with two cups of coffee in plastic holders.

'From a machine, I'm afraid,' he apologized, 'but at least there's a handle.'

Jim sat back on a semi-comfortable chair, of the type which looks domestic but is in fact only found in offices, and rested his feet on a low table, showing off his well-styled leather boots.

'We wondered if you'd come up with anything for us yet, Terry?'

Terry shifted in his seat and tugged at the strap of his wristwatch. 'Yeah, I have as it happens. I hope it's what you want.'

'What is it?'

'I've got three names, two in number 9 branch and one in number 15. The first one is called Bob Tuft, and he's an out-of-trade member. He talks right wing but in a confused sort of way, fascist almost, and he does not hang around with the rest of the right. A bit of a loner, probably just an eccentric with a thing about blacks, but you never know.'

'Sure.'

'The other in number 9 is called Gary Baker. He's a new member and he's wild. Talks really crazy.'

'Where's he work?'

'A firm called Michael's. You won't have heard of it; it's a back-lane, bread-and-dripping factory – employs about twenty lads, bad money, terrible conditions – you know the sort of thing.'

'Yeah, small contract work. Only the loonies join the union, the rest are too thick. What's the third one?'

'Yeah, he's the one from number 15. A guy called Jacko

James. He's only been around a few months. Talks about having been in the Forces – the Paras, or the SAS, or maybe the French Foreign Legion, depending on how the mood takes him. Mouths it off a lot in the branch. They say he's clever, but with a screw loose.'

'What's his line when he mouths off – Nazi stuff?'

'Surprisingly, no. Red revolution. Blood on the barricades. Reckons he got converted while doing time in a military gaol at Colchester, or maybe it was Sidi-bel-Abbès, or the River Kwai.'

'Colourful lad, eh? Where's he work?'

'Hardcoats.'

Well, well, well, Crispin. While you're on the nest, I think I've gone and found our man.

'Maybe he really was in the Army, then.'

'Yeah. In fact from your point of view he sounds like a government agent, doesn't he?'

Yes, fuck it, he does at that. Crispin with his bright ideas.

'We'll check them all out. It sounds a promising haul.'

'Incidentally, that last one, Jacko James, is a colourful character in more ways than one. He's tattooed all over like a cannibal chief.'

'Well, he should be easy to spot.'

Somebody looked in, apologized, and closed the door again.

'No problem,' Terry said, 'this room is free for another hour. Smoke?'

They lit cigarettes. Terry looked pleased with himself, having delivered the goods. Now comes the statutory talk about the old days, Jim thought. I might as well kick off.

'Chris sends his regards.'

'Where is he today?'

'Shagging.'

'What a bastard, eh? I'll tell you what, Jim, you've found a hell of a bloke to work with there. Chris is the 100% original pure-water bastard of all time.'

'You must have enjoyed working with him.'

'You what? It was something else. Chris, to me, was what it was all about – very sharp, very tough and a real grafter. He never got tired, you know? I've seen him go down to London overnight on a bus to a picket, stand on the line from dawn to noon, go and have a skinful of ale, get the coach back, and go straight from the bus to a meeting. And all the time on the coach, when everyone else was trying to sleep, he'd be working – drafting leaflets or whatever. Real organized he was. I'm surprised he never burnt himself out.'

'Which picket was that?'

Terry thought a moment.

'I'm not sure, to tell you the truth. We seemed to go on a fair few in those days. They all blur into each other. I remember daft things. Like waking up in the middle of the night – 2 am it was – at a motorway service station and going for a cup of tea with the rest of the lads and finding a thousand miners from Barnsley in there, all wanting bacon butties.'

'Going to the same place as you?'

'Sure. Rough as bears' arses they were. They didn't care where they were going. Their union had asked for volunteers and that was good enough for them. Mind you, I suppose it was better than working a shift down the pit.' He was warming to his own memories. 'Another time I remember getting to this picket early, the moon and the stars were still shining. We were giving the police on the gate some stick about what we'd do when our mates got there, and this sergeant says, we're not fucking bothered, lads, we're only the bleeding night shift, we're off in a minute, you should see *our* mates who'll be on in half an hour. They weren't wrong, either. Jesus, they were hard bastards.'

'Did they get rough?'

'It depends on what you mean by rough, Jim. It stands to reason when you get a few thousand big lads and a similar number of coppers, all pushing and shoving around a gate a few feet across, that you'll get a few injuries. Occasionally the police went over the top, but usually it was a fair fight. Actually, the worst bit was waiting in the cold for it to happen. You'd get dropped off maybe five o'clock or earlier, still dark, and you'd hang around shivering until something happened, which might be two hours later when the scabs reported for work. But you found ways to pass the time. March your banners up and down, that sort of thing. You'd get into a routine. Like I'd always have about eight pints afterwards, before I got on the bus. That way, I'd sleep most of the way home. It's a good technique.'

'Bit of a sacrifice if it was London beer, though?'

He found he was warming to Terry in spite of himself, allowing him to catch some reflected glory from Crispin. Well, there was plenty more where that came from. He could understand why Crispin himself hankered after that past. It had to beat what they were doing right now. Not to mention flogging antiques.

'Don't you miss them days, Terry?'

'Oh aye lad, I miss them all right, but like you miss your childhood. They aren't going to come back.'

'And we're not going to get out of this alive.'

'You're not wrong.'

'Do you fancy a pint?'

'Good idea. Kill the taste of that coffee, eh?'

They took the lift down to the ground again, leaving the eighth floor to its collective labour. With them rode the shade of Chris Powell, legendary revolutionary of Northburn in days gone by.

19

The first thing that struck Crispin on his official visit to ROF Hardcoats was how lax the security was, something he decided must have been an accidental side effect of privatization. A quick word with the guy on the gate with the peaked hat and the electric wall heater, and he was waved through. It was, admittedly, the first time that Crispin had ever thought of security as something you encountered getting into, as opposed to out of, a factory. Well, there was a first time for everything in this strange world.

Ted had obviously decided to make the best of a bad job, and was a mine of information and affability as he showed his guest around. Crispin for his part asked questions like a diplomat being shown round a collective farm – Where did these parts come from? How long did this process take to complete? What would happen if it was held up? – probing the system's defences, looking for its weaknesses.

Actually he was surprised at how cumbersome the production process was. It was not quite like watching cars go down an automated line, so many an hour. The stages seemed fragmented, with transporters dragging their product from shop to shop.

In fact by the time he was halfway through the guided tour, Crispin began to realize how naïve the comrades had been in selecting Hardcoats as a target. The idea of halting, even disrupting, production with a single, well-placed, explosive device was meaningless. It would have needed carpet-bombing by the Luftwaffe to do that.

A tank could spend a year and more trundling its way through the shops, maturing like a bottle of wine. Where did you stop it? During the initial fabrication? Or during the machining? Or the fitting? Each stage was a jumble of moves and operations. A more sophisticated process would have been more vulnerable to assault, but bugger up part of this and it would be child's play to bypass it temporarily. He was reminded of how primitive life forms could withstand attacks that would kill a mammal. They had picked an industrial starfish that could happily regenerate a blown-off limb.

Suitably depressed, he agreed to share a bacon sandwich and a pot of tea with his guide in the canteen. As if sensing his guest's mood, Ted was getting more cheerful by the moment. Crispin buried his face in his sandwich, trying to ignore his host, nodding or muttering agreement occasionally. When he reconnected with Ted's conversation, he was in mid-diatribe:

'. . . must be one of your shower. A real loony. But I defended him just the same. Broke the poor sod's nose. Pulled for fighting with a workmate, and it's harassment. I suppose you'd have agreed with him. Rubbish. But I still represented him. Not that I got any thanks for it. But we can't expect any credit from the likes of you, can we, blokes like myself?'

'What happened to him?' Crispin asked absent-mindedly. Ted was obviously boasting of his prowess and fair-mindedness as a convenor.

'I got him off with a warning. Good, eh?'

'Quite right. Look, it works both ways. I represented a Polish guy once. He worked on the nightshift. One night he pulled a knife on another bloke. Now he was a genuine Nazi. An émigré. Probably had a collection of ears at home. He made you look like a Trotskyite, Ted. Personally I'd have enjoyed watching him hang, but I represented the bastard. So it's quits.' He paused. 'Mind you, they sacked the cunt anyway.'

'You were never any good as a union man, Chris. Too busy with politics.'

'That's right,' said Crispin, refusing the bait. 'Who was this great revolutionary you saved to fight another day then?'

'Jacko James they call him. Ex-army lad and a real barrack-room lawyer. He's an electrician, works in number 18 shop, where they do the fitting. Mind you, he does more talking than working. His sort always do.'

'You've got something in common, then.' Crispin was all attention now. Small world, he thought – I've found our favourite headbanger, mad Jacko. The man, whom he had never met, was starting to assume a reality he would probably never match up to.

Maddeningly, Ted now changed the subject, insisting on discussing football for ten minutes, before suggesting that they resume their tour. But then Crispin had one of the amazing strokes of luck for which he had always been famous.

On the way out of the canteen they passed a line of men queuing with trays by the counter, one of whom nodded to Ted. Some instinct made Crispin check him over, police style, in the couple of seconds available to him. Caucasian, about six foot tall, thin, red hair, aged thirty or thereabouts, eyes not quite right – well, he would not be the first lad to spend his shifts blocked on drugs – ears sticking out a bit and tattoos, tattoos on every bit of him that was visible. Snakes twining up his arms. Flowers growing up his neck. A thought started to form in Crispin's mind.

'Talk of the devil,' said Ted, as they stepped outside. 'That was that bugger Jacko I mentioned before, standing in the line back there.'

'I thought you meant his politics, not his hair, when you

93

called him a red,' said Crispin, full of an irrational enthusiasm which bore little relation to his actual first impression of Jacko as a production-line, drugged-up psychopath. At that moment he would not have been unduly discomfited if Jacko had had two heads. He had assumed corporeal form – it was a start.

Ted saw the rest of the tour as essentially a mopping-up operation. All that remained to look at were a couple of shops situated between the canteen and the main entrance. That completed, he would be well positioned to see Crispin on his way.

The work being done in these shops was all fitting: less interesting to watch, less spectacular, than the fabrication or even the machining. Ted rattled off his statistics – how many components were involved, how many trades, right down to crap like how much paint they used in the specially designed paint-spraying equipment – the kind of figures that guides the world over invent as they go along.

Crispin had tended to share Ted's assessment of the final stages of his tour as a formality. He was no further forward with the actual target, but he had got a good fix on this man Jacko, and that was a bonus well worth the time and the money. It would do for the day. But then, suddenly, he had a vision. He saw a paint store hurling flames into the winter sky, destroying the adjacent shop and its contents in an uncontrollable rush of fire. The blaze would be localized, of course, causing no insuperable problems to production elsewhere in the works, but it would be fucking spectacular, a headline grabber, which was presumably the idea. I mean, you could not hush something like that up, with fire engines descending from the four corners of Northburn and the neighbours turning out to watch. Cracked it, he thought. With a little bit of work, and a lot of luck, we're there.

'How much paint do you store here, Ted?' he enquired innocently.

20

After the euphoria comes the arm-twisting. Jim was having doubts about Crispin's choice, both of target and assailant. They argued about it over the Formica-topped kitchen table, across the fish papers, and the beer cans and the uncapped sauce bottle, the overflowing ashtrays and yesterday's greasy plates. It was a perfect setting for a domestic squabble.

Much of the force of Crispin's argument was directed not at his partner, but at himself, because he recognized that his plan, and its intended executor, had an air of desperation about them. Both men were, in fact, full of fear. Jim was afraid that the plan would lead to disaster; Crispin's fear was a more immediate one of losing momentum.

Eventually Jim acquiesced reluctantly, for lack of an alternative, reflecting ruefully that this was exactly the basis on which he had won the initial agreement of the regional leadership for the whole enterprise. Having invoked the inertia principle himself, he now found himself powerless to resist its advance. They agreed to make a start on trying to contact Jacko the following day. However, the next day brought news that was to hold up their plans.

Down in Southdale Alan had died unexpectedly of a heart attack. Jim immediately decided that he wanted to attend the funeral. Crispin initially opposed this on security grounds, arguing that the police would obviously film the occasion and run a check on the mourners. But he soon relented in Jim's case, though not in his own, conceding that there was force in his argument that, since Jim would be expected anyway, his

95

absence might excite more attention than his presence.

He also recognized that Jim had two very valid reasons for attending that did not apply to himself. One was to pay his respects to a comrade from whom he had learnt some lessons and who had helped his political development; the other – in Crispin's view equally legitimate – reason was the young man's right to fight for his corner, even from his temporary exile. He could sense in his partner the possibly unrecognized attraction of a power struggle, the primal response of a political activist to the sweet smell of a fight over a leader's succession.

So they declared a two-day moratorium on contacting Jacko, and the next day Jim drove down to Southdale for Alan's funeral.

The crematorium was set in a small park on the edge of town. The chapel had seating for eighty. Designed to accommodate all faiths, but only if they were not too devoutly held, it could hardly have satisfied any. Jim found the compromises upon which the décor rested – exemplified by the stained glass with secular motifs – distasteful and vaguely sacrilegious. If you were religious you would presumably prefer to worship in a proper church or mosque or synagogue, and if you were an atheist you would not want to worship at all, so what useful purpose did this tarted-up waiting room fulfil? It disturbed him, as did the chimney beyond it with the unwelcoming smoke, an image he could not separate from memories of old newsreels of concentration camps. This is nothing to do with Alan's life, he thought: surely there has to be a better way of saying goodbye?

As Jim took his place between Martin and Bill in the row immediately behind Alan's family he reflected that only a few years before, the funeral of a comrade of Alan's stature would have filled the chapel and left a sizeable crowd outside the doors. But the slow death of industry, the repression and the fear, had thinned their ranks. The chapel was only half full.

As he listened to the oration, which was delivered by Frank, he checked on who was there and who was missing. There were a lot of absences from so-called prominent figures in the local movement. Even some leading Party members had not turned up. Where was that bastard Lou, for example? Celebrating his victory in that union election, no doubt. But this was where he should have been if he had any self-respect – in the symbolic front line, shoulder to shoulder with his comrades, living and dead. 'That bastard Lou' – the voice in his head was that of a new Jim, speaking in tones he had learnt from Crispin Pharaoh. The undifferentiated respect for experienced comrades which had been his a few weeks before was slipping.

And rightly so, he thought. Because people whose non-attendance would have excited no comment had made the effort and run the risk. Comrades or friends whom Alan had worked with, perhaps only briefly, over the years, in the workplace or the union or the locality, people with no position or reputation – some known to Jim, some not, and one or two of them looking quite ill or down at heel – *they* were there, shaming their leaders.

Then he realized that this was, in a sense, their day, as well as Alan's final triumph. A man's worth lay in his ability to impress and inspire not his peers, but those less close to him. Leaders were transitory, as good as their last victory only. What would endure, survive even the dark days they were in, were people like these whose festival this small funeral had become.

There were tears in Jim's eyes as he stepped out into the cold morning. From inside an unmarked car opposite the chapel the police were taking photographs. Impulsively he raised his fist in salute. Forward ever. Fuck you bastards.

After a few drinks in a nearby pub to take away the cold, Jim, Frank, Martin and Bill held a short meeting at the bookshop. They elected Martin as their new chairman, with Jim as his deputy. It was agreed that they should recommend to the regional committee at its next meeting the removal of Lou from the leadership and the cooption of two new members, if prior discussions with them proved satisfactory. Then, after approving a progress report from Jim on activities in Northburn, they dispersed.

Driving back to Northburn, Jim's thoughts were in a jumble. He was gratified, and genuinely surprised, by his elevation to the deputy chairmanship, though he had some doubts as to whether he would ever be around to actually fill the post. On the other hand, he had to face the evidence of the Party's continued decline. We bury our dead in semi-secrecy, check on who has reneged this week, and then piss off again. A nice, tidy shop with nothing on the shelves is what we run. I'm the new deputy of sod all.

All this was in his head, abstracted, emotionless. He felt drained of feeling. Had he known what Crispin had been up to in his absence, it might at least have got his adrenalin flowing.

Crispin had spent an hour debating with himself whether he should contact Tom. The idea was crazy and he knew it, a calculated exercise in how to make an already dangerous and complex situation even worse. But he was tempted, prompted by his certainty now that Tom had been the chief conspirator against him, by his proximity to his foe, by the fact that Jim, who would certainly and rightly have vetoed any contact, was absent. When he decided finally to postpone contacting him until the Hardcoats operation was properly set up, there was an element of compromise in his decision. Denied one treat, he would placate himself with another. He could still take advantage of Jim's absence by contacting Pamela instead.

Selling the idea to himself, he had intended to limit this contact to a lunchtime drink, but one thing led to another, and they ended up adjourning to his flat in order to snatch an hour of love in the middle of a working day. It was, of course, a crazy breach of security, a crossing of the Rubicon as total, in its way, as contacting Tom would have been. He had never admitted to her before that he was actually living in Northburn.

'Christ, Chris, you're slumming it a bit,' she commented as he let her in.

'Well, it's only temporary,' he said, helping her off with her coat and showing her straight into the bedroom.

'You could have made the bed, you pig,' she said, instinctively starting to straighten the sheets.

'Later,' he said, plugging in an electric blow heater in a belated attempt to defrost the air in the room. 'Come on, get them off.'

Undressed, they shivered in each other's arms, under the blankets in the narrow bed. Then they made love, urgently, without preliminaries, and after that the cold had gone.

But not the curiosity.

'Do you share this place with anyone, Chris?'

'Yeah, two bum boys, three Filipino au pairs and a small flock of sheep.'

'No, seriously.'

'A young comrade called Jim Carson I'm doing some work with.'

'Where's he now?'

'At a funeral in Southdale. That's why I took the opportunity to ring you while he was away. I don't think he would approve of all this frivolity.'

'Ah, so the Party provides you with a chaperone these days?'

'All part of the service, and some would say not before time.'

'I don't suppose you're going to tell me what you're up to here?'

'Only under torture. My lips are sealed.'

'Mm, I like a bit of mystery,' she said, running a fingernail up his spine. 'Look, I've got to be back at work in half an hour.'

'So what do we do with the other twenty five minutes?' he asked, cupping her breasts in his hands.

'We'll think of something.'

When he saw her down to her car it was with a strange sense of relief that they had finished before Jim's return. Perhaps this is what being underground is all about, he thought: you end up so that everything has to be hidden from everyone.

21

He was either a police agent or he wasn't, and there was no way of finding out except by taking your courage in your hands and approaching him. Once you had crossed that mental barrier, science did not really come into it, nor did subtlety. Making contact with Mad Jacko came down to a simple question of getting hold of him by himself in a quiet corner and saying, excuse me, but we're from the Party and it's time we had a chat. Simple, but there had to be a dozen ways of doing it dead wrong. It was the first open political contact they had had to make with a stranger since they came to Northburn, the sort of approach that has to be handled with care in the most ideal of conditions, and far more so in circumstances of near illegality. If they got it wrong, there might well not be a second chance.

So they sweated over it. And after a week of observation, shadowing him like a pair of private eyes until they no longer even felt self-conscious about it, they had a pretty good picture of his habits. He lived in a flat on a bleak concrete fortress of an estate a couple of miles from Hardcoats known as Hillside Terraces and he travelled to work by bus. He was an average time-keeper. He did not go out to the pub at lunchtime, though he might drop in after work if he had worked over, which he did twice during the week in question. There was a wife and young children in the flat, but he did not seem to spend a lot of time with them. In fact he went out on his own every night, to pubs – not a particular pub, just pubs – and he stayed in them till closing time. The picture they got was of someone who liked to be lonely in a crowd. He did not appear to have a girlfriend, or a regular set of mates.

Eventually they decided that the simplest way to introduce themselves was to give him a lift to work. They caught him at seven in the morning, standing by himself at the bus stop, dressed only in trainers, tight jeans and a denim jacket, despite the covering of snow on the ground. Jim wound down the car window.

'You work at Hardcoats, mate?'

'Yeah.'

'We're going that way. Want a lift?'

'Cheers.' He climbed into the back. His clothes were dirty and smelt of a mixture of stale sweat, oil and cannabis.

'Some fucking bus service, eh?' Crispin said over his shoulder.

'Fucking crap. Do you two work at Hardcoats? I haven't seen you before.'

'We used to,' said Jim, 'then we got the pedlar.'

'What for?'

100

'We didn't like gaffers,' said Crispin.

'What do you do now, then?' Jacko asked. His tone was one of innocent curiosity, rather at odds with his rough appearance.

'We're professional troublemakers,' said Jim.

'Straight up?'

'Yeah, and we'd like a chat with you sometime, Jacko,' said Crispin.

'How come you know my name?'

'We're from the Party. We've heard good reports of you. We want to check them out.'

'Fuck off. This is a put on.'

'No, it's not. We'd like a pint with you tonight.'

'Hey, look, I'm not sure about this.'

'You weren't planning to take your missus to the theatre, were you?' Crispin asked.

Jacko laughed. 'No way. But look, no offence, but I've never seen you blokes before. How do I know you aren't fuzz or something?'

'You know that bastard convenor of yours, Ted Atha?' Crispin asked.

'Yeah, right cunt.'

'Ask him if he knows Chris Powell. Ask him for a description if you like. He'll put you right. It'll be unprintable, but he'll tell you about me.'

'Ah, you're bullshitting me.'

'You ought to get wise,' said Jim. 'If you're serious about fucking up this system, you need some organization behind you.'

'Sounds like the frigging Army.'

'Yeah, the Red fucking Army.'

They had reached Hardcoats. Crispin stopped the car and turned round.

'Look, Jacko, I think you're more serious than you make out. Where are you going to be at eight o'clock tonight?' His tone was authoritative, brooking no argument.

Jacko paused, but only momentarily. 'OK. Do you know the Crooked Billet on Engine Street? That's where I'll be.' He got out of the car. 'Thanks for the ride.'

'See you then, mate. Do some for me.'

101

'What do you think?' asked Jim, watching Jacko walk off towards the factory gate as Crispin turned the car round in the road.

'I think he'll show.'

'But will he be any good?'

'That's jumping a few steps, isn't it? Look, at the moment I think he's a nutter. But then again, he'd have to be to even speak to us, wouldn't he? As far as I'm concerned right now, as long as he's a kosher nutter, that'll do.'

The Crooked Billet was a scruffy pub in the south of the city, mainly patronized by workers, or ex-workers, from a couple of run-down engineering works. Crispin assumed that Jacko must have worked around there at some stage; it was not, otherwise, a particularly obvious spot for a meeting. Even Crispin had to rack his brains to remember whether he had ever had a drink there before. Inside, it was obvious that the place had not been decorated, or even properly cleaned up, in years. Parts of the seating area (lounge would have been too grand a term) were shrouded in semi-darkness, and customers were thin on the ground. Altogether, Jacko could have picked a worse spot for their purpose.

When Jacko turned up, right on time, he had smartened himself up and was wearing a suit that looked like it was normally reserved for weddings and a shirt designed for playing championship snooker in.

'Well, he's bright-eyed and bushy-tailed tonight,' Jim remarked as he approached their table.

'Hello, Jacko,' said Crispin, feeling the cloth. 'What's up, mother-in-law died?'

'Didn't want you to think I was a scruff,' said Jacko, smiling.

'No danger.'

There then followed what could fairly be described as exploratory talks, helped on by ale.

Jacko talked about himself, freely, with the air of a man who was practised at telling all to strangers. He had been in the Paratroop Regiment, or the SAS, or possibly the one and then the other; his account was ambiguous. He had seen a lot of active service, and done some firing in anger. The Army had

102

been OK, but he did not like the class system underpinning it, or the discipline. He had been busted out after taking a knife to another squaddie, or possibly an NCO; again the account was vague when it came to details. The charge had started off as attempted murder, but they had reduced it to GBH so he had got off with a year in military prison and a dishonourable discharge. The prison had been tough – no chance to go running to the welfare office, everything done at the double and guaranteed total loss of remission: it was intended to break men, but in his case, of course, it had simply hardened him up.

On his release he had lived off his wits for a time, done a lot of drugs and a spot of reading. He had even written a bit – poems and stories about army life. Then he had got married and gone back to his home town. A few jobs at his trade in factories and on sites, and then the present one had come up. He had been bloody lucky; he never told them anything about his army service, just left that section of the application form blank, and fortunately they had never asked.

He had been interested in politics ever since he had seen through the bullshit and the brainwashing in the Forces. They weren't the first people he had met from the Party, but this was the first time he had had the chance of a proper discussion and he welcomed it.

The questions he asked were articulate. They showed a familiarity with political ideas, but in a muddled and idiosyncratic way, suggestive of a man who had developed his thinking in isolation. They also suggested an explosive, resentful temperament, shot through with violence and frustration, beneath a controlled façade. Crispin recognized the type – basically intelligent but unstable, with natural talents unrecognized and undeveloped which had never completely vanished but had become distorted as a result of neglect. The veneer of charm masked a personal, and hence political, psychopathy. He remembered what Lenin had said about revolutions attracting the very best and the very worst elements in the working class, and he remembered how many lads just like this he had turned away in his time.

But this time it was a mirror image of those earlier meetings with wild men. The answers he was giving Jacko now – instead of tending, gently but inexorably, towards the conclusion that the Party was too full to find a place for comrade James – were tailored instead to pander to his instability, to emphasize every violent, antisocial interpretation that could, at a pinch, be placed upon Party policy.

It's called stretching a point, he thought, and the damnable thing is I'm not half bad at it.

Of course they did not tell him what they were after. Instead they dropped dark hints about subversive activity at Hardcoats, mingled with instructions that he was to keep his head down until they told him otherwise. They relied on his imagination to do the rest. They also got an agreement that they should meet regularly to further his political education.

During a natural break, while Jacko was taking a leak, Crispin asked Jim his opinion.

'He's a headbanger, but I don't think he's a police agent.'

'So he'll do?'

'He'll have to, I suppose. I'll tell you something else, though.'

'What's that?'

'He drinks like an alcofrolic.'

Crispin realized at once that Jim was right. Every round Jacko had been rattling an empty glass when theirs were still half full, and the last round he had set up some shorts on the side. And he was starting to talk wilder, more aggressively, as the liquor took hold; they had had to ask him to lower his voice twice already.

'Be bloody funny if he suggested blowing up Hardcoats before we did.'

'Wouldn't it just.'

Ten minutes later he made precisely that offer, along with some suggestions for selective assassinations.

'Not just yet, eh, Jacko? Get your feet under the table first.'

At this stage the bell went for last orders, effectively providing the ultimate diversion. Jacko scuttled up to the bar and returned with four pints, one each for Jim and Crispin, and two for himself.

'Sorry I'm a bit short tonight,' he said, downing half of his first pint at a swallow, 'or I'd have doubled up all round.'

'You're all right,' said Jim. 'I was meaning to tell you – come

104

the revolution they'll stay open all night.'

They gave their new accomplice a lift home and he regaled them with a tuneless rendition of the Red Flag from the rear seat. Since he only knew the chorus, it was a bit repetitive.

Hillside Terraces was the sort of estate that ought to breed revolution, but normally produces despair and apathy and scripts for valium. It consisted of five long, narrow blocks of flats, each a couple of stories taller than the one in front, banked up a hillside. All the front doors faced out, across passageways and guard rails, down the hill. Bleak streets suspended in the air.

At night the place had a feral atmosphere. Its inhabitants mainly avoided each other; most of them stayed indoors, while an assertive minority pissed in lifts, dropped milk bottles off the walkways to shatter in the darkness, screwed standing up on pitch-black stairs or in stolen cars, or engaged in territorial feuding at ground level.

They did not hang around once they had dropped Jacko off.

'For Christ's sake don't crash any lights or squash any moggies,' said Jim. 'I'll bet the fuzz mark down anything coming out of there.'

'It always was a rough estate, that one,' said Crispin. 'They moved people there from the old back-to-backs. Then later they used it for bad payers. Now it's like going into a black hole – you don't get out of there alive.'

'Well, we've got our man, if we can keep him sober and stop him from starting the revolution without us.'

'Oh, there's never any problem getting lads like that. Capitalism ain't going to produce working-class leaders to order, but it churns out misfits like Jacko ten a penny. I'll tell you, Jim, this is the easiest job the Party has ever given me. Straight up.'

For a moment he almost meant it.

'You still think this strategy is misguided, don't you?'

'Sure, but even a wrong strategy has to be seen through. There are no short cuts, no easy way out.'

No way out? thought Crispin. What kind of old bollocks is that I'm talking? Crap disguised as Marxist theory for Jim's young and impressionable mind. There's always a way out. You just stop, that's all.

'We'll need to keep very close to that headbanger, Jim,' he went on, 'we haven't got much time to play with.'

22

They saw Jacko again twice during the snowy, fuddling week running up to the Xmas holidays, meeting him in different pubs, listening to his monologues, half deranged and half eager to please, trying to get his measure and gradually extending their influence over him. It had worked. Jacko was like a stray dog who had stumbled on a new master. Now all they had to do was train him.

But Xmas stood in their way. Crispin did some half-hearted shopping for presents for his family, things to carry home wrapped up in his dirty washing, taking Pamela with him for moral support. Strictly speaking, Jim had no home to go to in Southdale, but he had no great desire to stop in Northburn by himself. So he made a few phonecalls until he found a girl in Southdale called Janet who would otherwise have been spending a lonely Xmas too. On December 23rd Crispin and Jim went their separate ways, arranging to return on the 28th.

Jim had not seen Janet for the best part of a year, but his timing was immaculate because she turned out to be on the rebound from a love affair and it was easy enough for them to take things up from where they had left off. They went out together, hand in hand, to buy a turkey and bottles of wine and a television guide, just like a young married couple. Then they did not go out again at all for two days.

Lying in bed late on Boxing Day morning, Janet sleeping beside him and her two cats curled up at their feet, Jim pondered in comfort on his life style. It was the first time in a couple of years that he had spent more than one consecutive night with the same girl. He was twenty five years old, with no family ties, no trade, no job, little money and little luggage. Jim Carson, of no fixed abode. A real bohemian. A description that made him shudder to the depths of his serious-minded soul.

Like Crispin, he had become involved in socialist politics while still at school. But there the similarity ended. Crispin's domestic life had barely been affected by his politics. He had served his time as an engineering apprentice while living with his parents, done his National Service, got married in his early twenties when his girlfriend finally got pregnant, and settled down to a steady job and a rented flat. Apart from being a revolutionary there was little to distinguish Crispin from his contemporaries. True, he was out a lot at meetings, but he could just as easily have been out boozing or working his allotment. His, at least up till eight years ago, had been the conventional working-class lifestyle advocated as a universal model by the Party. And of course he had never really questioned it, even under the peculiar circumstances of working full time for the Party. Ignored it, yes, bent its parameters somewhat, but never questioned its validity.

The times had been different for Jim. He had left school a year later, if no better educated. By then National Service was a distant folk memory and apprenticeships were going the same way. Work had never been so central to his world as it was to Crispin's; he had done various jobs, fitting them in around his political activities. While at work, he worked well, but with no real sense of long-term commitment. Much the same was true of his personal life. Sex no longer led inexorably to pregnancy and marriage: the rules had changed, and he took reasonable advantage of this fact, too.

It would have been very easy, and quite predictable, for Jim to sink into the rôle of paid-up member of the new leisured class created by deindustrialization and efficient contraception, a sort of sub-proletarian punk intellectual. But labour movement traditions were a strong countervailing force in Southdale and these, coupled with his own personality which was intensely puritanical, pushed him in a different direction. He became a full-time, if unpaid, activist for the Party, always available to go where needed; a very together, disciplined young man, using the time that society had given him, in thoughtless plenty, to organize its downfall.

But working with Crispin had shaken some of his preconceptions. On a purely stylistic level, Crispin seemed to get away with things that were logically forbidden. He seemed to have gone beyond the rules that, ostensibly, he had lived by. He was a one-off, an eccentric, who did not give a fuck for anybody or anything. He was also, disconcertingly, the most chillingly effective revolutionary Jim had ever worked with. Crispin had moved beyond the necessities of analysis and expectation into a world of freedom where he could operate unrestrained by fear or inhibition. The weeks spent with him had left Jim confused; he no longer knew what model he was following. Perhaps, indeed, there were none. Each to his own, and all for the cause.

Janet stirred beside him, rubbing him with her bottom. A good lass, Janet. A year or so younger than him, tall, good-looking, of West Indian parentage, she worked as a secretary for a finance company and had got herself a smart flat together. In fact she had a lot more to show for her efforts than he had. Not that he was jealous – just realistic. She was the sort of girl he ought to be settling down with, rather than using as a port in a storm. But that was pure fantasy. It did not fit into his plans at all. A few days holed up here avoiding political contact was fine, but in the New Year a new, and terrifying, phase of struggle beckoned. And there was no way he could tell Janet about that.

He got out of bed to make them a cup of tea. It was a short and painless journey to the kitchen. Janet's flat was small, but it had everything the place in Northburn lacked – carpets, hot water on stream, central heating, a deep freeze and a good stereo. Yes, she had got it together all right.

He plugged the kettle in, seized a mouthful of cold turkey and stuffing from the fridge, and padded back into the living room, where he put a record on – something classical she had played him the night before and which had done the trick then. Cats rubbed against his legs, demanding to be fed. He moved back towards the kitchen. He knew there would be abundant tins of cat food and at least three can openers in working order. The domesticity of women never ceased to amaze him. Going into their houses you felt like a Goth exploring his first villa.

'Is that you up, love?' Janet asked sleepily.

'No, it's your friendly neighbourhood rapist. Happy Boxing Day.'

'What are you doing?'

'Mashing some tea and feeding your moggies. Then I'm coming back to bed to show you what I'm made of.'

'Fetch us a mince pie, then.'

'Your word is my command.'

23

Crispin approached the journey home to Carlton with all the single-mindedness of a skid-row drunk in transit. He boarded the 125 Inter-City Express straight after the cleaners had done their work, and a good half-hour before it was due to depart. For the journey to London, which was scheduled to take less than three hours, he had provided himself with newspapers, magazines, sandwiches, a bottle of aspirin, a volume of mind-numbingly boring articles and speeches by Togliatti, a half-bottle of whisky and four cans of strong, German-style lager.

His objective in arriving early was simple. Most seats on the 125 were arranged in fours, two pairs facing each other across a table. In such circumstances strangers thrown together would tend to fall into conversation, and this he wanted to avoid at all costs – not for security reasons, though this provided a good rationale, but on grounds of general unsociability. Crispin, too mean to reserve a place of his choosing, was anxious to secure a seat in one of the occasional isolated pairs found at the rear of the compartments.

Having found just such a pair with no reservation tickets on them (he just had to hope that these had not been accidentally removed, as sometimes happened, leading to disputes later) he stationed himself in the outside of the two seats, placing his belongings on the window seat beside him. It was a challenge. People would readily ask anyone sitting by themselves in the window seat if the place next to them was taken, but somehow it was psychologically more difficult when it was the other seat that was vacant, especially if access to the seat in question was barred by a large man with a lot of drink in front of him and an expression saying 'adios amigo'.

The stratagem worked. Two days before Xmas the 125 was full of punters heading home from exile in the North, but none of them breached Crispin's exclusion zone.

Crispin thoroughly enjoyed this stage of the journey. He skim-read Togliatti with eye, but not brain, engaged while he drank in a steady rhythm. Take a good mouthful of ale. Wait two minutes. Uncap the whisky – the bottle still in its brown paper bag to show you're a serious drinker – take a shot, replace the cap. Wait two minutes. Repeat the sequence from the top, first the beer, then the scotch. Vary occasionally by taking a sandwich, or a look out of the window.

He finished the whisky at Hitchin, the last can of lager somewhere near Wood Green, and arrived at Kings Cross well drunk.

The next stage of the journey was perilous. Before braving the tube journey across central London, he visited the station delicatessen and pharmacist to purchase more cans of beer, more sandwiches and another bottle of whisky in a brown paper bag. Then he took the Circle Line to Embankment, the route he always used in order to avoid changing lines. Safely arrived at Charing Cross station, he celebrated by having, for the sake of variety, a pint of draught bitter in a buffet frequented by a mixed clientele of railway staff, resident down-and-outs, and bona fide travellers like himself.

After that he settled down to an interminable ride in an antediluvian boneshaker of a train – so unlike the 125 they barely seemed to belong to the same service – that limped its way through every suburb and hamlet from the Thames to the South Coast. By now his drinking was becoming more unreal. He no longer needed to discourage human contact; he had acquired an invisible aura of unapproachability.

When he got out at Carlton it was snowing and the little station was unmanned and deserted. Fortunately there was a public phone at the station and it was in working order. He rang

Mary and told her he had arrived, then he sat in the bleak waiting room, surrounded by a century's carved initials, staring morosely at the place where there would have been an open fire blazing in the glorious days of steam and manned stations, and swigging scotch desperately.

He regained his spirits as soon as Mary turned up.

'Christ, love,' he said, climbing into the passenger seat, 'I'm glad you're here. I feel a bit lonely.'

'And a bit smashed?'

'Totally bombed out, to be honest.'

'Yeah, I can smell it.'

'I always was a bad traveller. All those strangers, and having to remember where to change tubes. It's too much hassle.' She looked at him quizzically. 'You poor, neurotic, drunken clown, it's good to see you in one piece.'

And probably it was, though by now Crispin had irretrievably set the tone – psychologically, spiritually and probably metabolically – for the whole short holiday. He knew this as soon as he got back to their house and sat warming himself in front of the fire, brandy in one hand and a sandwich in the other, as a preliminary to falling asleep in the chair.

He knew there would be good bits – chatting to Mary over drinks as she worked in the kitchen, lying warm and instinctively at home in the curves of her sleeping form – mild therapy for bone-weary outlaws. But otherwise it would be boredom blurred by drink, the recipe as before, and he would be glad when it was over. He had business to finish and would not be happy until it was done. Mentally he needed to remain in the greater reality of Northburn, back in his personal Liang Shan P'o.

Over the next few days the considerable quantities of drink taken were to have an ambiguous effect on his personality. At one extreme, as on Xmas Day when he all but collapsed during their lunch, it made him morose and withdrawn. At the other, like on the final day when he stayed up all night carousing with a comrade who had driven over to see him from a town a few miles away, it enabled him to enter into a never-never land of wit and good cheer. But always it was a prop for unreality; an antidote to frustration at being thus becalmed.

111

In retrospect he could identify, and remember with something approaching awe, one break – real or illusory – in this endless catalogue of boozing. So atypical was it that it was to become, paradoxically, his symbol of the brief holiday.

It occurred on Boxing Day morning when, no doubt still intoxicated from the day before, he felt moved to action as soon as he drew the curtains by the sight of the fresh snow on the ground, reflecting the cold sunlight, and the feel of chill in the air. He dug through a cupboard for his old walking boots with the thick socks still stuffed in the tops, the anorak and the stick, and dressed himself in them for the first time since the autumn – noting as he did so one of the skeletal leaves from his last outing still trapped in the dried mud on the boot soles. Quite the squire today, he thought, briefly inspecting himself in this equipment in a mirror, before setting out for a brisk walk in the Kent countryside.

He strode down the lane away from the house, which at that moment seemed a place of danger, crossed a stile, and joined the old road used by medieval pilgrims and, before them, travellers since prehistory. Taking deep and visible breaths of cold air, he tramped through the snow, following from memory what would usually have been a well-defined path up the side of a hill into the woods which covered the ridge top for a stretch of several miles with only an occasional break. Well, pilgrim, he said under his breath, you've got the world to yourself this morning.

He stopped at the first break in the trees to look down at the valley. Easy to smile indulgently at picture-postcard farms and churches and oast houses, but there was rich soil below the snow, land worth fighting over and most of it still firmly in the grip of its last – Norman – conquerors. A pretty scene, but deadly.

Funny how plans fail to work out. He had seen his retirement place, his break from the city, in terms of a stone-built terraced house in a northern market town, with working people in the pubs and a mountain looking down on them. Instead, as retirement drew nearer, he found himself stuck in this fertile rural wasteland. Unless, unless. Better not to think of it.

And difficult to think, looking down on agribusiness and tourist board Kent, that he had work to do back in the badlands where he had spent most of his days. Changed lands now – ravaged by cynically created depression, gripped by a very British, perfectly legal, slightly incongruous repression; populated, as far as he was concerned, by enemies, traitors and men with guns and prisons. It was all unreal, as unreal as the virgin snow before him, the only untrodden territory left in these islands, bar the sands when the tide runs out. Yes, old lad, he thought, every fucking square foot was bought and sold and bled over before you were born. You came into the game late in the day.

He walked on into the woods, dead silent except for the occasional fall of accumulated snow from a branch. So soothingly, numbingly monotonous was the scene, that when some tiny movement caught his eye, he instinctively stopped. About fifty yards ahead, standing square on the path, was a full-grown deer. He looked at it with a degree of awe. The woods were full of deer, he knew that, but they were creatures that you glimpsed moving through the foliage, so momentarily that you wondered whether they had really been there or not. He had never seen one full frontal before.

They stood and looked at each other for a long, silent couple of minutes. I'm privileged, thought Crispin; in fact I've got to have some peasant in me to have been given this sight of you. But be not afraid. You are safe with me. Unlike my murderous neighbours, I carry no gun. I am far too urban to be interested in killing animals.

When the deer moved off he felt like waving farewell. It was a moment of magic in all the madness.

Back at the house he found Mary in the kitchen, carving slices of cold pork and turkey for a salad lunch. Once he had taken his boots off, he poured a gin for himself, neat with ice, and a sherry for his wife and they sat with their drinks at the kitchen table.

'Enjoy your walk, love?'

'Yeah. I saw a deer. It just stood on the path and looked at me. Amazing.'

'Begging for some local fascist to shoot it.'

'That's right. I told the bugger, sorry, old son, but I only shoot landowners. On your bike.'

113

He sat for a moment in silence, wriggling his toes in the thick socks, smelling the sweat and tasting the gin. Then he continued:

'How would you feel if I suggested selling up the business and taking the money and running? Going abroad somewhere.'

'Are you serious?'

'Well, it's been going well enough, but we never intended it to last for ever, did we? And the kids don't want it as far as I know.'

'This is true. The business is dispensable. I just can't see you going abroad, Chris. Where would you go – the GDR? Cuba? You always hated foreign holidays. Frankly, I can't think of anywhere where they speak English that would be likely to take us. Anyway, would we get passports? We'd have to use our real names, wouldn't we?'

Good old Mary, practical to the last.

'I don't know. Anywhere that's not here.'

She took his hand.

'You're in trouble, aren't you? Look, it doesn't matter, Chris. If we have to go abroad, we'll go. It doesn't make any difference.'

'Thanks,' he squeezed her hand. 'I never thought I'd be talking about going into exile.' She gave him the same quizzical look he had seen on her face when she had met him at the station.

'Chris, love, you've been in exile all your life.'

24

December 27th. A day with no name. Two days worse than Xmas, and that's saying some, thought Jacko. He sat at the kitchen table, sucking the last scorching dregs of a blast out of a roach and disgorging the smoke into an empty beer glass for reinhalation. Waste not want not. How did that old tune go?

'Zonked at breakfast,
stoned in the evening,
bombed at supper time;
be my little sugar
and love me all the time'

Love? I should be so frigging lucky.

Around him was the accumulated debris of the holiday period, not only the box of empty bottles and the plastic sack of balled-up wrapping paper, but all their unfinished business: hers, the sinkful of dishes, the washing machine overflowing with dirty clothes and topped off with the sheets from the beds the kids had wet the night before, the chair piled high with ironing: his, the broken steam iron, radio and electronic toys, pointedly awaiting repair on the table.

The high passed into a wave of irrational, paranoid fury. What a pissy dump! Why can't the lazy slag keep the place clean? She expects me to repair this junk. Fuck that for a scene. I spend all lousy week doing exactly that for the man. Why waste my holidays doing the same for free, just so the bitch can go and break them all over again? She probably does it on purpose to get out of doing the ironing and that. And can't she for Christ's sake keep them fucking kids quiet?

Jacko's two young children were squabbling in the next room. Their voices, mingled with the soundtrack from the television and clarified by the dope, carried through the hardboard wall. Jacko's personal hi-fi lay with the other broken things. There was no way of blotting them out.

Slipping an oven glove over his right hand, Jacko began to torment the cat, a young tortoiseshell queen, swinging at her, poking her, provoking her to claw and bite with futile savagery at the padded glove.

'Come on, you fur-coated bitch. Come on, I'll break your goddam neck, you vicious bastard.'

Lyn, his wife, chose this moment to enter the room. Thin and nervy, looking like there would be lucky to be six stone of her under her jeans and t-shirt, she rooted round the table, searching for a cigarette, ignored by Jacko.

'Jesus, Jacko, can't you stop tormenting that beast?'

115

'Take some more valium, woman, and go back to sleep. Give some to the fucking kids while you're on.'

'Jesus, you shitty lousy fucking rotten bastard. I'm surprised you've even fucking noticed we've got fucking kids.'

She was clinging to his left arm and screeching in his ear, desperate with frustration. Jacko felt a degree of calm settle on his mind. He slipped his right hand out of the glove, leaving the cat to savage it at will as she dragged it over the floor. Then he turned round and slapped Lyn across the face with the back of his hand.

She fell into an old sofa set up against the wall and sat there for a moment, a trickle of blood at the corner of her mouth, with a surprised expression on her face. Then she started sobbing, an open-mouthed, gasping cry of pain.

That's your second mistake, bitch, thought Jacko, his mind still calm; first you aggravate me, then you play for sympathy. One for the money, two for the show, fuck you baby, here we go.

He seized her by the hair with his left hand, pulled her to her feet, then punched her twice in the face, knocking her back down again. In the next room the children had fallen silent. Well, I've found something that works, he thought. On the couch Lyn wimpered, covering her face, curling into a foetal ball.

'I'm going to the pub,' he said, matter-of-fact, pulling on his jacket. Then he went out, not even slamming the door behind him.

Surprisingly, for a holiday, the lift was working. He listened to its creaking approach, then he heard the urine swilling round inside it as the doors opened. Fuck that, he thought, I'll use the stairs.

You needed to watch where you put your feet on the stairs, too. Dog shit and vomit in dark corners. Broken syringes and knotted condoms. Not to mention graffiti to chill the blood.

Outside it was cold. Jacko turned up his collar, stuck his hands in his pockets and set off down the path through Hillside Terraces, calculating angles of fire as he did so. What had Connolly said about a street being simply a defile through a city? Even better with flats than houses. Station snipers every-where. Pin the bastards down.

116

There were more kids outside than grown ups. Young lads showing off their new bikes. Slightly older lads smashing up what was left of an abandoned car. A group of teenagers hanging round the entrance to a passageway. One of them shouted over.

'Are we on for today, Jacko?'

'Not today, try Steve.'

Decisive action. I've got to turn over a new leaf. For the Party. In fact I ought to try and get myself fit for the Party while I'm on. He stepped up his pace until he was almost jogging.

It was a pity Chris and Jim were away for Xmas. In the few days since he had last seen them a million questions had come into his head. He ought to start writing them down before he forgot them. Be systematic about it. Because Marxism was a systematic business, he had sussed that out. Those guys had the answers, no doubt about that, and he needed to get them off them. Otherwise he would not be equipped to do a job for the Party, whatever that job might be.

Chris and Jim had been vague on that one. Not that you could really blame them. They had to be sure he was reliable, fair dos, and he had to make sure he was ready. Well, he would be ready all right. However difficult, however dangerous, however violent it turned out to be, he would do what the Party required of him.

He wished he could have a drink with Chris or Jim right now. His usual mates, unable to share his new obsession, irritated him, with their heads full of booze and drugs and pornography to the exclusion of any new excitement. Still, they were a damn sight better than staying at home. He turned into the Eight Bells.

There was nobody in the bar he especially wanted to talk to. So he sat down with a pint, took out a pamphlet from his pocket and started reading. This was an act unusual enough in itself to cause one or two heads to turn. Then they saw, or somebody told them, that Jacko had got politics, much as he might have got religion or got leprosy, and they looked away again. Nobody tried to engage him in argument, or even pull his leg. Times had changed. Politics was no longer a joke or a drag. Politics was positively bad news.

117

The words swam on the paper in front of Jacko's eyes. He could have used a boost of speed or dope to help him along. He had already read one or two books that Jim had given him – *The Communist Manifesto*, Connolly's *Revolutionary Warfare* – and they had not been too bad, but this latest one – Lenin's *State and Revolution* – was heavy stuff. But he was going to persevere. If that was what they wanted, fair enough: there had to be something in it. And when they met to discuss the pamphlet, he would see if he couldn't persuade a couple of his mates from work to come along. The more he showed willing, he figured, the sooner he would get a chance to win his spurs.

The words did not get any easier, but after a while his man showed up and he scored. Speed and dope for himself, the last of his holiday pay blown, but this time no smack for the kids. He was turning over a new leaf, preparing for the revolution.

25

Xmas is a flat and vulgar season, busy but empty, when it's your karma to be an old man's fancy – not even his kept woman, which might just be fun, but the lawfully wedded second wife of a man old enough to be your father, with no children to care for and everything material you need indoors, along with quite a lot you don't.

Pamela lay in bed, feigning sleep as her husband padded round the bedroom in his pyjamas, coughing quietly, looking for his cigarettes. Pathetic. If I was human I'd get up and give him a hand. No, I might as well make the most of this, she thought, today is going to be quite long enough as it is without volunteering for an extension. More entertaining to do. His daughter coming for the day, with her wimpish husband and her obnoxious children, who ought to have been gassed at birth. God, I'll be glad to get back to work. And even gladder when

118

Chris gets back. He jokes about my bourgeois lifestyle. He ought to try it for a week.

And for what seemed like the millionth time, the same hackneyed question ran through her head: how did I get into this? Well, actually, I blame the Party. The Party, comrade? Yes, comrade, the Party. You see, I joined it as a shy, bookish girl from a respectable working-class home. And it changed my life. Gave me a taste for older men, and the confidence to pull one with a bit of class. Well, allegedly. My case rests. It's all the Party's fault, I tell you.

The Party. My finishing school. Where I spent what were definitely the happiest days of my life. It didn't do much for me politically, I have to admit, because I remain to this day an unrepentant soggy liberal, able to tolerate even my high Tory husband and his fascistic relatives. But my God it was good for the rest of me. There I was, the bricklayer's daughter who never fitted in at grammar school, who did not really trust anything I had not read in a book, and suddenly I found myself in this exciting and dangerous world, where it was possible to be clever, and tough, and sexy, and anything else you wanted to be, and still keep your accent. You could even talk to your family about it. They might not exactly agree with you, what with their residual Catholicism and their Labour voting, but at least it was partially within their experience, unlike 'A' level Latin and your smartarse grammar school friends. Yes, happy days.

And the Party had this way of both using, and developing, your talents. They did it in a subtle, gentle way. I used to take minutes at meetings longhand, in a big hard-backed book. God knows why, I don't think anyone except me ever read them. But it broke me in. Then they got me to speak at Party meetings. Opening the political discussion, they called it. You had to familiarize yourself with the Party's analysis of current affairs, and then make a speech about it which the other comrades would then chew over. From there I progressed to representing the Party at public meetings, actually getting up on my hind legs in front of strangers in cold halls and giving them the Party line on anything from proportional representation to the non-aligned movement. I think of that sometimes these days when

119

I'm in the witness box in front of some geriatric judge. Don't try to rattle me, you old bastard, I think: I've done this before and there's nothing to be scared of. In fact, now I've learnt to be an exhibitionist, I rather enjoy it.

It was such a full life. Every spare moment you seemed to be doing something connected with the Party – attending a meeting, handing out leaflets, reading a book, it was all Party work. Even if you went to a party, it was usually to raise funds for the organization – a Party party we called those socials, and if anyone wondered what we meant we'd sing the chorus from that Beatles' song, 'yeah we're going to a party party', as a sort of private joke. Chances were you'd been involved in organizing the bugger, anyway.

Yes, a full life indeed. And then there was Chris. I had to come to that. My long, exciting, dangerous love affair with Chris – half guru, half thug, as I saw him then, and, of course, half mine. I was such a slow developer, wasn't I? I used to go round in awe of him, even when we were lovers. God knows what he got out of me; I must have seemed like some sort of sycophantic vampire.

And when we stopped being lovers, I found that the Party was over for me. Oh, not all at once, it does not work like that in real life. I flirted with the opposition to him for a while, out of spite disguised as principle I suppose, and then, once he had departed for Kent, I just gradually drifted away from politics. I started reading the *Guardian* and going to films on general release. Growing up at last.

Then eight years later I pick up the phone and there he is, growling away, as large as life, asking me out to lunch and checking on my bra size. Of course I had to go. There isn't room in the world for the sort of curiosity I was feeling.

My husband has switched on the radio downstairs. What he still persists in calling the 'Light Programme'. Barry Manilow and Mantovani. My old man, who put the M in MOR. This reverie has been pleasant, but it can't go on too long. My bladder is irritatingly full.

The second date with Chris was harder than the first. A drive out into the country, a logical transition between a restaurant date and a bedroom date. Not because I had any doubts about

120

going, just because I wasn't sure how to play it. I remember sitting at that dressing table over there, saying to myself, 'Well, OK, girl, but what am I supposed to let him do this time? Feel my breasts? Put his hand down my tights? I really don't know. I need advice, I'm out of practice.' Etiquette is a tricky area. I was glad when we got through the courtship preliminaries and down to some serious adultery.

It's a crazy affair and I know it makes no sense, but nobody turns me on like Chris. He's the only man in the world who can make me laugh, really laugh. A hard man, but intelligent, witty and full of surprises.

Like just the other day we're sitting in a pub, talking about Freud, who Chris thoroughly disapproves of on principle, although he has never read him. 'OK then,' he says, 'if dreams have a meaning, explain this one I had last night. I'm back in my old office where we used to hold the meetings when I was organizer, and I've got this bailiff in, trying to dun me.' 'That sounds authentic,' I say. 'Right. But would you believe I had a gorilla sitting beside me? "And another thing," says the bailiff in my dream, all self-righteous, "you can get rid of that gorilla. No pets – the lease says so." Now, this is the good bit. The gorilla gets up from its seat, takes the bailiff by the collar and slings him straight through the door and down the stairs. "Up yours, you speciesist bastard," he says. "Good lad," I say, pouring us both a drink, "here's to a working alliance. Now what are we going to do about that door?" What do you think your man Freud would have made of that one?'

I laughed till I almost wet my knickers. Chris Powell, my revolutionary antique dealer, telling me about his crazy dreams. God knows what he's really up to, him and his sharp young partner, but I'm glad he came back.

It's no good, I'll have to go. Pamela pulled her nightgown on and started exploring the area round the bed with her toes, searching for her slippers.

Well, Chris, I fell in love with you once, and it looks like I've gone and done it again. I could leave my old man for you, Chris. Did you know that? You've only got to ask.

121

26

After two more days of serious drinking, culminating in an all-night session with a comrade who called in to see him, Crispin's Xmas holiday was at an end. He headed back up North on December 28th. It was not the best of trips.

He started out with the firm belief, stated emphatically to Mary when he said goodbye to her at the station, that he had drunk himself sober in the course of the night. Certainly he felt none the worse for drink on the journey to London, as he swayed about in the creaking compartment, feet resting on the seat opposite, looking out on the still snowbound fields – a little light-headed, perhaps, a trifle detached, the stomach a bit upset, but nothing out of the ordinary. He had a half-bottle of whisky on him, but he took nothing more than an exploratory sip all the way from Carlton to Kings Cross, braving even the underground with relaxed equanimity.

The trouble started almost as soon as the northbound 125 left the station. Crispin was sitting, carelessly and uncharacteristically, at a table with three old ladies, trying to ignore their crosstalk about their families and feigning an interest in his copy of Togliatti, when he began to feel unwell.

At first it was no more than a feeling of nausea and faintness, which he attributed to the fact that he had eaten little during the preceding twenty four hours. He undid the top button of his shirt and loosened his tie, put down his book and looked out at the scenery in an attempt to distract himself, noting that the snow was now less in evidence than it had been in Kent. But it was no good. He still felt unwell. In fact he felt worse. Within a

122

few minutes he began to be gripped by anxiety, panic, indefinable terror.

It was no time to be surrounded by old ladies. He made his way to the lavatory and locked himself in. Then he bent double as the stomach cramps hit him. His hands were suddenly shaking uncontrollably. He knew he needed a drink, but doubted his ability to take one without vomiting.

But with no valium to hand there was no real alternative except to get worse. Sitting on the floor, too frightened to feel degraded, he took a massive swig of whisky, holding the bottle in both hands, and with curious empathy his body accepted the drink without complaint or argument. He felt just fractionally better as he splashed some water on his face, which meant that he felt like hell. He could have gulped down a gallon of the water which a sign warned him was undrinkable. Somehow he felt inclined to take signs like that terribly seriously, though. Jesus shit, he thought, what a scenario. A middle-aged revolutionary on active service, trapped on an express train with a bad dose of the shakes.

Leaving the lavatory, he positioned himself by the train door and lowered the window slightly to let some air in. There he stood with his head bent to catch the air as the cramps came and went, grappling with his fear, while the door to the compartment opened and shut automatically, its nervous system apparently as shattered as his own.

He had a full range of paranoias to choose from. Fear of the door opening and propelling him on to the line. Fear of some passing guard or traveller detecting his condition, and its cause, and trying to get involved. Fear of fear itself. Three or four times in the course of the journey he had to return to the lavatory, which he never let out of his sight, like a wounded, cornered animal, to drink down the worst of his physical symptoms.

It got no better but after a while he did adjust to the situation which, while filled with horror, was not, in the strictest sense, unbearable. After all, it was finite and he did have the whisky. Without those two comforts, unbearable would have been a fair description, he decided. Grimly, he measured the declining contents of the bottle against the train's progress. It ran late, but no worse than might be expected halfway between Xmas and New Year. Eventually it passed through a station which he knew to be about ten minutes' run from Northburn. It was time to make the effort of will to get back from his corridor perch to the compartment and retrieve his luggage.

'Don't forget your book, dear,' said one of the old ladies, as he lifted his bag down from the rack. The bloody Togliatti.

'Thank you,' he said, putting it into his bag, imagining them thinking, 'Dear, dear, that awful man, he was a communist, you know, and very drunk, you could smell it on his breath.' His voice sounded thick and distant. Contact with old ladies was much too much to handle.

At Northburn he was one of the first off the train and through the barrier. Leaving the station, he walked half the way home, allowing the sense of freedom to work on his nerves until he had calmed down sufficiently to tackle catching a bus. By this stage the shakes had gone, and the cramps had subsided into a dull, steady pain.

On the bus he sat behind a fat gypsy woman who smelt of a combination of piss and patchouli. Accompanied by three young children whom she cajoled and threatened alternately, she seemed to be at the end of her tether. Crispin felt sorry for her in a maudlin, self-projecting way that he found distasteful. He felt an irrational impulse to give her money or offer to help amuse the children, despite his own precarious emotional condition. He started to persuade himself that the children reminded him of his own at a similar age. Any excuse for self torture.

Christ, I've been a lousy father, he thought. One minute they're tiny and left with Mary for her to cope with God knows how, just like this poor cow sitting in front, while I'm off out doing important things for the Party. Next minute, so it seems, they're gone, grown up somehow and survived, little damn thanks to me. I did not even see them this Xmas; just muttered a few drunken commonplaces over the phone on Xmas morning. My paternal duty done.

Suddenly he realized there was a very real chance he might never see his children again.

He was glad to get back to the flat. It felt more like home than home did, and much of his remaining anxiety subsided as he walked through the door, like an animal finding itself back on familiar ground. Jim was already back.

'Good trip?' he asked.

'I've had better. Any beer in the house?'

27

Hogmanay is a collective birthday party, the year's big marker – a time for looking back with discretion and forward in fear and trembling. It is also, of course, an occasion for serious drinking.

Crispin and Jim left the flat early in order to be sure of getting a seat in the pub. They took with them, concealed in coat pockets, the traditional half-bottles of whisky for surreptitiously topping up the miserable and over-priced pub measures.

Standing at the flat door, checking his pockets for his key before he finally closed it, Crispin experienced a bitter-sweet pang of nostalgia, suitable for the season. His mother had always done the same thing when she left the house. Her ritual had been to take the key from her purse, hold it aloft, and then recite aloud, in order to recommit it to memory, her Co-op Society dividend number – 81899. As a small boy he had always assumed that the two acts, checking the key and repeating the number, were part of a single magic ceremony, the correct performance of which was essential if they were to expect readmittance on their return. How these little acts form us, he thought. I'll bet young Jim never went to the Co-op with his mother every single day when he was a toddler. Nearly fifty years later I remember that Co-op number more readily than I can remember my bank account or my National Insurance number now. And, mother, you would not believe the things I've done since then, but I still shop at the Co-op, though not, admittedly, every day.

It was obvious to Crispin, from the moment they got settled down behind their pints and chasers, that his partner had a bone to pick with him before the real drinking started.

'OK, Jim,' he said, 'let's have it, what's on your mind?'

'Chris, you're the strongest comrade politically I've ever worked with, and you've probably forgotten more than I'll ever know about this game, but on a job like this, where there's no room for error, we need to be straight with each other, right?'

Jim paused. Resisting the urge to tell him to get on with it, Crispin nodded agreement.

'So there are a couple of things I'm not happy about,' Jim continued. 'In a way they're personal, so I hope you won't take this wrong.'

'Criticism is the essence of comradeship.' It was the sort of instant quote Crispin had learnt to manufacture to order over the years.

'That's right. Well, look, the first thing is the drinking. I mean, we both like a drink and if you like one a little bit more than me, that's your business. But beyond a certain point, the way we're working together, it could affect me too. It seemed to me, when you got back from Carlton, that you had been drinking far too much. I couldn't even see the whites of your eyes, Chris, and you were all over the place in your head. Now, that's my problem too, isn't it?'

'Yes, of course it is, Jim, and I accept the point you're making. I'd been on the booze over Xmas. I'm not on the wagon now, but it's under control and it'll stay that way until we're finished here. Does that help you?'

'Sure. Look, Chris, I don't want to pry into your private life, and I realize that I'm at fault in a way in dragging you out of retirement and disrupting your home life, but if there's anything personal you want to discuss, or you think I could help with, just say the word.'

'Thanks. But it's not really like that, Jim. I guess I'm just an old boozer and I got carried away for a while. It's a bit dull down there, you know, not much in the way of action. When this is over, I promise you I'll take Mary on a proper holiday. In fact I should have written it into my contract, the Party could always have swung a couple of weeks on the Black Sea for me. Now what's the other point?'

'This is even heavier. Bluntly, Chris, it's Pamela. Now please don't misunderstand me; who you sleep with is entirely your

126

business. But she knows you of old, still calls you Chris Powell. She's no longer in the Party, she's married to someone who is hardly likely to wish us well and you seeing her has to be a security risk. Look, I stayed with a lass in Southdale over Xmas, so I'm not getting moralistic, but I swear I didn't tell her a word about where I was staying or what I was doing. Now when I find you bringing Pamela back to the flat, I've got to get worried about security.'

Crispin had noticed before how hard it was to get mad with Jim. The boy had far too much sincerity and a charm all of his own. But my Christ he could be a right puritanical young bastard. Cromwell and him would have got on like a house on fire. No papists, no royalists, and for sure no festivities at Xmas. And yours truly would be down as one of the ranting crew. Well, let's take the line of least resistance, grin and bear it and promise to be a good boy in future. Mea culpa. Mea maxima culpa.

'You're right again, Jim. Being in the Party doesn't immunize you against the corruption of the society we live in, and I suppose I'm a pretty averagely flawed product of capitalism. As a matter of fact, you're being too soft on me. My affair with Pamela is morally dishonest as well as being a security problem. I'd already decided to fuck her off before you raised the matter. The only problem is timing. Do it prematurely and it could be counterproductive, if you follow me. So let me work on it, eh? Meantime I promise you I won't use the flat in future, and it goes without saying I won't mention any of our business to her. Is that OK?'

'Sure. Look, I'm sorry I had to raise this, Chris.'

'Not at all. You did right.'

He ruffled the back of Jim's hair playfully, noting the tensed muscles in the young man's neck. Time you got some therapy, he thought. He felt the desire to make a speech, however incoherent.

'Moral questions, questions of how we live, *are* important. These days I don't think we give enough attention to values in the Party. There's a feeling that anything goes, and the kind of values I recognize – solidarity, honesty, discipline, courage – are denigrated and sneered at. And that sort of approach leads

127

straight to political opportunism; you end up as just another more or less bent trade union bureaucrat or social democrat politician.'

'It's down to abandoning Marxism, isn't it?'

'Absolutely. You see it many times. They blame the working class because it gets demoralized and won't fight, as if there was anything surprising about that, as if the class had been specially created to take endless clog at the whim of its so-called leaders. The bastards don't understand history, Jim. The working class understands history because at the end of the day it *is* history and it deserves better leaders than a shower of opportunists slagging it off.' He took a swig of beer, warming to his theme. 'Cuba is a good example. Everyone had it wrong there except Castro because he was the only one who understood the historical process at work. You know, when Castro attacked the Moncada barracks his followers were armed with .22 rifles, bloody fairground shooters, toys really, and naturally they were wiped out. But Castro wasn't bothered, and for sure he didn't blame the people for failing to support him. "History will absolve me," he said in court. A few years later he's back in action, landing from Mexico in the Gramna. And what happens? They walk straight into an ambush. Only about eight of them escape, but they include Fidel and Raul, Che Guevara and Cienfuegos. Makes you realize how circumstances create leaders rather than vice versa, doesn't it? I mean if Che had died and Pedro Soap had survived, then Pedro Soap would have been famous today, just like Plekhanov says. Anyway, the odds against them are impossible, but they fight on. And it doesn't matter that they're hopelessly outnumbered, because history is on their side. Batista's society is collapsing, leaving a vacuum, and the people gradually turn to the guerrillas. In a couple of years their armies are occupying Havana in triumph. Moral of this story – don't let the odds scare you into opportunism. If history is on your side, you have nothing to fear. Just stick to your guns and sooner or later you'll win through. And history is on our side, Jim, I'm sure of that.'

'Even if we're following a wrong strategy?'

'*Especially* if we're following a wrong strategy. Remember Moncada.'

Jim went to get another round in. Crispin was on form. It was going to be a good night. He felt vindicated. Crispin had accepted his criticism like a true revolutionary. He had been right to raise the matters.

Crispin noticed that the pub was starting to fill up. We're going public. Time to stop haranguing each other. Time for excessive drinking and talking nonsense.

28

They had been a bit taken aback when Jacko announced, with great pride, that he had got a couple of his workmates interested in the idea of political education. It was not quite what they had had in mind, and it seemed to create a potentially proliferating security problem. But there did not seem any way out of it without taking Jacko more into their confidence than they had planned at this stage. So they adjusted their plans accordingly and made the necessary arrangements.

The room above the pub, booked in the name of a non-existent model train enthusiasts' society, was dingy and scruffy, with full ashtrays and dirty glasses left behind from a previous letting. The one thing to be said in its favour was that it was free, a sprat to catch a mackerel of extra custom, offered by a landlord whose business was bad. He looked a bit hurt when he realized that the model train club only had five members, but cheered up somewhat when he got sight of Jacko's rate of consumption.

Jacko's two workmates turned out to be an articulate, but slightly deranged, Scot, a plater by trade, and a young labourer who said little when introduced. They soon had the three of them settled down upstairs, ready to be educated. Jim was going to lead a class on Lenin's *State and Revolution* with some assistance from Crispin. It was, Crispin reflected, a slightly odd way to spend an evening, even on licensed premises, but no odder than playing with toy trains.

Jim's introduction was competent and as lively as could reasonably be expected, given that the subject matter was nobody's idea of a bundle of laughs. He described the pamphlet under discussion as the classic restatement of where Marx and Engels had stood on the central questions of the state, the dictatorship of the proletariat, the transition from capitalism to socialism and from socialism to communism, drawing together all their scattered thoughts and remarks on the subject. He located the work in the context of 1917 when it was written, showing how the external crisis of the war in which Russia was then engaged had been reflected in a crisis within Marxist theory. Crispin smiled at the obvious if unstated parallel with their own experience. Opportunism within British Marxism had flourished during the long years of comparative peace and prosperity, when Macmillan had told them they had never had it so good and Rab Butler had positively delighted in educating the children of the masses. Now the hard times were back, and they were experiencing, like the Bolsheviks, both a political crisis outside and a theoretical crisis within.

As usual with this text, the audience warmed up a bit when Jim got on to Lenin's treatment of bourgeois democracy, show-ing it to be largely a sham and a con trick, and his argument for its replacement by an avowedly partisan workers' government. This always touched a nerve. People who never seemed to get what they wanted when they voted for MPs or councillors liked to hear their suspicions and prejudices confirmed. They also liked to hear of an alternative rooted, not in abstract notions of democracy and freedom which always seemed to benefit some bugger else, but in the rough justice of sticking together and getting your own back. It appealed to all their best, or worst, instincts, depending on which side you were on. It was the eternal cry for less crap and more tumbrils.

Crispin flicked through the pamphlet, looking for a passage he wanted to refer to in discussion. His copy was a genuine curiosity, custom-made for an antique dealer. Printed in October 1919 and costing what must then have been the very substantial sum of one shilling and sixpence, the author's name

130

was given as V.I. Ulyanov, the pseudonym, Lenin, presumably not being then in universal use. Lenin, Stalin, Crispin, he thought, you can't be a real revolutionary if you use your real name.

The flyleaf showed that Crispin's copy had originally belonged to the man who had become Northburn's first Labour mayor. Crispin remembered him as a decent, self-educated, worker, deep-rooted in the labour movement. He was no revolutionary, but he had been interested enough in what had happened in Russia in 1919 to spend one and sixpence to find out more. His marginal comments, in neat pencil writing, were typical of the man – dictionary glosses of unfamiliar words rather than political judgements. But something had seeped through somewhere, because the same man's daughter had later developed into a real revolutionary, trained at a special university in Moscow in the days of the Comintern, when the principle of internationalism was interpreted literally. Father and daughter were both dead now, the book a link with what suddenly seemed an unimaginably distant past.

What would they have made of all this, he wondered? How much relevance did it have to the task in hand? You did not need much political education to plant a bomb. If you were half crackers to start with, you had all the necessary qualifications.

Mind you, he thought, Jacko was trying. He had brought his two mates along even if it was a case of the blind leading the blind. And he did appear to have read the text – no mean feat in itself. He would not necessarily have understood it, but the effort of ploughing through it would mean that something would have sunk in subliminally. Probably the wrong bits, mind – the footnotes, quotations, parentheses and appendices in which Lenin always buried his argument, Lenin, that most discursive of writers, whose hatred kept driving him off the point and whose activism prevented him from ever revising or withdrawing a word written in anger. Yes, it was nailed on. Jacko would remember the names of all the nobodies Lenin had shat on from a great height. But would he remember the argument?

There is a kind of pattern to classes like these, related to the capacity of the human mind to absorb new information. The

131

speaker speaks. The audience asks questions. Then they repeat in their own words one or two of the arguments that particularly appeal to them. The speaker asks if they agree with these arguments, and they say they do. They have thus become Leninists. They then start talking about current affairs or problems at their place of work. This discussion bears little or no relationship to the introduction. It is entered into with a sense of relief at getting back to familiar territory and, as a result, is usually lively and well informed.

The Scotsman was speaking.

'I take Lenin's point about the poor being squeezed out of politics. I think a working man is occupied full time in keeping his belly full and his weans clothed and a roof over his head, forby any talk of politics. It's wrong, of course, when folk don't bother to vote and that, just like it's wrong when people don't go to their union branch, but it happens, and my God it suits the bosses and the ruling class to keep it that way.'

'And anything they give you, they can take away,' Jacko interjected. 'Look at the Health Service. We took that for granted, didn't we? Thought it would last for ever. Then one morning we woke up and it was gone.'

'Aye, of course, but be fair, Jacko, we still get free medical treatment, don't we, on that scheme the firm pays in for? Same as we still get the protected pension, even though we're no longer civil servants.'

'Yeah, but that's not the fucking point, is it? Anyway, it's not guaranteed. If you remember back a couple of years to when we were privatized, we nearly lost the pension, the health scheme, the lot.'

'You've got to say that for Ted Atha. He got it written into that agreement that whatever happened, the pension scheme was carried over. They would not have got privatization through otherwise.'

'Fucking bollocks, Jock. That sodding deal cost us two hundred jobs. That was the price of going private. Voluntary fucking redundancies. The rest was window-dressing.'

'Aye, well, there's two sides to that one I reckon.'

Jacko and the Scotsman were back at work, killing time with a private and essentially pointless argument. Then the labourer spoke for the first time.

'One thing I don't quite understand. The work we do is for the government, right? When I started they actually paid your wages. You signed the Official Secrets Act and, like you were saying, you got the civil service pension. OK, now it's supposed to be private, but that's a load of crap – the work is still for the government even if some bugger is skimming off the profits. Now, if we didn't make the tanks and that for the government, they wouldn't be able to put people down, right? So does that make us workers, or part of the state?'

Hole in one, thought Crispin. Over to you, Jim.

'Och, we're workers,' said the Scotsman, 'platers, electricians and that. I used to make ships up on the Clyde. It's no different to making tanks. It's just how a man earns a living. Your bairns can't eat principles.'

'But you could say the same thing about the police or the army, couldn't you? Or prison officers. Those bastards have even got a trade union. If tanks are used to kill workers at the end of the day, I don't see how we can get off scot-free for making them.'

'That's right,' said Jim. 'The point is, what are we going to do about it?'

29

Morning. When the coffee works at a man's bowels. Jim farted at an intensity dangerously close to shitting himself and answered Crispin's question.

'The Jock was as daft as Jacko. But that young labourer was good – a right thoughtful lad. He could be useful to us.'

'He could, if we were doing anything useful. As it is, I think he's better off out of it. Save him for better times. Jacko will do nicely for cannon fodder. Just like us.'

133

'Can I have your bacon rind?'

'Help yourself.'

Breakfast *chez* the partners. Crispin swept the crispy rinds from his plate to Jim's, then returned to his scrambled egg.

'Mind you, Chris, that Jacko isn't a joey. He was on top of the text last night; he'd obviously done the reading.'

'I've never said he was stupid. Crackers, yes, but not stupid. He's exactly the type of headbanger I spent my political career fucking off. So you could say he was ideal for our present purposes.'

'Cynical bastard.'

'Well, I'm alive, though maybe that's under negotiation.'

'Do you ever get scared, Chris?'

'Right now, my son, with three weeks to go to blast off, I'm shitting myself. No word of a lie. Mind you, I'm quieter about it than some people.'

Crispin reached for the brown bread and marmalade with steady hands. It was Saturday. Jim was down to have a dutiful lunchtime drink with Jacko. And Crispin was taking the weekend off.

'Where are you taking Pamela?'

'Would you believe a stately home?'

'A stately home?'

'Yeah, bad planning, I know. I made the tactical error of asking her what she wanted to do.'

'It's a good job one of us is doing some work today.'

'Having a pint with Jacko, work?'

'Bloody hard graft, if you ask me.'

'Well, that's the price you pay for reaching the dazzling heights of regional vice-chairman. It's all responsibility from now on in, kid.'

'If that's high-flying, it feels more like going nowhere fast.'

'A quick spin in a hot-air balloon, with the labour movement as ballast.'

'Very profound for breakfast-time.'

'Well, let's look on the bright side, Jim. We could have won, and then we'd have really been fucked. At least this way we might get a second chance.'

As he had made clear to his partner, the visit to the stately home was a penance for Crispin. Neither its history nor its architecture nor its contents interested him in the slightest and, if anything, the need to display his professional expertise in the field of antiques made the exercise even drearier. These old buildings seemed indistinguishable to him, identikit prefabs for the aristos – if you'd seen one set of rooms with ropes round the furniture, you had seen them all. You could not even fantasize about the workers taking them over. My Christ, when that happened they would probably be forced to visit the buggers. Anyway, as a matter of sober fact, the labour movement already owned the odd minor stately home, just like pop singers or the Maharishi. He had been to conferences and schools at them which, blessedly, had always degenerated into drinking bouts. No doubt just like the old days.

After their guided tour they drove back to a cottage just outside of Northburn which Pamela had borrowed from a friend for the weekend. There they spent the afternoon in that combination of frantic sexual activity and intense conversation which characterizes relationships in an early and uncertain stage. Then they quarrelled.

They both wanted to go to a restaurant for a late dinner and their table was booked. But Crispin wanted to go to a pub first, while Pamela had decided there was a film she must see at a cinema in town. Eventually they reached a sort of sulky compromise. They went to the cinema, a tiny studio with dirty furniture and bad acoustics, but Crispin bought a half-bottle of gin before they went in, which he sucked at ostentatiously through a straw during the performance, like a Prohibition-era jazzman, much to Pamela's disgust. The film was American, a sort of existential comedy, which everybody in the audience except Crispin found highly entertaining.

'Why do you have to act like an ill-educated boor?' she asked in exasperation when they got outside.

'Habit. Anyway, I am ill-educated, remember?'

'Bullshit. You're the cleverest man in town and you know it.'

'In that case I don't need to prove it. Look, I just haven't got your sense of humour. I haven't laughed in a cinema since I saw a newsreel of Kennedy getting shot.'

'Well, *I* enjoyed the film, you pig. Thank you for taking me.'

135

'My pleasure. Do you fancy a drink before your meal?'

'No, I'm starving. Let's eat.'

'OK. I can always order a bottle of gin with the meal. I've always fancied doing that.'

'Very colonial. I don't know how you drink so much and stay standing.'

'You reach a level and stay there, that's all. The only problem is having to stop.'

'I see: "Chris's basis for homeostasis".'

Jesus, we are getting clever tonight, he thought. Poncy films and fancy words. It's a good job she fucks as well. Homeostasis. Christ, what kind of word is that? Not the sort you pick up turning metal into parts or junk into antiques. I'd have to read *New Society* or *Socialism Today* to learn shit like that. Useless learning – as useless to me, flogging furniture and playing at anarchists, as to you, laying hands on social cripples and entertaining for some pig philistine businessman. We're both whores and fools and we don't need to turn clever rhymes to emphasize the point.

He goosed her. Fondly.

'Women's Lib has a lot to answer for. I always said you had too much brains for a woman.'

'How do you like your women, then, Chris?' she asked, as he took her into his arms, standing in the car park.

'With damp panties and taut nipples.'

'You're obscene, and I'm hungry. Let's go to this restaurant.'

She thought about her relationship with the man sitting next to her, wrapped in smoke and gin fumes, as she drove them to the restaurant. All these years and I've learnt nothing. Back he comes and off I go. Just as much in love, just as overawed by this big, ruthless bastard as when I was a daft young girl who thought she was a revolutionary. But he really is a revolutionary. He doesn't belong in bourgeois Britain at all. He'd burn the whole world down if it got in his way, without remorse or conscience. He wouldn't give quarter or express sympathy, and he would not expect them either. And the damnable thing is I love to be with him. I like to talk to him, serious or silly, drunk or sober. I like to force him to go round country houses or to watch arty films. And I like the feel of him in me and on me.

That above all.

She raised the matter, sitting at the restaurant table over the chilled wine and devilled whitebait.

'I've decided you're a psychopath.'

'Well, that sounds impressively bad, social welfare lady. What does it mean?'

'It means you'll get what you want, whatever the cost.'

'Yeah, I think that would be about right, apart from one slight catch.'

'What's that?'

'I've no fucking idea what it is I'm supposed to want.'

'I'll rephrase that: what the Party wants, I mean.'

'Well, OK, so I'm the Party's official psychopath. A great honour I'm sure. Mind you, I wouldn't bet your shirt the Party knows what it wants either.'

She bit the head off a fish, delicately, and swallowed it, holding the body impaled on a fork in midair.

'No, but whatever it was provisionally, whatever you'd got a line on at the last meeting, you'd go for that like it was eternal truth.'

'Oh aye, that's right. But think of the alternative, Pamela.'

'Which is?'

'Pissing around like the rest of humanity, playing games with home computers and letting the bastards win. The Party destroys you all right, but it enables you to be destroyed with your dignity intact and that's important. It may not be much, but it's all I've got and I'm sticking with it.' He squeezed her hand. 'Now, I'm sick of sermonizing. Finish your little fishes and we'll have some raw steak and claret. Then I'll take you back to the cottage and give you the benefit of my long experience.'

'OK.' She smiled. OK because I fear this is going to be over soon for another ten years, and I want to make the most of it. And if I'm wrong, I still want to make the most of it. OK because I'm human, too.

Back at the cottage they made love like teenagers who had just discovered how. The cottage was cold, and the mattress on the bed lumpy – an old one relegated to the second home. Crispin woke at dawn with a raw penis burrowing into Pamela's

137

bottom, arthritic pains in his back and fragments of a dream in his head. A blaze up at t'mill, lad, and we're going to keep on hitting you until you sign the confession. Yes, we know you did it, you Luddite bastard. Your pal Tom put the finger on you.

You old bastard. All those years ago. I'll kill you.

30

Sunday evening is an unreal time of the week, designed by Christians as a punishment for unbelievers, the time when buses run slow rather than fast in order to keep to their schedules and drinkers ease off in anticipation of Monday morning. If you had to pick an entirely suitable place to spend Sunday evening, Jim decided, then the waiting area of a police station was as good a choice as any. Not that he was enjoying being there. The place gave him the creeps, when it was not scaring the hell out of him. Crispin, sod the bastard, had picked a fucking good time to be out of circulation.

The pay phone in the flat did not ring very often, particularly at 5 pm on a Sunday. Jim assumed it would be Crispin, or a wrong number. When the voice, which sounded bored, told him it was Northburn Central Police Station, his first thought was that it must be a wind up. But it was not. They had a Mr James in custody and were charging him with a breach of the peace. There was a question of bailing him to a safe address. Mr James had given them his number as a close friend and could he assist? By this time he had realized that Mr James meant Jacko.

As far as he could understand the story, it seemed that Jacko had been thrown out by his wife, either during or after a drinking bout, and had then caused some sort of public disturbance leading to his arrest.

His instinct was to deny all knowledge of Mr James and his domestic problems. He shuddered to think of what Jacko might

138

have had on him, or what he might have said to the police. But the option of denial was closed. If it was a trap, the bugger was already sprung. So he left a message for Crispin and drove down to the station, full of mounting fear. It was one job he would gladly have swung on to his partner.

Keep your cool, he kept saying to himself. That's what Chris would do. These things are 90% psychology. It's down to style. Not too cocky, not too servile. Don't give them an opening either way. Shit, you've been in nicks before, it's no big deal. Yeah, but not with a headbanger like Jacko, not three weeks before blast off, and not, he suddenly remembered, in this particular nick with its grisly reputation, where suspects had a bad habit of dying accidentally, even in the old days when such things were frowned on. *Keep cool.* They don't know you. And Jacko doesn't know exactly what we're up to yet. They probably just see him as a troublesome drunk to get rid of with the minimum of hassle after they've given him a kicking. Check your pockets before you go in. No incriminating documents or offensive weapons. And make sure you park in the right place.

The nick was of the type built in the 1970s in anticipation of subsequent urban unrest. A solid mass of a building, physically isolated from surrounding office blocks, it was designed, literally, as a keep, a place of defence to be ringed, in times of trouble, by a curtain wall of barbed wire and armoured vehicles. Like any keep, the entrance was several floors up and reached by an external staircase.

Apart from one tramp, who appeared to be hanging round on the off chance of being arrested, Jim had the waiting area to himself. Once he had announced his arrival through the bullet-proof glass of the tiny reception hatch, he was left to his own devices and his fantasies. Life went on in the interior of the station behind the electronically operated door. Occasionally patrols went in or out, all guns and leather, giving him the automatic once-over. Otherwise nothing. He was there for an hour.

He was screwing up his nerve to speak to the reception hatch again, when a plain-clothes officer emerged from the door and took him inside, down corridors and past offices which at that time of day had an unreal, dead air about them. They had Jacko

139

sitting at a table in an interview room. He had obviously been beaten up and must have found it a sobering experience. Jacko was not arguing with anyone.

The formalities were brief. The arresting officer explained that he had signed a statement about the incident and would be summoned to appear in court in due course. His wife would not take him back. The police simply needed an address where he could be contacted between now and the court hearing. If Jim would just sign the form he could be released immediately, and keep off the beer, that's a good lad, eh?

Not without some trepidation, Jim signed. Then Jacko signed for the return of his property – a belt, a comb and a few coins – and they were escorted out. All quite painless.

'Thanks, mate,' said Jacko, when they got into the car. This was the first conversation directly between them.

'What a fucking state,' said Jim, looking him over. 'Did they give you a kicking?'

'Just a bit. Then the cunts started dropping hints about resisting arrest and assaulting the police, so it seemed like a good idea to put my name to a breach of the peace. They rang my missus and she wouldn't stand bail. That's when I gave them your number. Hey, thanks for coming. The breakfast in that place isn't quite my scene. They put milk in the cornflakes.'

'How did it start?'

'I got drunk last night. Never went home. Then I went straight to the pub this morning. In between times I'd been dropping speed. When I got home this afternoon, she'd put my suitcase by the door. That was the bell for round one. I smashed a window, she called the cops, I was shouting my mouth off. End of story.'

'Did the police find any speed on you?'

'No, I'd dropped the lot by then.'

'Who did you tell the law me and Chris were?'

'I just said you were mates from down the pub who worked on the buildings. Come on, I'm not going to tell those fascist bastards anything, am I? They'd had their fun by then, and they just wanted shot of me. If I'd given them Attila the Hun's number for surety, they'd have taken it.'

'I guess so.'

140

'Can you pull over a second, Jim?'

He did so, and Jacko opened the door and vomited into the gutter.

'Fuck,' he said, as he straightened up again, 'one of the cunts must have breathed on me.'

Crispin was waiting for them back at the flat. If he was worried, it did not show.

'Uh-huh,' he said, inspecting the bruising on Jacko's face, 'looks like they hit you with the hard end.'

'Bastards,' said Jacko, with more than a hint of pride in his voice. 'Still, I bet you've had some in your time, eh, Chris?'

Fuck me, thought Jim, he thinks he's been on the barricades. The crazy bugger really thinks he has won his spurs with us now.

'Well, it's what revolutionaries like us would expect, isn't it?' said Crispin, off-handedly. 'Do you fancy a drink?'

'Yeah, I could use one.'

Crispin poured whisky into three coffee mugs and passed them round. As he leant over Jacko, who was sitting down, to hand Jim his cup, he winked at him.

'He didn't say anything to the police,' said Jim, picking up the silent cue.

'I knew he wouldn't. Which is just as well, because the Party is going to need you for something important soon, Jacko.'

'Yeah?' He looked flattered. 'It doesn't involve blowing up a police station, does it?'

'Not quite,' said Crispin evenly. 'It doesn't involve bunking your old lady off, either. But it will need brains and nerve. So I want you to keep yourself straight in the meantime. Know what I mean?' He squeezed his shoulder.

'Sure.'

'Want another?'

'I wouldn't mind.'

Jim cast an eye over Jacko, trying to be as objective as possible. He looked terrible. His shoes and trousers were covered in mud. His shirt was bloodstained and torn, half the buttons were missing and it hung open revealing the dragon tattooed on his chest. His face looked worse by the minute and he smelt bad, too – a mixture of sweat, booze and vomit. And in a few minutes' time he's going to be legless and bragging his head off.

'Should I go and get a Chinese takeaway?' he suggested. Make the bloody dragon feel at home.

'Good idea, I'm getting peckish,' said Crispin. They both assumed that Jacko would be fed in the manner of the idiot on the wagon train.

He left Crispin talking to Jacko like an overindulgent father to a favourite but errant son. Good old Charlie Chan. It was an impressive, if rather cruel, performance, Jim decided, but necessary. At this stage they either upped their stake in Jacko, or they got out of the game. And it was a bit late to get out of the game, now the police had got their number.

31

Jacko got very drunk very quickly, a process which a tinfoil container of chow mein did little to arrest. He ended up crashed out on a settee, snoring loudly. In the morning he claimed to feel fine, although his face looked as if it had walked into a wall in a hurry. Jim drove him to work, dressed in an assortment of borrowed clothes. He came back at teatime, tired, but not obviously the worse for drink or drugs. In fact he was acting the model citizen, and by the middle of the week he had even got back together with his wife. Jacko was being a good boy, just as Crispin had asked him to be. But it was the following week before they told him what he was being a good boy for.

In the meantime they lived through a sort of phoney war, experiencing that particular combination of tension and boredom peculiar to positional warfare. They monitored Jacko's personal progress and fed him scraps of political wisdom. Jim went to Southdale to give and receive a progress report. Pamela phoned Crispin several times and lunched with him once.

142

Crispin, full of bad memories of rail travel, bought a second-hand car ready for his departure from Northburn. Nothing had been done yet but it felt as if their work was almost over.

They finally put the proposition to Jacko sitting next to a loud and well-fed jukebox in the deserted backroom of a pub in that quiet, change-over part of the evening when pubs tend to empty out, between the first rush of custom after work and the later social drinking. Crispin did most of the talking: he described what they were after with a due sense of its historical moment, and Jacko heard him out with corresponding seriousness. His questions afterwards were all to do with practicalities.

'It has to be February 1st to tie in with what's going on elsewhere?'

'Yeah, that's very important from a propaganda point of view. It's the anniversary of the introduction of the Domestic Emergencies Act, the first step on the road to fascism in Britain. It's a historic occasion, Jacko. Some workers will be striking, some demonstrating, and we'll be lighting the fuse that starts the revolution. That sounds dramatic, but it's the truth. This will be the first symbolic act of armed struggle, just like the storming of the Winter Palace.'

You should be on the stage, Jim thought, you'd get a bleeding Oscar. It's just far enough over the top to work. *Only twenty-four hours from Tulsa*, sang the voice from the jukebox. A golden oldie selection.

'February 1st. That's not far off. Does the time of day matter?'

'No. Obviously we don't want casualties if they can be avoided. That could affect timing.'

Only one day away from your arms . . .

'The best thing would be to plant it the night before, timed to go off in the early hours of Friday morning. No bugger will be around then.'

I hate to do this to you . . .

'Perfect,' said Jim, 'it'll be on the news all day.'

'How easy would it be to plant it the night before?' Crispin asked.

'It would be the easiest time, after the production men have gone home. I'll have the place to myself practically. All I have to

143

do is swing some overtime, clock out for half an hour to get some tea, pick up the bomb and clock back in.' He was starting to sound enthusiastic, thinking out loud as he mentally filled in the details of the operation. On the jukebox the record had reached an instrumental passage.

'Any problem getting overtime?'

'Nah, there's always something going wrong on the electrical side these days, what with undermanning and flexible working. If necessary I'll fuck something up on purpose. It wouldn't be the first time.'

'That sounds OK.'

'I'd need to meet your explosives expert to go over the details. I know quite a bit about explosives, as it happens, but I'd want to get the lowdown on what I'm handling.'

Jim and Crispin exchanged glances. *But I love somebody new . . .*

'It sounds reasonable,' Jim said. 'I'll check it out.'

'Now, how do you make sure the bomb doesn't get traced back to me?'

'Oh, I'm sure you'll be questioned about it. You and a few others with big mouths. You just say it's not your scene, you know nothing about it, and stick to that. They can't prove anything. At most, if they really dug around, they might be able to show that you knew us – a couple of education classes, a bit of bail. Big deal. Look, if they pull Jim or me, the first thing I'll do is finger that bastard Ted Atha.'

Silence suddenly surrounded them, followed by clicking noises as the jukebox changed records. Instinctively they all paused until it started again.

'Ted Atha?'

'Yeah, Ted Atha. I can prove he took me round the factory to reconnoitre it – there must be scores of witnesses to that. I can prove he was in my pay, and if any fucker is going to cop for this one it's Ted. I've got him bang to rights. Look at that, if you don't believe me.'

He slapped down the photograph on the table. The force and style of the gesture reminded Jim of West Indian players he had seen, producing the crucial domino in a game. The picture was the one he had taken of Crispin giving Ted the money.

'Neat,' said Jacko, all admiration. It was not all that obvious to Jim how the photograph took Jacko off the hook, but he said nothing.

'The bastard should have opened the box when he had the choice,' said Crispin.

A pause fell on the proceedings, filled up by the voice of Otis Redding. Another golden oldie. Crispin spoke again.

'So what do you think, Jacko?'

Jacko lit a cigarette before answering. His hand was trembling slightly more than usual.

'It's a good plan. Smart. It'll make a big bang, no doubt about that. Scare the shit out of the cunts. Yeah, I like it,' he breathed out some smoke, 'and I've got the bottle to do it. No sweat.'

'Then what's the problem?' asked Crispin, responding to his hesitation.

'Well, the thing is, I wonder if I'm politically reliable enough. Don't get me wrong. I'd plant the bomb all right and if the bastards caught me they wouldn't get a thing out of me. They tried to break me once before and it only made me harder. I tell you, I walked out of the prison laughing. But look, you said it yourself just before, Chris, I've got a big mouth. I've been a bit of an alcofrolic on the side, and a speed artist too. I've had problems with the missus and problems with the law. When you add it all up, it doesn't sound like a description of steel-hard cadre, does it? I'm just not sure whether I'm the best man the Party can get for the job.'

And I believe you mean that, too, Jim thought.

'Ah, Jacko,' said Crispin philosophically, 'if life was a rock and roll band, you'd be well equipped for playing in it. Damn shame it isn't really. But with life the way it is, deadly serious and tending towards tedium, there can be problems in finding your own personal niche in it, and I think you've had some. Jacko, take it from me, you were made for this one. I knew that from the word go. This is for you. You're the comrade the Party needs for this job. Nobody else. You.'

'Yeah, I'd like to have been in a band. Or written plays for television. I had a good imagination as a kid. Can you believe that? Instead I ended up being taught to kill people for the ruling class. Just like a fucking mercenary.' He took a drink

145

from a long-empty glass. 'You're right, Chris. This one is for me. I'll do a job for the Party.'

'That's good.' Crispin squeezed his shoulder.

Jim felt pangs of guilt, mixed with sympathy. Jacko wasn't a bad bloke, just a mess – a mixture of intelligence and madness, innocence and guile, high-flown fantasy and downbeat wit. Morally, this was his finest hour, and their worst. No, morality did not really come into it, or at least it was not taking sides in the matter. It was a tragedy: his that they were setting him up; theirs that they had no better use for him.

Yeah, and somebody was mother of them all.

'I'm going to get some drinks in,' said Jacko. He wanted to celebrate his final acceptance into the brotherhood.

'That went well,' said Jim, when Jacko had gone through to the bar, safely at the other side of a wall of noise.

'Did you get it all?'

Jim produced a small tape recorder from his pocket, detaching the lapel microphone as he did so.

'Yeah, it should be OK. The sound quality will be terrible obviously, with that jukebox booming away by the door, but we should have the whole conversation down here.'

'Good. We can have a listen later. Put it away now before Jacko gets back.'

'I should be in MI5, do you know that?'

Crispin gave him a mock-serious look. 'Funny you should say that, comrade, but I've had my suspicions for some time.'

32

The last week. Monday morning. Thursday they would plant
the bomb. Friday it would go off. They were almost there. Time
to wrap up some loose ends.

Clever invention the phone. Any time during the last eight
years, anywhere in the country, you could have picked the
bastard up and spoken to Tom. Told him exactly what you felt,
got it off your chest without any of the complications of having
him within arm's reach. But you didn't. No, you tiptoed round
the magic handset while the other comrades died or gave back
word and the pain and hatred festered in your heart. Clever
invention my arsehole. You took your time getting round to
using it. Even now it's taken you weeks to dial those six digits.

'Chris. Chris Powell. It's a long time since I've heard from
you, comrade.' The voice sounded older and weaker than he
remembered it. It also sounded guarded and defensive. 'Where
are you calling from?'

'Northburn. I'm back up here for a few days on business.
How are you keeping, old mate?'

'Not so good, Chris. I've got this bad heart. The docs tell me
it could conk out any time, so I have to take it easy. To tell you
the truth, since the wife died I haven't gone out much any more.
I'm not my old self at all.'

Thank Christ for small mercies, then.

'Do you have much to do with the Party these days, Tom?'

'They don't have much to do with me, is more like it. Don't
get old, Chris, it's not worth it. I can't be active because of my
health and I haven't got much money to spare since I took this

147

retirement, so nobody from the Party wants to see me. I get no literature, I hear no news. All those years I worked for the Party and now I'm an unperson. The Party has lost my address, Chris, they don't come to see me any more.'

Then they've learnt some sense in their old age.

'I'll come and see you while I'm up here, if you like – for old time's sake.'

The voice went cautious again. 'Yeah, I'd like that, Chris.'

'How about this Wednesday, then?'

'Fine. I'm not going anywhere. Don't make it too early in the day, Chris. I sleep late in the mornings now.'

'Typical bloody engineer. I'll call round in the afternoon.'

'Engineer? I used to be that. Time-served and section one member. I'm nothing now – just an old has-been. Yes, come in the afternoon if you want. You can tell me what's been going on in the world since I got off.'

'Good. I'll see you then. Keep smiling.'

He put the phone down with a strange feeling of exhilaration. You self-pitying old bastard, he thought, you've just done the impossible. You've made me hate you a little bit more. You had the nerve to sell me up the river and then this is how you end up, whining about how hard life has treated you. What did you expect to get out of it – the Order of Lenin and a band of disciples?

But you shouldn't have let me hear you going on like that. You don't know what I'm made of, old son. If you thought I was down and out thanks to you, then you couldn't have been more wrong. I just got on with my life, same story, new chapter, and I've done very nicely. No, you don't know where I'm at. But I know exactly what you're made of now, from your own mouth – soft shit and pure water. Roll on Wednesday. I'm going to enjoy seeing you like this.

With these thoughts charging him up, Crispin set off on his second task of the day. Another loose end to tie up. It was time to bid a fond farewell to Pamela. Well, that was what it was going to amount to, even if she wasn't to know just yet. End of holiday, end of romance. Those were the rules. If any rules applied in this unreal business.

At the beginning he had looked Pamela up for old time's sake, because she was part of the past he seemed to be pursuing like some great white whale. Then, inevitably, their meetings had taken on a momentum of their own. He barely connected the woman he was having an affair with now with the one of ten years before. The surrounding circumstances were too different. If they had one thing in common, it was that both were transitory, as this whole crazy episode was transitory. Permanence, or the fantasy of permanence, was keeping house for him elsewhere. It was Mary's job to bury him, wherever he fell. That was different. That was for keeps.

Pamela had not been sure what time she would be free for lunch as she was involved in a case in the juvenile court, so she had asked him to look out for her in the foyer of the building where the court sat. The idea was bizarre enough to appeal to him, and besides, he could not object without sounding paranoid. But he took care not to mention it to his partner.

Once there, he explained his legitimate purpose to an usher, found a seat in the corridor and sat back to enjoy the show. Courts fascinated him, with their violent juxtaposition of pomp and squalor, tedium and drama. They were a reflection of society, but a distorted one. To follow the game you had to know the rules and what each player's function was. He tried to work out who all the waiting people were and why they were here.

Right opposite him sat a rather gawky girl of about fourteen, flanked by a big-chested platinum blonde in her mid-thirties and a harassed-looking, chain-smoking woman about twenty years her senior, whom Crispin gradually identified from their conversation as being, respectively, the girl's foster mother and natural mother. Next to the older woman was a florid-faced man who seemed to be the girl's father, and next to him a smartly dressed young solicitor. Two social workers, a young woman and an older man, sat next to the foster mother. All were engaged in an animated and apparently friendly discussion which centred, both physically and in terms of its subject matter, on the teenager. This is your moment of drama, kid, Crispin thought, centre stage with the super trouper full on you. If you weren't fucked up before you got here, you'll sure as hell get fucked up by all this unnatural attention. Go on. Have a smoke. Have a cry. Have some therapy. This is your big day.

149

But the girl was not the only person under observation.

'It's Chris Powell, isn't it?'

That's a hell of a question. Supposing I said not? The speaker had sat down next to Crispin. He was a police inspector, in uniform, and he was offering Crispin a cigarette.

'Thanks. Yes, that's me. It's a fair cop, governor, or whatever you say these days.'

'Inspector Blackman. I don't suppose you remember me. I did you for obstruction, oh, it must have been fifteen years ago. I was a young constable, still wet behind the ears, and you gave me a hell of a going-over on my evidence in court. Taught me a lesson, actually.'

'Yeah, I do remember, now you come to mention it. Fifteen years ago, eh? As I recall it, it still cost me ten notes, even if I did give you a hard time on the way. Well, it can't have done you any harm if you've made Inspector.'

'It's funny, Chris, after all these years I can remember the case quite clearly.'

'Don't need to refer to your notebook, then?'

'Not this time. No, you were really sharp. You'd been leafleting a factory when I lifted you. It was a clothing place and you tried to trip me up on the time of the arrest because they started work half an hour earlier than the engineering ones.'

Crispin laughed, despite himself. 'I remember that.'

'Then you had me on the width of the pavement, all sorts of details. I was a right sloppy bugger with evidence till then. I'd made a few collars, but they'd all been like taking candy from a baby. You taught me not to assume I was smarter than the other bloke.'

A moral for us all there somewhere.

'Still, the bench was on your side.'

'Only just, that day. What are you doing now, anyway? Still fomenting revolution?'

'No, I've grown out of that. Anyway, it was getting a bit heavy. I'm running a little engineering business down in Southdale these days. Becoming a right capitalist in my old age.'

The Inspector was coming on friendly but he wasn't taking his eyes off him. Crispin wasn't convinced that he had believed the story.

150

'So what are you doing in court? Can I put in a word for you?'

'I don't think it would help. Tell you the truth, I've been going round with this lass who works here. I don't think she'd want to know my lurid past. I'm not sure she'd want to know I'm married, either.'

'Oh, I see. Say no more, you old ram. I better be off then.'

'Nice seeing you. I'll drive carefully. Honest.'

'See you, Chris.'

Inspector Blackman proceeded on his way, leaving Crispin to his paranoia. Jesus, he's going to have me through the computer. Make a few enquiries. And even if he doesn't do so immediately, bells are going to start ringing in his head this Friday, as soon as the mushroom cloud goes up over Hardcoats. Just my luck. I should have pleaded guilty fifteen years ago and saved myself the grief.

When Pamela showed up, elegantly dressed in suit and blouse, with a flower in her buttonhole and a cardboard file under her arm, Crispin was too preoccupied with the likely consequences of his meeting with Inspector Blackman to pay much more than nominal attention to what she was saying.

But he gathered she was concerned about the court's decision in some child care proceedings she had just been involved in. From the fragments of her account that penetrated his consciousness as they walked to the restaurant, it seemed fairly obvious to Crispin that the kid in question's parents were unfit to care for a mentally deficient guinea pig, and he said so. This turned out to be a mistake, because she then proceeded to tell him the other side of the story in great detail, reliving the dilemma of her, and the court's, decision-making.

So Crispin found himself trying to eat Chinese food with chopsticks and drinking lager, with a head full of Inspector Blackman and an earful of social problems. It was not quite what he had had in mind.

'I wouldn't fancy your job. It seems to involve maximizing complexity, always looking for the catch, I mean.'

'But it *is* complex, Chris. You can't just look at one aspect in isolation, you should know that as a Marxist. I mean, come on, what would you do in this case? Find someone to blame and chop their hands off?'

151

'Why not? You can agonize too long over decisions and end up like Pilate, dithering over the nature of truth when all society wants is a well-run Palestine.'

Had he got that analogy right? He was not sure. Did it matter, for fuck's sake? He was only half-conscious of what he was saying; aware, though, that she was taking his offhand remarks very seriously, and aware that they were annoying her, but not sufficiently in control of the situation to do anything about it.

'Jesus, for a revolutionary you're bloody primitive at times, Chris. Right now you sound as bad as my husband.'

'I don't think I want to know about your husband.'

Damn these chopsticks, they weren't designed for big, clumsy hands like mine.

'Well, he's a man like you, he's barbaric like you, and I'm thinking of leaving him.'

'Are you thinking of leaving me too, then?'

It was a cruel and unnecessary remark. He saw her eyes fill with tears and her hands begin to shake with anger. Her sacrifice, her secret, was out and at once rejected, devalued, betrayed. Then she composed herself, folded her napkin, laid it by her plate and got up.

'I'm sorry, Chris, I've got some paperwork to do arising from this court case this morning. I'll have to get back to the office. I'll ring you later.'

'OK.' Strung up by his own desire for a smart answer, he lacked the energy to apologize and start again. It was a hell of a way to say goodbye, but it was going to have to do.

He watched her rear as she walked out of the restaurant. She had turned into a well-made woman. Tiring of her pig husband, too. Fuck you, Inspector Blackman, for spoiling my afternoon.

On his way back to his car he watched a couple of young policemen harassing a drunk who had been braving the cold on a bench in the small garden surrounding the war memorial. They asked him to stand up and when he did so, stumbling drunkenly against one of them, they used this as a pretext to arrest him. The drunk was led off to a waiting police car, casting longing backward glances at the bottle of cider sitting forlornly

152

beneath the bench. Go quietly, Crispin thought, don't make it
hard on yourself. You've got a whole life in front of you.

33

Tuesday. A crucial day. Tuesday was when it got hairy.
Tuesday they had to collect the bomb.

Party HQ wanted as few people involved in the collection as
possible. They agreed to Jacko being there, with Jim as his
guarantor. HQ was sending Steve Brown who was, of course,
familiar with their plans, along with an explosives expert to run
through the technicalities with Jacko. The expert had been
given the name of Harris. It was good to know that someone
down there had a sense of humour.

For unexplained reasons the meeting place chosen was a
hotel in a small town on the coast. It could hardly have been
picked for their convenience since Northburn was about as
inland as anywhere in the British Isles could reasonably be.
Obviously it must have made sense to HQ in terms of security
considerations and their general itinerary, but HQ was not
giving any details.

Jacko, liberated from work for the day and, Jim suspected,
well speeded up, was not the ideal motoring companion. It was
like travelling with a character from a beatnik novel. He talked
incessantly in a sort of politicobabble, blending theory and
paranoia and personal hang-ups into an unending monologue.
After a time Jim dissociated himself from the voice in his ear and
concentrated on the landscape.

The weather had improved. It was a mild, spring-like day
with the sky clear. A good day for a drive.

The first part of the journey took them through the northern
fringe of the local coalfield. There was something instantly
recognizable about a pit village, Jim thought, even if the pit had

153

closed and the winding gear been dismantled a decade before, even if the place itself was now a suburban postal district and none of the inhabitants was engaged in winning coal any more. It was something to do with the straightness of the streets and the uniformity of the houses and the size of the Co-op store, and something a bit more indefinable.

And yet each village had a fiercely individual character. Jim had first discovered this in his teens when he had gone canvassing for the Party in a village near Southdale. On the surface there had been nothing very unusual about the place. It looked industrial yet not fully urban – an ordinary working village. But then he had started knocking on doors, and soon discovered that the place was like nothing he had ever encountered before, a throwback to an earlier, or imaginary, epoch. He had expected flashes of isolated, spontaneous militancy. Instead he found the real thing. Every other household had seemed to be able, effortlessly, to produce an articulate advocate of class politics to test his revolutionary credentials on the doorstep.

By the time his day's canvassing was over he was convinced that the whole coalfield must be like that – a revolutionary sea into which he had chanced to poke his toe. It was an inspiring thought and it kept him buoyed up until a few weeks later, when he had tried canvassing in an adjacent village and rapidly found that nobody would give him the time of day. His demoralization was exacerbated when he mentioned his experience to old-timers in his Party branch, who laughed at his naïveté and gave him the folklore about the village:

– Half the bastards blacklegged in '26.
– They called it scabs' row for years.
– They've been under the priest's thumb for ages.
– The lodge secretary is bent as a nine-bob note.

From then on he learnt not to generalize about pit villages and their politics, and it had turned out to be a useful lesson.

Pit villages and rhubarb fields started to give way to rich agricultural land. It was enemy country, a reminder that the same bastards had been in power a long time and weren't going to depart in a hurry. They pushed their money from coal to engineering, from property speculation in decaying British cities to industrial investment in Taiwan or South Korea, as the

154

fashion changed, but the reservoir of their wealth and power lay in fields like these, Jim decided. Land was a finite commodity; there was not much more to be discovered in a country like England. And this kind of territory was the archetype: all walled estates and Norman churches and village greens, an eternal Keep Out notice directed at people like himself.

He was glad when its fertility gave way in its turn to the open moorland which he knew would continue right through to the coast. It was desolate country in winter even on a fine day. Pockets of snow lingered on the higher ground, and the sheep by the roadside looked like they were begging you to take them home.

'What's that over there, Jim?' Jacko asked, pointing to some futuristic domes and radar dishes surrounded by barbed wire fencing over on the horizon a mile or so away.

'That's where the bastards track nuclear missiles, so we'll know when we're going to die.'

And so it was. A bleak, apparently uninhabited, station where technology kept silent tabs on man's ability to rage and kill, and prepared for the destruction that was to follow destruction.

'No way I'd want to know I had four minutes to live.'

'Not unless I was within shooting distance of the prime minister.'

'Chance would be a fine thing.'

They ran into fog as they got nearer the coast. Nevertheless, they had no difficulty in finding the Royal George Hotel, which was on a headland overlooking what had once been a fishing community and which now depended on tourism in summer and state benefits in winter. And there, as arranged, over an unfashionably heavy roast beef lunch in the hotel dining room, which they had to themselves, they met Steve Brown and Mr Harris.

Jim had fantasized with Crispin about what Harris would be like. His own fantasy was that he would be Irish, wearing dark glasses and black leather gloves with a party of Special Branch men in tow. Crispin had plumped for a geriatric veteran of the Spanish Civil War who had last handled explosives as a Home Guard instructor in 1940. Their fantasies were an expression of

155

a genuine worry. The Party, as far as they knew, had no recent home-grown expertise to draw on. They only hoped it could import the best available on the international circuit without an unacceptable risk of security.

A glance at Mr Harris in the flesh restored Jim's confidence on one score at least: he looked like someone familiar with death and destruction. In fact, put next to the anaemic Steve Brown, you inevitably thought of an organ-grinder with his monkey. Jim wondered, as they were introduced, what on earth the two men found to talk about.

Harris was taller than Jim, well over six foot and bulky in build without carrying an ounce of spare flesh. Aged about thirty, he was dark enough in complexion for Jim to start speculating about his nationality. It certainly would not have surprised him to learn that he came from the Middle East. However, whatever his origins might have been, he spoke English with a public school accent. His face, with a scar on one cheek and a broken nose, the hair cut militarily short and greased down to show off protruding ears and a neck thick with muscle, was striking, but not as striking as his hands, which were enormous in their spread, covered in thick black hair and with broken knuckles. They were hands that looked like they were designed for killing people, that made weapons super-fluous, and Jim found his eyes returning to them as they ate lunch.

The meal was uneventful. Jim watched the waiter, formally dressed, carve slices from a large side of beef on a serving dish and found himself wondering whether they roasted a fresh joint every day to pander to such a meagre clientele and what in God's name they did with the surplus. Ah well, he thought, I'm not paying. Jacko kept mercifully quiet, perhaps a little over-awed by Harris, perhaps merely uncomfortable in the shabby genteel setting of the dining room. The others conducted a general conversation which revealed nothing of their various feelings or intentions. Jim found himself surprised that Harris could talk sensibly about the weather and the seasons and their effect on the countryside. He did not look like he was designed for normal human intercourse.

After lunch they went upstairs to Harris's room to inspect the

156

bomb, which turned out to be a device about the size and shape of a shoe box but considerably heavier – not exactly disappointing, but certainly unspectacular.

'Great,' said Jacko, after the initial inspection, his enthusiasm breaking out, 'that'll go in my tool-bag. If I tape an aerial to the end and wrap it up in a plastic carrier bag, I can pass it off as a radio if I'm stopped.'

Harris demonstrated the workings of the bomb to Jacko, explaining how to activate it and how to use the timing mechanism, and then got him to run through the whole procedure to show that he had understood the briefing. Jacko performed perfectly, showing not only an instant grasp of the device's technology, but a surprising degree of confidence in actually handling it.

Whether this was attributable to his claimed familiarity with explosives or to his general electrical training was hard for Jim, with no experience in either field, to judge. It was noticeable that he was keeping quiet about his military credentials for once – but then, so was Harris.

Jim was relieved that Jacko's performance was so credible. After all, his own credibility was on the line too. On the other hand, he felt isolated by this display of expertise. Jacko had been his and Crispin's discovery, almost their creation. Now, as he and Harris played with this deadly toy, he had a rôle from which Jim felt quite excluded. It was a military takeover in microcosm; the politicians were being left impotent on the sidelines. I know this is all my responsibility, he thought, but where the hell do I figure in it now?

The next stage was for Harris to go over the actual operation with Jacko in some detail, concentrating especially on the timing and the exact nature of the target, before declaring himself satisfied.

'You better tell them to have some buckets of water round when that goes off,' he said, producing a bottle of brandy and glasses from a bedside cupboard, 'you're going to have a big bang and a big fire on your hands, my friends.'

'Fine. It'll all be more overtime, cleaning up the mess,' said Jacko.

Steve then gave Jim a telephone number.

'Ring this as soon as you have confirmation that the bomb is planted.'

'OK. What happens if we hit any problems?'

Harris answered that one. 'If you don't use it on Friday, then get shot of it quick. Those things aren't like wine, they don't improve with age. And don't, for Christ's sake, try to dismantle it or tamper with it once it's been set.'

'Booby-trapped?' Jacko asked.

Harris nodded. 'I'll explain the system to you, but frankly it's best left well alone.'

Jesus, Jim thought, this thing really is dangerous. Remind me to drive carefully on the way back.

34

Enter the dragon. The beast flaunted its multi-coloured coils at the grimy mirror propped precariously above the handbasin as Jacko struggled to shave in lukewarm water with an ageing blade. Eventually he abandoned the attempt, rinsed his face, wiped it cursorily with a towel and pulled on the day before yesterday's singlet. That served to banish the dragon which covered most of Jacko's chest along with the geishas who adorned his back. The designs on his arms and hands – serpents, a dagger, tigers, a shark – remained visible, as did the floral pattern on his neck.

Wednesday. Come-down day. Back to work for Jacko. No more excitement until tomorrow. Just keep cool till then. He switched the light on in the kitchen and lit a cigarette as he waited for the kettle to boil for a cup of coffee. It was still dark and the rest of the household was asleep. He had a few minutes to spare before he needed to leave to catch his bus.

He had liked that Harris. He was the business, a real professional. That was important. It was a matter of credibility.

This far in he wouldn't have liked to find out he was working with a bunch of amateurs. But everything was fine on that front. He was with the right team. They were going places. He was damn lucky to get in on the ground floor.

The thing that had worried him at first had been the politics. These guys seemed to know so much, and try as he might, he could not see himself catching them up. But that did not matter so much now. Jim had the theory, but he had seen his face yesterday, looking at the bomb like it was going to bite him. They needed him for this part. He had come into his own. It was quits.

Of course, this operation was going to be dangerous, he had to accept that. Not so much the business of getting the bomb inside the works and planting it – he had got all that planned in his mind and it wasn't too tricky. No, the problems were going to start after the bomb went off. From that moment on, he was going to have to keep super-cool.

First thing they're going to do is search the flat, he thought, casting his eyes over the routine squalor of the kitchen. Plenty for them to go at in this dump. I'll go over it with a toothcomb beforehand. No drugs, no weapons. I'll even dump my political pamphlets and the Teach Yourself Russian cassette I've had lying around for ages. They'll find this place cleaner than clean.

And, of course, I'll be questioned. I'm prepared for that. Got my story worked out. I'll swear on a pile of bibles I'm a pacifist. Love and peace, man. Wouldn't have anything to do with bombs. And if they pull my teeth out I won't say anything different. I can take it. No sweat.

What have they got to go on with me? Fuck-all really. Just my views, and they aren't a crime. OK, under this new Act they can hold me on suspicion for twenty-eight days. That'll be a holiday. There's not a thing politically I've ever done they can hold against me.

Anyway, it's worth a little pain. Things are going to be hotting up. When I'm in the clear on this one, the Party will be making contact with me again. I've thought this one out. I'll be tried and tested and proved reliable, but at the same time I'll be a marked man. So it stands to reason they'll be asking me to go underground, simply because there's nowhere else for me to go.

159

And they won't be making a mistake, because that's what I'm cut out for. Going where I please, doing the Party's work, footloose and fancy-free like Crispin and Jim, or maybe more like that Harris bloke. No wife, no kids, no mind-numbing work. Just me and the revolution.

Time to be going. He took the aspirin bottle out of the kitchen drawer and shook the contents into his hand. Three speed tablets and a couple of pellets of dope wrapped in tinfoil. Getting low. I ought to replenish, but maybe I'd better keep clean until this is over.

He recapped the aspirin bottle and stuffed it into the pocket of his jeans. Then he put his jacket on and stepped outside on to the still-dark landing. As he walked along the landing to the lift, he felt the damp air seeping into his clothes and hair. A real downer of a morning.

Pamela was spending Wednesday morning writing a progress report on a fifteen-year-old girl. Since the girl had been living quietly in a small children's home for the past two years and, like most of her charges who chose to live quietly, had consequently seen little of Pamela in that time, there wasn't really much to add to her last report, prepared six months before. However, when the state assumes responsibility for your welfare, it has to be kept informed of your progress, so there was no getting out of writing the report. Pamela was at the stage where imagination was required, but inspiration was sadly lacking.

Pamela worked in the sort of open-plan office loved by supervisors and loathed by their staff. Over a period of time she had done her best to modify her environment, barricading her desk with filing cabinets piled high with exotic plants and books in an attempt to put herself out of sight and sound of her colleagues. But at moments of stalled creativity like this, fragments of a dozen phone conversations and face-to-face discussions broke through. It was hopeless trying to concentrate in this zoo. She would have to finish the reports at home.

Her thoughts wandered back to her last lunch with Crispin. She had not seen him since, and he had not contacted her. Now the question was starting to grow in her mind – had she blown it? She had phoned him a couple of times and got no reply. Nothing unusual in that. Nor in the fact that he had not phoned her. Nevertheless, she was worried.

For all she knew he could have buggered off back to Kent by now. Their relationship was founded on that degree of uncertainty. She simply did not know, had never been told, how long he intended to stay in Northburn or whether he intended to return to Mary afterwards. The truth was that she really did not know what he was doing in Northburn anyway, him or his young sidekick, Jim, whom she had never met. Something political, he had told her, with the implication that he meant something illegal and she had better ask no questions. So she hadn't. But she had to admit that he could have been working as a white slaver's agent for all she knew. She had taken a lot on trust and as a result her doubts and fantasies were running riot now.

She decided to go and visit a schizophrenic lady and try to persuade her to take her three-year-old son to a day nursery, despite the lady's firm conviction that the matron in charge of the nursery was literally an agent of the devil. It was a decision smacking of desperation.

There has to be more to it than this, she thought, as she threaded her way through her fellow workers' personal boundary markers towards the lift. Sticking bandaids on social casualties all day and entertaining my husband's cronies in my so-called spare time, a part of the problem masquerading as part of the solution. Damn it, Crispin, I need you to rescue me. You've done it before. And now you've given me a taste of freedom again, surely you can't let me down?

Too late. She watched the lift door shut. A couple of minutes to get it back up here. Knickers. It's a bonus. Before I go out I'll try his number just one more time.

A flat soon gets to feel uninhabitable when you're intending to flit from it the next day; it starts to suffer from a sort of personalized planning blight, all its defects on show, with no possibility of any of them ever being remedied. It also gets to feel small and vulnerable when you're sharing it with a bomb.

161

A bomb called Porky, for that was the pet name which Crispin had given the damn thing. Why, because it goes off in warm weather? Jim had asked. No, because it kills pigs, he had replied. It was the sort of laboured humour popular among the killing classes throughout the ages.

Jim had toyed with the idea of leaving Porky in the boot of his car, but the thought of explaining things to the police, let alone Party HQ, if the car got stolen, dissuaded him. So instead it rested uneasily in a cupboard in the kitchen, waiting for its time to come.

Crispin lay on the couch, half-listening to some music on the radio, trying to kill time, conscious that a bomb was capable of detonating at any moment, with all too imaginable force, a few feet from his head. Try as he might, he was incapable of rationalizing away his fear. To do so would have involved ignoring two basic lessons of experience, that flesh is vulnerable and technology imperfect. Anyway, he reasoned, his situation should not be seen as an accidental occurrence. Rather, correctly interpreted, it seemed to symbolize the central dilemma of his life: which did he fear the most – death or boredom?

'Just keep calm there, Porky,' he said.

'Talking to yourself again, Chris?' Jim interjected from across the room, where he was sitting in an armchair sewing a button on to a shirt.

'It's one way to get a sensible conversation.'

Just then the pay-phone rang in the hall. Jim laid his shirt on the arm of the chair, drove the needle into the upholstery, and got up to answer it.

'If it's Pamela, I'm out,' said his partner.

35

'I still think it's bad news going to see the old bastard this soon before blast-off.'

It was Wednesday afternoon and Jim was speaking to Crispin, who was just setting out to see his old chairman, Tom. 'Do you really have to visit him at this stage, Chris? You know he's guilty. From what you say he's dying anyway. What good is it going to do you seeing the old chuff?'

'Satisfaction. Simple as that. You've heard of revolutions betrayed? Well, he betrayed mine. It's all so clear to me now. I've got to see him face to face one more time before it's too late.'

'Just make sure he doesn't betray you again.'

'Stop fussing,' said Crispin, tossing his partner a cigarette, 'and make sure you've got my tea ready for me when I get back.'

'Yes, ma'am.'

The area where Tom lived had not changed much in eight years: a little more double-glazing and a few more frosted-glass doors, but basically they were still the same timeless, red-brick terraces that had once covered much of the city – a small, uncleared, reminder of the original urban forest.

Tom, however, had changed a lot. The man who answered the door was a shrunken, diminished version of his old chairman. Stooped, his face sunken and his eyes watering, his complexion pallid and his hair reduced to a few grey strands, he struck Crispin at once as a dying man. His handshake was cold and weak and he gasped for breath as he said hello. It was not only death that hung about him, but neglect and decay in all

163

their little revealing details – the stubble on the face, the piss stains on the trousers, the worn-out carpet slippers.

Tom led Crispin down the passage past one closed door into the back parlour.

'I live in here these days, Chris. Hardly go in the front room since the wife died.'

She had a name, he thought. She was called Jean. I don't remember them using the front room much even when she was alive, only for entertaining special guests. Perhaps he nursed her there.

'Well, it's cosy in here,' said Crispin, warming his hands at a single-bar electric fire of a type which was almost collectable.

'Fancy a pot of tea? I'll mash some.'

'Yeah, that would be good, Tom.'

Tom shuffled through into the kitchen, leaving Crispin to survey his old adversary's lair. Except that he was not simply his adversary any more. Complexity had reared its ugly heads. He was Tom, who used to be married to Jean, a real person for all his faults, and one he badly needed to come to terms with.

It was a room caught in a time-warp, like the wedding photograph of Tom and his bride on the sideboard. Everything about it, the furniture – a sideboard, table and easy chair – the ornaments and clock on the mantlepiece, the budgerigar serving out its time in a cage on a stand, seemed to belong to an earlier epoch. Crispin had always seen Tom as more or less his contemporary, but a yawning chasm of an age-gap now seemed to have opened between them. Tom had got old and was not going to get much older. He had retreated from active life into this shell of domesticity, which must have been unknown territory to him in his prime. The place felt claustrophobic. Although he had hardly spoken to Tom yet, he already felt trapped with him and his dying.

He went over to have a look at the shelf of books next to the fireplace. They were a monument to the old values that had once united them as comrades – Marx, Lenin and, yes, the long-proscribed selected works of Stalin in its cloth-covered, wartime edition; Hewlett Johnson's *Socialist Sixth of the World*; the Webbs' *Soviet Communism*; a few Left Book Club titles but none of the rare ones; a few later paperbacks – Fanon, Guevara,

Mao – and an assortment of no longer topical pamphlets. It could have been Crispin's own library; in fact he probably possessed, or had possessed, every book on the shelf.

He had no desire to reread a single word of them but their presence made him feel nostalgic. The books belonged to an era before the Party got buried in waves of anarchic opportunism – feminism, gay liberation, black consciousness and all. The values they embodied were old, simple and to both men true – working-class solidarity, working-class internationalism and beyond those semi-sloganized phrases the basic reality they embodied – courage, discipline and brotherhood in the face of a harsh world that belonged to a usurper. Bloody good values too, Crispin thought, before the courage and the brotherhood ran out.

It took Tom a long time to make the tea. By the time he got back from the kitchen the last of Crispin's hatred had drained away. He had looked his dying enemy in the face and that would do. Forgiveness and vengeance were now equally pointless.

So they sat, Crispin at the table, Tom in his easy chair, and drank their tea and talked. Mainly they spoke of Tom's current ailments and grievances much as they had done on the phone. Tom showed little interest either in Crispin's current activities or, perhaps more surprisingly, in reminiscing about the old days. They alluded to his wife's death in passing, but both men were part of a culture of emotional restraint that inhibited them from discussing it in any detail. It was therefore both a stilted and a depressing conversation, with a man who had rejected both past and future and retreated for safety into a solipsistic present.

He saved the important question till near the end.

'Tell me, Tom, to ease my curiosity. We worked together bloody close through a lot of hard times. So why did you turn against me? I mean, it was you that was decisive in that – Alex, Pamela, Ian even, they were neither here nor there, it was you that was crucial. But why? It wasn't politics: you agreed with me more than you ever agreed with the barmpots that came after me. It wasn't personal: we were long-time mates. So what was it?'

165

Tom looked at him in a slightly bemused way, as if the question was indicative of terminal idiocy.

'You were out of step. You had to be cloched. I was chairman, so it was my job to do it. You'd have done the same, wouldn't you?'

'Simple as that?'

'Simple as that.'

He could not resist the next remark.

'It doesn't seem to have done you much good.'

'No. These things don't necessarily.'

There's no answer to that, Crispin thought.

'Well, don't do it again.'

Tom smiled for the first time. 'No danger.'

They chatted for a bit longer, then Crispin decided it was time to go.

'I've got to be off, Tom, old lad. It's been nice seeing you again. I get up this way occasionally on business. I'll look you up next time I'm through.'

'Do that, Chris. I never see any bugger these days.'

They both knew Crispin was lying: they were not going to meet again, ever.

Well, it's over, he thought, getting into the car. Not quite what I expected, but at least it's an ending. He glanced in the mirror as he fastened his seat belt. No kids playing in the street. No washing hung across it, for that matter. The little signs of change, like the row of parked cars along the kerb and the fact that they've tarmac'd over the cobbles. Life goes on indoors, but the streets are dead. Dead as my passion. I'm buggered if I didn't feel sorry for him. Can't get much deader than that.

Tom's pathetic figure framed in the doorway – then the door closed. Now the real shooting can start, thought Crispin, switching on the engine.

166

36

'I warmed to him a bit, you know, for all his moaning. It was just his way of disguising his fear.' Crispin was speaking.

'Fear?' Jim asked. They had just finished tea.

'Yeah, he's afraid of dying, that's all.' His eyes had the slightly distanced look of someone who intended to speak at length. 'Everyone is afraid of dying when you get down to it. If you live long enough to get old, I think whatever contentment you won in your middle age turns to a cloud of depression.

'I remember we had this comrade called Benny. One of the best. Cab driver by trade. Spent his whole life fighting religion. Parked his cab outside the synagogue and sat inside it eating bacon butties, that sort of thing. Then came the Six Day frigging War. His wife got a bad dose of Zionism, and pretty soon after, she got religion too. Next thing, he finds she has him put down for a kosher burial – twenty-four hour job, candles, the works. He comes into my office, poor old chuff, with a few bevvies inside him, and starts weeping about it. Imagine it, this tough old bolshevik literally weeping about a kosher funeral.

'It's ridiculous, of course, and I say so to him. Jesus, Benny, you're supposed to be a materialist, what the fuck does it matter to you what your missus does to you when you're dead? If it makes her happy, she could have you stuffed for all you would know about it.

'But that's not the point and I know it. The point is, he loves his wife, or at least feels easy with her, and there she is, behind his back, making the necessary arrangements for them to spend eternity together in a kosher heaven – no Arabs, no shiksas need

167

apply – and all she's doing is reminding him that he's going nowhere, with or without her. That's why he's weeping. If I wanted to comfort him I'd have to say, look, there's a let-out clause, Benny, old son. Marx didn't really mean it, you're going to live for ever.' He paused to light a cigarette. 'And somehow I don't think he'd have bought that one.'

'So Tom wasn't scared of you?' Jim returned him to the present.

'No way. Just of The Reaper.'

'Are you scared of dying, Chris?'

'Yeah. Sure. Fuck, yeah, of course I am. But, on balance, not as much as I'm scared of the alternatives, if they amount to eating shit and living like a zombie. Taking risks is the price you pay, once you step out of doors.'

'Amen. All this is a shade too profound for me. Let's go and meet Jacko. I'll tell you what, I bet that's one man who isn't afraid of dying.'

They had arranged to meet Jacko that evening for a final check on details. Crispin laughed.

'No, you're probably right there. I just hope we don't get to find out.'

'Fuck it, stop being morbid. Where are you planning to head for once we've delivered the bomb tomorrow?'

'Christ knows. I really haven't thought about it much. I suppose I'll lie low somewhere until the situation is clearer. I've arranged to phone Mary at a call box in the village on Friday night. How about you?'

'Well, I'm not as cosmopolitan as you. I'll stay in Southdale. Keep my head down for a bit same as you. Hope they don't question Jacko too hard, or check that bail form too far.'

And he doesn't even know about Inspector Blackman. Well, ignorance is bliss.

'We're a couple of bloody amateurs when you get down to it, aren't we, Jim? They'd fucking laugh at us places where they're used to armed struggle. Serves us bloody right, really – we've had it too cushy too long.'

'Still, we didn't do too bad for beginners, did we?'

'If the others have done as well, I'll be surprised.'

'And you know what? I enjoyed it.'

168

'Me too, mate.'

It was suddenly an emotional moment, and the right one to disengage at.

'Jacko.'

'Right. Let's go. Where did we say we'd meet him?'

'Green's.'

'Christ. The Worst Bar in the World.'

Every town has one pub of legendary and enduring awfulness. Such places are clearly regarded by the breweries that own them as some kind of necessary sacrifice to the gods of alcohol: certainly they never seem to be closed or upgraded, however notoriously unpopular they become. Nor do they ever entirely lack a clientele – some degraded or lunatic regulars can always be found in them. Moreover a really bad, as opposed to a merely mediocre pub will always attract the occasional party of sightseers – hardened pub-crawlers who enjoy a challenge, perhaps, or bright young students on a slumming expedition, about to acquire a permanently distorted picture of urban proletarian life.

Situated between a railway bridge and a Salvation Army Men's Hostel, most of whose residents were far too discriminating to be seen dead there, Green's Hotel, named, Crispin reckoned, after some long-forgotten Victorian poisoner, was Northburn's contribution to the *genre*. It had rickety tables where none of the chairs matched, lino on the floor and nothing on the walls except grime. The beer was not so much undrinkable as unspeakable. Nobody had ever risked the sandwiches, displayed like curiosities in a glass case. Those were its strong points; otherwise it had nothing to commend it.

When Crispin and Jim arrived, Green's had three customers; a tramp who was conducting an astonishingly foul-mouthed dialogue with the demons in his skull, and a couple of punks, presumably one of each gender, in bondage gear and peacock haircuts. The punks soon left.

Jacko arrived shortly afterwards and joined them in a can of lager, which seemed about the safest thing to drink. In marked contrast to his surroundings, Jacko was in the sort of high mood that verges on euphoria.

'Yeah,' he said, in answer to Jim's question, 'I feel good about

169

tomorrow. It's going to go well.'

'No trouble about the overtime?'

'You won't believe this, but they *asked* me today if I'd work over tomorrow and Friday. Christ, I thought, tomorrow's OK, but I could be tied up Friday. No, but you should have seen me, seriously. I made like I was a right grabbing cunt – yes, boss, you put up the cash and I'll work all weekend too. Come to think of it, if that bomb blows a few fuses, I might just be on for that.'

'Somebody up there must love us.'

'Comrade Lenin doing the honours as usual.'

'So what time do you want to pick up your parcel?' Crispin asked.

'About four. If I'm going back in as everyone else clocks off, nobody is going to notice if I'm carrying a three-piece suite, never mind a small bomb.'

'Good. I'll be parked just round the corner from the main gate. What time do you expect to clock off finally?'

'About seven.'

'OK. I'll be parked in the same place then.'

'We should be on for a few drinks, eh?'

'Yeah. Mind, I want you clear-headed the morning after as you pick your way through the debris.'

Jacko was all smiles. 'I reckon I've got that bit sussed too. If they pull me in for questioning, I'm going to act dumb until they spell out what happened. Then I'm going to turn all horror-struck and tell them I'm a pacifist.'

'Working in a fucking tank factory?'

Jacko looked crestfallen. He had obviously been working on the idea. He scratched a small tiger on his arm reflectively and swilled some lager round in his mouth. Then he cheered up again. 'No, I'll tell them I hate terrorists. Go on about how they killed my best mate in the Army. They can check that.'

'That's good. I'd stick to that.'

A wave of ear-crunching, hideously distorted sound swept over them. Somebody had activated a disco on a low stage, which none of them had noticed before, at the end of the bar room. Behind a barricade of speakers and flashing lights, the disc jockey, a huge black man, was operating twin turntables.

'Jesus,' Crispin shouted over the racket, 'a disco in this place? I don't believe it. Who's going to dance in here, for fuck's sake?'

By way of answer, the tramp marched over to the area in front of the speakers reserved for dancing and began a grotesque jig, howling obscenities as he did so.

'He should get an agent,' said Jacko.

'I don't know who's more loony in this dump – the customers or the management. Hiring that lot must cost a week's takings,' said Jim.

'I've heard enough,' said Crispin. 'Let's go somewhere else.'

Green's as a venue had been Jacko's idea, but he expressed no objection to a move. Basking in the anticipation of revolutionary glory, riding on a gentle but unassailable high, he would have gone anywhere the comrades suggested.

'Yeah,' he said, his face all innocence like a schoolboy, 'I fancy a good night out.'

37

Thursday. The last day. 8.30 am. Crispin stood in his underwear in the cold bedroom. Spread out on the lumpy mattress – one thing he would definitely be glad to see the back of – was the new set of clothes he had bought for the occasion. His going-into-hiding outfit, garments to get lost in: blazer, tight-cut trousers and shirt, a good pair of shoes and a complete range of accessories – tie, belt, cuff links, patterned handkerchiefs. The Party had coughed up without too much argument. Necessary expenses. Go to hell and if it's absolutely essential, go there smartly turned out.

He dressed quickly with a sense of purpose, inspecting the result in the speckled murk of the dressing-table mirror. Yes, that will do nicely, son.

Next he packed his luggage, such as it was, into a holdall. The important items he left until last – his phone book; the tape of Jacko agreeing to do the dirty deed with jukebox accompaniment; the photographs of Ted Atha taking the money. He then did a quick scout round the flat to make sure he had not left anything of importance behind, but all he came up with was a toothbrush. Not much of a haul.

9 am. He was just making some coffee when the phone rang. I'd better answer it, he thought, in case it's Jacko ringing to tell me he's broken his leg. He did, in fact, feel nervous. At this stage any hitch would be a nightmare.

It was Pamela.

'You must be psychic, kid, I was just on my way out the door. Another second and you'd have missed me.'

Encouraged by his tone, she carried on. 'I just wondered if you fancied lunch today. We left things a bit up in the air last time.'

'True. Thing is though, Pamela, I'm a bit tied up the next day or two. Can I come back to you on it?'

Like maybe in another ten years.

'Sure, I'd like that. Can I ring you at the weekend?'

'Yeah, why not do that.'

'It's nice speaking to you again, love.'

'And you.'

'Look after yourself, Chris.'

'Bye.'

'Bye.'

End of a beautiful friendship. No time even to think about it now.

9.30 am. He had almost finished his coffee when the phone rang again. Jesus, we're in demand today. Jim, who had been sitting on the edge of his chair chain-smoking, jumped up.

'My turn,' he said.

'Probably a wrong number.'

But it was not, and when Jim reentered the room a couple of minutes later, he looked as if he had been kicked in the balls.

'What's up?'

'That was Martin from Region. He's had a message from HQ. It's all off.'

'It's off?' Crispin stood up, knocking his empty cup off the arm of the chair, feeling a rush of incredulity and anger. 'What the fucking hell do you mean, it's off?'

'Well, the National Executive apparently held an emergency meeting last night. It went on into the early hours, which is why we've only got the message now. There seems to have been some sort of shift in the balance of forces. Armed actions are now premature and adventurist. Strikes are OK.'

He sounded mechanically bitter. Crispin was less restrained.

'Strikes are OK? That shower of shit couldn't organize a strike at a shop stewards' reunion. Adventurist? Crossing a road would be an adventure for them cunts. They've bottled out, that's all. Fuck the sodding bastards! I'll tell you what, Jim, this is fuck all to do with politics and political differences. I know these bastards. They're all piss and wind. I'll bet you and me are their entire national campaign. I'll bet no bastard elsewhere has come up with the goods. Come Friday morning there would be one explosion in Northburn – where the bastards haven't even got an organization since they sacked me – and everywhere else, fuck all. That's the truth, Jim, and they can't face it. Bastards!'

Crispin was pacing up and down. Jim had been shaken, if secretly a little relieved, by the phone call, but the strength of Crispin's reaction disturbed and upset him. He knew it was not an act. Crispin, who really did think the bombing was adventurist and had been prepared to say so when others were nodding it through, had nevertheless put his loyalty behind it and, once again, he had been betrayed. He felt for him. And he could see that there might well be some truth in his practical assessment. He had accepted the reality of a national campaign as given. He had not expected to be given any details and he had not asked for any. Now he saw that he had been naïve. Other Jims elsewhere might not have had a Crispin to make the idea a reality. They really might be on their own.

'Yeah, it's a fuck up.'

'Fuck up? I'll tell you what, Jim, I'm not taking this from the messenger boy. That little cunt Steve Brown should have rung us, not Martin.'

'Well, that's typical.'

'Yeah, well, I'm going to ring him whether he likes it or not.'

And, to Jim's amazement, armed with nothing more than the coins in his pocket, some remembered numbers, and a soul on fire, he tracked Steve down and crucified him, a performance all the more remarkable because, with due regard for security, the entire conversation was conducted in coded generalities.

'Well, I was right on one thing,' said Crispin when he was done, collapsing into a chair, lighting a cigarette and leaning forward again, 'reading between the lines, I'm bloody positive now we were the only attack actually set up. I mean, let's be right, looking back on it we were left to our own devices, weren't we? Fucking leadership they call it – it's a pissing joke. So I reckon comrades started to panic on the Executive, and then the opposition, who could be anyone the way things are, used it as an excuse to abort the whole shebang.'

Jim passed him a scotch in a coffee mug. 'Have a drink. You deserve it, I reckon. You were magnificent on the phone.'

Crispin did not feel magnificent at all. He felt crushed. Because, however he looked at it, history was repeating itself. He had been set up and let down yet again. Unbelievable, but he had had a second opinion and it was true. He had not yet had the chance to sit down calmly and assess things, but the verdict was obvious.

Obvious and twofold. Firstly, on a practical level, he had been proven to be stupid. He should have seen it coming. It was not the first time after all. Daft bastard, he had been too busy brooding over the last betrayal to foresee this one, even when it had been staring him in the face. But there was a second level, a moral one, where he had to record a guilty verdict too. He was confronted by a mirror. The mirror said: this happened to you, mug, because you are a perfectly appropriate person for it to happen to. You are just as bad as the people who did it to you. You would have done the same. You bloody well have, times many. Live by the sword and perish by it. Except that the mirror had not got it quite right. Definitions of good and bad, and who was which, had got all jumbled up. The depressing fact was that they had seen him as being as bad as them and, unfortunately for him, he had not lived up to their expectations.

He drank off the whisky which went down easy and good. He

had to say that for his partner – he bought the right brand and he poured a decent measure.

'Well, that's that then. Back to the drawing board. Put back the date of the revolution yet again. What does your guru Martin want us to do now?'

'He said I was to go to Southdale this morning. Meet him there at one o'clock for further instructions. Meanwhile we're to wrap things up here. Get rid of Porky. Pay off Jacko. Vacate the flat as planned.'

Pay off Jacko. It suddenly struck Crispin that Jacko could well turn nasty when he heard the news. Christ, he felt angry enough himself and he was more or less sane. I'll have to tell him in person, he thought, or he'll go berserk.

'Well if you've got to go and see Martin, I'll see Jacko. I reckon that gives me the best of the deal. I'll drop Porky in the canal en route and kill two birds with one stone.'

Since the phone call the bomb had been mentally disarmed. For the first time since Jim had carried it through the front door, Crispin was not expecting it to blow up the next minute.

Silence fell on both men for a few moments.

'I'll tell you what, Chris, I feel fucking bad now for having dragged you into this mess. It's a fucking daft business.'

'What a fucking Party, eh? Bunch of wankers.'

'Still, you thought the whole idea was daft from the start. I reckon you were right. It's a moral victory for you.'

'Wonderful. I need victories like that like I need a hole in the head.'

Another pause.

'So that's it, then,' Jim said. 'End of a beautiful partnership. Pension off Jacko and Porky and hit the trail.'

'For two pins I'd go ahead as planned. Show the bastards we could do the job, even if they couldn't.'

'You're not serious, Chris?'

A slight hesitation. 'No, but you've got to admit it would show the bastards.'

38

Jim left at 11.45 am after a low-key, anticlimactic farewell to Crispin. The war was almost over. No reason now why he should not see Crispin again sometime. And no reason to believe he would.

The traffic was steady as he negotiated the commercial heart of Northburn. Who was it who said that places looked better looking back? A line from a song in an old movie. Well, maybe it would. He had never warmed to Northburn's town centre, so different in feel to Southdale's; a soulless place, he found it, dedicated to the naked making of money rather than the creation of real wealth in the form of things of value. 'Office to Let' signs proliferated, and the speculators' response was to build more offices and argue that this would force down rent levels and encourage occupancy. And they wondered why they had a depression. Well, it was that sort of place.

Over the river was another world – the pay-off for the diversion of resources out of industry and into the maw of the financial houses with their computers and telex machines. Once there had been factories, surrounded by houses, pubs and shops. First they had demolished the houses and moved their inhabitants to new estates leaving the factories and the occasional pub in splendid isolation. Then they had shut and boarded up the factories, or demolished them completely. What remained was a vast area of desolation, a sort of understocked urban nature reserve, threaded by roads all leading to the motorways out of town.

Looking just like I feel this merry day, thought Jim.

Once he was on the motorway heading south, with thirty minutes of near automatic driving ahead of him, Jim began to think about the job he had left his partner to finish. It had not been a fair division of labour at all. All he had to do was talk to Martin – something, it suddenly struck him, he was going to have to do a lot of as vice-chairman to chairman in times to come. Meanwhile Crispin had to dispose of a deadly bomb and a possibly not much less deadly Jacko. He had lumbered his partner with the heavy work, as always.

But at least he knew Crispin could handle it. He had set the operation up and three hours before he had been in no doubt that it was going to work. Now, equally, he was the ideal person to dismantle the scheme safely – Jacko, Porky and all. Despite his sometime indiscipline, despite his eight years voluntarily spent in the wilderness, despite his womanizing and his boozing and his daft obsessions with old quarrels, Crispin could do no wrong.

It was not obvious to him why he felt this way about Crispin. He knew his stuff politically, certainly, and in his own odd way he was a brilliant organizer, but he was scarcely unique, in Jim's experience, in these respects. No, it was something to do with Crispin's personality that marked him off from the leading comrades – many of them Crispin's contemporaries and trained in the same vigorous school – with whom he had previously associated. Crispin was warmer, more flamboyant, less predictable, more *real*. He also lacked the caution that was their collective hallmark. Unconsciously, Jim had stumbled on the right man for the job. For all his cynicism, Crispin was a hundred-percenter; he did not know what half measures were.

It was curious, but he was not really looking forward to seeing Martin and assuming the mantle of dutiful young heir apparent. Martin would greet him as one who had done well, but he actually felt like a failure, sharing, at least in part, Crispin's sense of frustration. A few weeks ago Martin had been his natural point of reference politically, the comrade he sat next to at meetings and cadged cigarettes off. He wondered if he would now detect the gulf that lay between them.

At 12.30 Crispin walked out to his car with the holdall in his left hand and the bomb tucked, heavy and uncomfortable, under his right arm. At that moment he had two things on his mind. One was the prospect of being blown to eternity. He had no idea of how stable the bomb was, or how it might react if, for example, he tripped and fell, but he had a pretty good idea of what he would look like afterwards. The other was the admittedly remote possibility of bumping into his landlord or his son. He had already given notice and paid a month's rent in advance, but he did not want the time of his departure too closely pinpointed, just in case.

He had decided to meet Jacko at 4 pm as planned, so in a sense there was no urgency. But who the hell wants to spend any longer than necessary in the company of high explosives? He would go to the canal now and dump the bomb. He knew a good spot to park, next to a derelict mill and by a bridge. It was well off the beaten track and nobody would see him or disturb him.

Anyway, he thought, as he drove to the spot, look on it as a going-away treat. He had wanted to spend some time by the canal ever since he had come back to Northburn. This was his last chance, before circumstances once more banished him from the place he loved.

He found the place and parked. Some youngsters were playing on the towpath below him, rearing up on the back wheels of their BMX bikes as they described tight circles inches from the edge. Better wait until they've gone. No rush. Have a smoke. It's been a trying morning. He suddenly felt rather tired.

Canals were important to Crispin, a symbol of continuity in a crumbling world. Built, navigated, at the very beginning of the industrial revolution, they had seen it through to the bitter end, their engineering still good to service today's surviving trade of renting narrow boats to holiday-makers.

'First in, last out,' he said to nobody in particular, lighting a cigarette.

From here you could follow this canal all the way over the mountains to the sea. A real trip down the memory lane of industrial archaeology. It was a good way to see some of the things that used to be, their remnants well hidden unless you took the trouble to explore these backwaters. Jesus, he thought, mills like this one next to me were typical. Look at those rows of windows, all the glass long gone. So many levels of concentrated productivity, as much floor space as any factory left working in town, more economically arranged with all the hands crammed under the one roof. What *happened* to all that work and the people who did it? They built everything and ultimately got nothing. Tricked out of power and written out of history, and now being broken up like old machinery.

Declassed and deindustrialized, as the sociologists say. Aye, buggered from arsehole to breakfast-time, just like yours truly. No doubt it will come together again, somewhere, some time. But fucked if I can see any sign of it at the moment.

He felt the rage returning, generalized and then specific. Why not use the bomb he had with him? Just for the hell of it. Give me one good reason why not? For two bloody pins I'd do it and show the bastards.

When Jim got to the shop at 1 pm he found Martin already there, sitting behind the desk in the upstairs office, where he still half expected to see Alan. The office had the advantage of being free of the snails and beetles which haunted the downstairs meeting room, though it did offer lodging to a tribe of mice who would periodically make nests of shredded paper in wastepaper baskets or filing cabinet drawers and gnaw their way through boxes of tea bags.

Martin's greeting was warm, almost overfriendly.

'It's good to see you back safe and sound, comrade.'

'It's good to be back.'

'Before I forget, we've made arrangements for you to stay with Mike Arkwright until you get something else fixed. Do you know where he lives?'

He could have done worse. Mike was a nice enough lad who would not ask too many questions.

'Sure. I can find it.'

'Now Jim, everything has happened in a bit of a rush. Have you made all the necessary arrangements in Northburn – I mean to call off the operation and dispose of the evidence?'

'Crispin should have dumped the bomb by now. He'll be seeing Jacko at four o'clock to tell him it's off. That ought to about wrap things up at that end.'

'Ah, I thought you might have got rid of the bomb yourself.' A hint of anxiety in his voice.

'Crispin said he would do both jobs while he was on. No problem, is there?'

'No, no. You're quite happy he can handle it?'

'Frankly I'm glad it's him doing it, not me. Bombs can go off, and Jacko can be an awkward bastard.'

'Ah yes.' He still sounded worried. 'Well, fair enough. Did he get the cash, by the way?'

Crispin's demand for a final payment to kit himself out with some new clothes had rankled with the Party, as he had fully expected it would.

'Yes, he got it. He's dressed like the oldest swinger in town today. Chris the dude.'

'Where's the bugger off to then – back to his business?'

'I suppose so. I don't think he was in any special hurry.'

'Sounds like Chris. Well, did you find Northburn educational?'

'I found working with Crispin educational. He's still got a lot of good contacts and there is some potential. We met one very good lad at Hardcoats, for example, that we could not do very much about since we weren't involving him in the other business. It might be worth following up sometime.'

He had reverted to the orthodox manner of reporting on a routine political assignment, like visiting a potential recruit. Martin nodded. They both knew it was pissing in the wind.

'It must have been a bit hairy at times. Are you glad it's over?'

He seemed to be probing for something.

Jim thought for a second. 'I'm not sure. I've got mixed feelings.'

'You mean about the Party calling it off?'

'Yes. Not so much the fact that they called it off as the way they did it – no consultation, no warning. Yes, we felt a bit let down over that.'

'Well, you appreciate it's not the sort of decision you could take at a delegate conference.'

'No, but tell me this, Martin. Was the original decision really worked for in the Party? Chris and me were ready to go this morning, ready to risk our necks back there – did any bugger else do a job on it?'

Martin caught his bitterness. He shrugged his shoulders. 'Your guess is as good as mine. Maybe not. Yes, probably not, if you want me to state a personal opinion. Look, I know you worked hard, Jim, but does it matter now?'

'It matters to me.'

'And Crispin?'

'Yes.'

What was Martin driving at?

Martin leaned forward over the desk. He looked older and tired, not his usual jokey self.

'Let me give you a bit of advice, Jim, as a friend and as somebody a wee bit older than you. Maybe you disagree with this decision, or how it was taken, or maybe both. And you could be right, let's face it. But it's a National Executive decision, and you've got a position here as regional vice-chairman. What I'm saying is, don't make too much of your disagreement after today. These are difficult times. We need to stick together.'

'How do you mean, exactly?' he asked, knowing exactly what Martin meant.

'There's been a bit,' he paused, searching for the right euphemism, 'a bit of a shift on the National Executive. The decision had a good majority.'

Meaning heads of dissidents are likely to roll in celebration. Meaning those who loyally risked their necks had better loyally keep their traps shut.

Martin continued. 'It doesn't do any good getting sore at these things. I heard about Chris mouthing it off to Steve Brown this morning. Stupid.'

He shook his head sadly. Jim felt an irrational urge to hurt him, even though he realized he was trying to be helpful.

'Chris was just pissed off because of the way he got the news. He thought he should have heard it from the organ-grinder.'

'Not the bleeding monkey,' Martin chimed in. 'Thanks, comrade.'

181

They both laughed. 'Sorry'.

'Look, Jim, I know you admire Chris, and he's a mate of mine from way back as well, don't forget, and nobody knows better than me that he's got the heart of a lion but he does have a tendency to go off at tangents. Frankly, we wouldn't have let him go back to Northburn unless you had been there to keep an eye on him.' Jim raised his eyebrows at this. It was not quite how he remembered it. 'So don't let him lead you into bad ways, kid. You've got a future here in the Party, whereas Chris, all credit to the comrade for what he's done, is really just a one-off these days.'

And that's all the thanks you get in this man's Party.

'Thanks for the advice, Martin. I've said my piece. I intend to take my job as vice-chairman seriously and carry on doing whatever the Party asks me to do, which is precisely what I – and Crispin – did this time, don't forget. But I'll say this just once for the record, so you understand me; there are times when I think Steve Brown and Co are a bunch of shit-houses and Crispin Pharaoh, for all his faults, is worth a hundred of them.'

'Then don't give them an excuse to hammer you. Come on, you've been working too hard. I'll buy you a pint. It's good to see you back in one piece, kid.'

It was 1.30 pm. Crispin still had not made his move from the car. He had been sitting there for nearly an hour now, lost in his thoughts.

He watched a rat, wet-backed and furtive, scuttle across the towpath and lose itself in the vegetation, thick even in winter, that ringed the walls of the mill. Vegetation always seemed to run riot along canal banks. It was a contradiction – as they became more sterile, so they became more fertile. In that sense they were the forerunners of those latter-day nature reserves, the motorway verges.

Nature versus technology – to date it had been no contest, he reckoned. Whole civilizations had vanished beneath desert sands, or under jungle, like Machu Picchu. Any old tame English suburban grass, more used to the lawn mower than the machete, would fuck up your tarmac, given a clear run. What we called civilization was, to a large extent, a matter of pride. In its developed form it was marked not just by an ability to destroy large numbers of human beings – we had had that capacity as a species since time immemorial – but by its ability to wipe out their natural environment as well. Our desire to outface nature had its harmless aspects, like the antiques he dealt in, but it had a dark side, too. The bomb that turned cities to glass, that could kill everything down to the microbes in the earth and call a halt to the basic process of photosynthesis, that was our revenge on nature for daring to appear stronger than us.

But don't get into that. You've been through all that, and it's beside the point. Your matter of pride is just a stupid political squabble. Don't try to seek comfort or comparisons in lofty philosophizing.

He pushed his thoughts away from violence and vengeance, towards his meeting with Jacko. It was not going to be easy.

He lit a cigarette and let the smoke fill the car. Perhaps he won't show up at all, he said out loud. Yes, that has to be the solution. He'll have knocked work for sure today. Gone down with chickenpox or yellow jaundice. He's crackers, but not crackers enough to turn up for this.

Oh yes he is, echoed, like a pantomime audience, isn't he, boys and girls? He's exactly that crackers, and well psyched-up for action. Positively raring to go. He'll show up all right.

And why shouldn't he? That was the question, morally speaking, wasn't it?

After all, he was expecting something out of this. They both were. A thrill. A sense of purpose or importance. A challenge. An adjunct to feeling young and crazy, or an antidote for being old and frustrated. Stupid maybe, but human. You couldn't blame Jacko. He wasn't to know the bastards would fuck you round the way they always did.

And I'm supposed to be the one to tell him.

But first I've got to take the bomb and drop it in the canal. One heave and it'll be gone for ever, down among the detritus, the silt of bikes and prams and bathtubs and all the other junk that folk dump in canals. It'll be safe enough there for a while,

183

just as long as some daft sodding Sunday fisherman doesn't pull it out again.

Yes, that's what I'll do. Any minute now.

And the voice echoed in his head. *The hell you will.*

2 pm. The first pint of the day tasted good, but something was worrying Jim.

'You sounded a bit anxious back there, Martin, about my leaving Crispin to clear up. Was there some problem?'

'No. I just thought you might have seen the –' he glanced round in case anyone was listening, 'package off yourself before you left. I mean in case anything went wrong.'

Then the penny dropped, and he heard Crispin's harsh voice again. *For two pins I'd go ahead as planned. You've got to admit it would show the bastards.*

'Oh hell, Martin, you don't think Chris would do anything daft, do you?'

'Well, after what he said to Steve Brown this morning, I must admit I did wonder,' he laughed apologetically, 'but you've satisfied me. So forget it. Come on, tell me about this new lass of yours.'

Martin was happy. He did not mention the matter again. He stayed for a couple of quick pints, chatting casually about this and that, and was gone by 2.30.

But the idea was now firmly planted in Jim's mind and the conviction that he was right grew as the clock edged its way towards the afternoon closing hour of 3 pm.

I'd go ahead . . . show the bastards.

Which left him with only one thing to do. He could not sit supping ale till closing time and waiting to hear the bang. He had to drive back to Northburn straight away, get to Hardcoats by four, and physically prise Crispin and Jacko off the bomb if necessary.

As he drank up, he caught the sound of familiar lyrics from the jukebox. *Only one day away from your arms.* That golden oldie again, 'Twenty-four hours from Tulsa'.

Jesus, he thought, how the hell did I get into this mess?

He got back into his car, feeling slightly drunk. He had never had the strongest of heads for alcohol, but it would have to do.

184

No Crispin to bail him out this time.

For two pins I'd go ahead as planned.

He switched on the engine. Straight back to Northburn. With just one quick stop to buy something which might prove useful.

At 3 pm Crispin finally got out of the car. He stretched, feeling the stiffness in his joints as he straightened up.

'Jesus, you're getting old. It'll be the boneyard for you soon.'

He took a few steps and flicked his cigarette into the canal. A flash of blue across the grey water caught his eye. Unmistakably a kingfisher in action. It took him a few moments to locate the spot where it had come to rest, perched on an overhanging tree branch on the far side of the canal. Age is taking away my eyes too. At one time I could have counted its feathers; now I can't even see if he caught anything. Amazing bird. It hardly seemed to belong on an industrial waterway in the bleakness of winter. You ought to be in India, mate, he thought, where there's better weather and bigger sticklebacks for the taking.

He made his way back to the car, opened the boot and took the bomb out. No, Porky, I'm not going to waste you, he muttered protectively. Back in the car he sat with it beside him on the passenger seat, covered by his coat, feeling now no fear. The branch with the kingfisher on was still in view. He focused with some difficulty on the patch of colour, emptying his head of thought and feeling, preparing for what was to come.

185

39

4.12. Jesus suffering Christ, just don't let me be too late. Not now.

Jim had been held up by a routine police traffic check. Waved over into a queue of stationary vehicles as he came off the motorway. He had sat drumming his fingers on the steering wheel and wondering what Crispin would have done in the same situation.

You've got to admit it would show the bastards.

Shat himself if he'd had any brains, if his sense of danger had not got fatally scrambled years before. Instead he tried to educate me in the dangerous art of indifference. Despite the cold weather Jim was sweating. I'm going to end up as the best documented underground revolutionary in history, he thought. And I'm not sure I could pass a breath test right now.

Eventually it was his turn. A young policewoman, trying her best to be an android, asked him a few questions. Starting point. Destination. Purpose of journey. Keeping the peace, believe me, lady. She noted his answers on a form on a clipboard, checked his licence, and then he was on his way again.

I'd go ahead as planned.

He had driven the rest of the way to Hardcoats as fast as he could manage and now he was turning the corner into the road where Crispin had arranged to make the handover. There was Crispin's car all right. Empty. Now what the hell did that mean? He parked behind it and got out, thinking suddenly, what if Chris and Jacko have been arrested, what if this is a stakeout? Well, you'll soon find out.

But by now Crispin had emerged from a shop where he had been buying cigarettes. Jim was the last person he had expected to see, and it showed on his face. They met on the pavement.

'Chris, have you seen Jacko yet?'

'Yes, he's just gone back into work.'

Now the real question.

'Did you dump the bomb?'

A pause.

'No, it's with Jacko.'

'Oh, fuck it, Chris, I knew it. What have you done?'

His voice sounded desperate, near to tears.

'Go back to Southdale, Jim, this is my game now.'

'The hell it bloody is. We're both in this, and it's still Party business. We've got to talk.'

'OK,' said Cripsin resignedly, 'let's get into my car. We don't want the whole street to hear.'

Inside the car they sat for a minute in silence, each afraid to make the first move.

'My head has been going round all afternoon, Jim, trying to work this one out,' said Crispin at last. 'They shouldn't have called it off, not after all that work, and not without an explanation. I've been fucked around too many times. We risked our necks and they did fuck all. So why listen to them now?'

'You're risking your neck now.'

'Why not? It's not worth much, and it might just shake the bastards up a bit.'

'Which bastards, Chris – the Party or the bosses?'

'Both. What the hell!' He stubbed out a half-smoked cigarette.

'But Chris, that bloody thing is going to go off now, first thing tomorrow morning. People may get hurt. They won't be in either camp. How are you going to square that?'

'Wrong, son, wrong. It's well too late, and you're well too compromised, to start pleading conscientious objection. You should have put that argument yesterday. Killing people can't be right one day and wrong the next, just because a scum-bag like Steve Brown says so.'

Just for a moment Jim felt diminished. His line of argument

had been a cheap shot. But there was no time for regrets now.

'That cuts both ways. You had all the arguments against doing this. The Party came round to agreeing with you. You won, damn it. Now you're just being perverse, Chris.'

'Yeah, that's right. I put my tactical skill at the service of the Party's strategic imbecility. And it stays there. I'm being perverse as hell. These are gunslinger's rules, Jim, if you start a job you finish the bugger.'

'No. No. No. Chris, when we watch this on television tomorrow morning, we're going to hate ourselves.'

I always said, nobody could use a plural better than you, partner. I'm going to have to give in. You won't leave me alone, and I can't drag you down with me.

A long silence filled the car, into which Jim, very sensibly, did not intrude.

'OK so what do you want me to do?'

'Let's go to Security and get them to call Jacko to the gate,' he said, the relief showing in his voice.

'That won't work. Suppose he refuses to cooperate? I mean, that was always a possibility. He's crazy enough, and I'll tell you he was raring to go ten minutes ago. No, we'll only get one shot at this and we'll have to get it right. We can't really have a slanging match through a twelve-foot gate, can we?'

'So?'

'We'll have to get inside the factory and get the bomb off him there.'

'How do we do that?'

'Only one way. We get hold of Ted Atha again and make him take us in.'

'That sounds risky.'

'Got any better ideas?'

'No.'

Crispin always had a monopoly on dangerous solutions to impossible problems.

'We better do it quick, as well.'

'Jacko said he was working till seven.'

'Yes, but once he's set the bomb it might be difficult to unset the bastard. Didn't they tell you it was booby-trapped?'

Didn't they just.

'Come on,' Crispin continued, 'Ted will be home by now. Let's go and get him. We'll leave your car here.'

He moved to switch the engine on.

'Chris, I'm glad you're going to help.' Suddenly he grinned. 'I won't be needing this now.' He produced from his pocket the gun he had bought while half-cut before leaving Southdale.

'Jesus, is that thing real?'

It looked real enough, a heavy revolver with a full-length barrel.

'No, it's a replica, but you weren't forced to know that.'

'Damn clever, these Japanese. Keep it, it might come in useful.'

4.45 pm. Ted's wife, a neat woman in an apron, had answered the door of the pebble-dashed, pre-war bungalow.

'Two friends to see you, Ted,' she said by way of explanation to her husband, who had come into the hall in his slippers and braces. 'They say it's urgent.'

I suppose I must have met his wife sometime before, Crispin thought, but she obviously does not remember me.

'A quick word, Ted.'

'In the front room, then.' He ushered them through officiously.

As soon as the door closed behind them, Crispin wheeled to confront Ted, towering over him, fanning out the incriminating photographs Port Said style, and whispering with an intensity of hatred that cut through the fear in the room.

'One good look at them, you bent little cunt, then get your slippers off and your shoes on. I don't suppose you were doing anything tonight, but if you were, it's cancelled. I want to get into the ROF. I want to see your man Jacko James. I want to see him like about five minutes ago, so don't fuck me around.'

From Ted's face, it seemed that the words and pictures were well synchronized.

'He means it,' said Jim, realizing that he was not going to need to show him the gun.

189

'I mean it like I should have killed you thirty years ago, and tonight I might just make up for lost time.'

'It's not that easy, Chris,' Ted said, baffled and frightened, his composure gone.

'Oh yes it is,' said Crispin.

At that point Ted's wife put her head round the door.

'Would you like a cup of tea?'

'No, love,' said Ted. 'I'm going to have to go back to work with these lads now.'

'We won't be long,' said Jim, charming as ever.

'Let's go then,' said Crispin. 'With a bit of luck you'll be back in time for Coronation Street.'

5.30 pm. By now it was dark. Crispin and Jim stood with their faces averted, but within earshot, as Ted Atha squared things with the security man at the gate.

'OK,' he said at last, 'come and sign the visitors' book.'

Crispin took the book and pointedly printed 'E.Edwards' in as illiterate a hand as possible in the column indicated, then passed it to his partner. 'Right then, Martin,' he said, 'make your mark.'

Once inside they walked down the path in silence. Ted had had Jacko called up from the gate. When they got to the shop where he worked he was standing outside waiting for them. He looked puzzled, which in Jacko's case was not a pretty sight. Keep calm, Crispin thought, but he did not feel it. His throat had gone dry and his stomach was churning. He was not at all sure how he was going to keep the situation under control.

'Can we have a word in private?' he asked.

'Come into the paint store,' said Jacko. 'It's open. I've just been doing a bit of work there.'

'Wait here with Ted,' Crispin said to Jim, wishing he could take him with him.

Crispin looked round the store as Jacko switched the light on. It was a big place. The area where they stood, by the door, was clear for quite a distance in. There were signs, from the rubbish on the floor, that this area was sometimes used as an improvised workshop for small jobs. When the paint supplies did start, they

190

stretched away into the darkness, large drums stacked up to the ceiling. Crispin spotted Jacko's bag with the bomb inside it lying about fifteen yards away on the periphery of a stack of cans. It concentrated his mind. He must have been working on it when we arrived, he thought. Has he set the bastard yet?

Then he turned his attention to Jacko. He noticed that he was sweating, even in the cold of the store, and shaking. Something was getting to him. He could be a hard man to reason with right now, he decided.

'What are you doing here with that cunt Ted?' he asked. 'What the fuck's going on?'

'Ted is only here to get us in and out. The thing is I need the bomb back. The operation is off.'

'Off?' Jacko's bloodshot eyes had narrowed into cruel slits of suspicion. 'Who says?'

'The Party. There's been a change of plan. There's –'

Damn it, I haven't handled this right, a voice was saying in the back of his head. I've lost him. He's going to blow.

'This is a set-up. A fucking set-up.'

He heard a click as the knife opened.

'Hang on, Jacko, let's – '

'No fucking way.'

Jacko slashed at him with the blade. Crispin moved back, noticing that he was cut off from the door, skidded through a pool of oil on the floor and fell almost in a splits position. Now is the time to be terribly cool. You're dealing with a mean, crazy bastard. So see him off, and quick. His hand closed on a strip of thin metal about three foot long, an off cut from a sheet, which was lying among the other shit on the floor, and he came up from his knees swinging it wildly.

He caught Jacko over the eye and at once blood was splashing everywhere. He sidestepped. Took care with his footing amongst the oil. Then kicked for the crotch. Not hard or accurate enough. He connected with something, but nothing vital. He was off balance now and panting, and Jacko was on him, one hand sweeping blood from his eyes, the other wielding the knife, cutting into the fabric of his blazer.

He's twenty years younger than you. He did time for using a

191

shiv once. He's mad and dangerous and you've got to kill the bastard. No messing. Just kill him.

Crispin came back at his opponent, ignoring the knife. Head-butted him. Then followed him down. Got him by the ears, thumbs well hooked in. Yanked up his head and banged it down as hard as he could manage on the concrete, as if he were trying to crack open a coconut. Once. Twice. A sickening, hollow thud.

But then, somehow, Jacko had thrown him off. He lay for a moment, puzzled and exhausted, as Jacko rolled over. Still with the knife. Jesus, only a real loony could still be fighting. I'm in trouble now.

'Drop it. Just fucking drop it. Or you're frigging dead.'

Thank Christ, partner, you came in just in time.

Jim was holding the phoney gun to the side of Jacko's head, sliding it down his cheek towards his mouth. Jacko released the knife and raised his hands to his head, trying to stop the blood pumping, his eyes bewildered.

Crispin moved on to his knees, panting for breath, as he stretched out to take the knife.

'You – better – stay awake – long enough – to fettle – that – fucking bomb.'

Jacko bent his head.

'No sweat, Chris,' he said. 'I haven't set the bastard yet.'

Now he fucking tells me.

They left Jacko in a lavatory in the store with a running tap and a pile of paper towels.

'Let's get back to Ted,' said Crispin. He felt as if he was going to collapse if he did not get out of the ROF soon. At the same time he felt irrationally exultant. You didn't do so bad, you old bastard, he thought.

Even in the darkness he must have looked fairly rough – tie adrift, half his shirt buttons gone, not to mention the blood stains.

'What the hell has been going on?' asked Ted when he saw him.

'He forgot to pay his dues,' said Crispin, gesturing with his thumb towards the store. 'Come on, take this, and let's get back through reception.' He handed Ted the bag. 'Careful, it's heavy.'

'What the – ?'

'Just take the bugger, Ted, it's been a long day. Besides, Jim here might shoot you.'

I know you're bent, Crispin thought, I've just got to hope that Security are used to seeing you walking out with swag under your arm.

Obviously they were. They got through reception without incident, Crispin taking care to stay in the shadows. The clock at the gate said six. Outside the street was deserted. It was starting to rain.

'Do I get a lift home?' Ted asked.

'Take a fucking taxi,' said Crispin. 'Here,' he pointed at Jacko's bag, 'I'll swop that for your filthy photographs while you're on. Hand it over and piss off.'

Ted held out the bag. Crispin took it, and threw him the envelope contemptuously.

'No need to be like that,' said Ted, huffily.

'Jesus,' said Crispin, swinging a blow at his head.

Jim stepped in his partner's way as Ted scuttled off. Then he started to laugh at the incongruity of the whole situation, still immensely dangerous, but also farcical. Unreal. It broke the tension. Crispin handed him a cigarette and he worked his lighter.

'There you are,' he said, 'light the blue paper and retire.' They both laughed.

He took a look at Crispin. His new clothes were all messed up. Oil on his strides and blood on his shirt. His knuckles scraped and his face bruised. Not quite how he had planned it.

'What next?' he asked.

'We split. Pronto. Get away from this fucking place. I'm going to dump the bomb and clean myself up. Then I'll hit the road and keep moving. A new town would look nice right now.'

It still seemed unreal. He opened his car door.

'Well, so long then.'

'We're making a habit of this goodbye business,' said Crispin.

'I hope we meet up again soon, Chris.' Jim held out his hand.

193

Crispin took it. 'Oh, we will, partner. Somewhere out in the fucking West with the other cowboys.'

'We didn't do too bad, did we?'

'Not too bad? What do you mean not too bad? We fucking showed them, kid.'

They drove in convoy to the end of the street. Then their ways parted. As Jim turned to head South, Crispin gave a honk of his horn, and made for the river.